Upbound

Peter Hassebroek

Upbound Solutions

Also by Peter Hassebroek

Melange and Other I. T. Stories

The Dancer's Spell

Greenplays

Thylacine

Upbound

Upbound

Published by
Upbound Solutions
Whitby, Ontario, Canada

ISBN: 978-0-9866640-8-3

A previous version of this novel was published in 2008.

www.peterhassebroek.com

Upbound

/1\

Karl Stevenson, snugly bundled in a tight curl underneath the blue flannel sheets and his thick Sylvester and Tweety Bird comforter, hears the soft, familiar thud of a palm against his bedroom door, followed by a faint whoosh, and a whisper.

"Time to get up, dear."

He shifts his bum and shoulders back and forth, as if still asleep, as if he hasn't heard a thing.

"Come on now. I know you're awake."

With on purpose slowness he uncurls, stretches his fingers, and slinks like a worm—no, a snake—up over his pillow until his hair brushes against the hard wood of the headboard. He rolls the sheets down to his chest, pauses, before rubbing sleep from his eyes.

The dim hallway light reveals a slender figure he knows so well at his door, a blurry yet eerie shadow watching him, sort of. The way her head leans, up and out toward the window, it's as if his mother is trying to get his attention and avoid him at the same time. When she flicks on the bedroom light, the brightness catches him by surprise. He ducks back under the covers.

"No games, Karl Philip. I don't want you to be late."

He pokes his head out and—blah—she looked better with the light off, when darkness hid the pale face and baggy eyes and dry lips. Everyone always says how pretty his mom is but they wouldn't if they saw her now. Not even Uncle Douglas. Her brown hair, normally smooth and wavy, is all jumbled up. It's hard to tell where the hair ends and her torn and ugly old brown robe begins. If she were a jigsaw puzzle, that section would be as hard to finish as any body of water, clear blue sky, or dry grassy field.

"Do I have to go?" he says, only partly joking.

They stare at each other. For a moment, it looks like she might let him stay home. But then she smiles her impossible to fool smile.

"Stop being silly, you love school."

"I know, but—"

"Then snap to it."

"Mom, I'm pooped. Can't I stay in bed?"

"How can you be so tired? How much sleep do you need?"

"Huh?"

"You don't remember yesterday? The game? You barely made it through the third quarter."

The game. He rubs his eyes again, shakes his head a couple of times before it comes back to him. How could he have forgotten? The Super Bowl, Super Bowl Six—or Super Bowl Vee Eye, as his dad called it—and Uncle Douglas's surprise visit.

Karl was so busy choosing a puzzle he almost didn't hear the big and loud LTD bounce over the curb and onto the driveway. When he did, he almost spilled all the pieces in his rush to the door. First, the big hello hug, then the snowman self-portraits in the backyard, followed by a snowball fight, and the challenge from his uncle that Karl couldn't finish his puzzle before halftime. That started Karl's flurry of puzzle piece sorting, fitting, inspecting, discarding, re-sorting, all the while keeping one eye on the television, silently cheering time outs, penalties, incomplete passes, even injuries and commercials: anything that stopped the clock. Karl would have finished on time except for that last piece which, as he always did, Uncle Douglas concealed in his shirt pocket. For a long while they wrestled for it until finally, just before halftime ended, his uncle gave it up, letting Karl finish the puzzle all by himself. Suddenly tired, Karl went to bed.

No wonder she's surprised, after all that sleep she thinks he had. Of course he can't say anything about his midnight walk, seeing the mess, and . . .

"Has Daddy gone to work already?"

"No, they won't be up for a long while."

"They? Do you mean—?"

The look on her face is just like the one last week at the grocery store when the cashier gave her too little change. Only this time she shakes her head and grins.

"Nice try, but I'm afraid not, young man. Besides, you don't want to miss your special breakfast."

As if by magic, the frying pan sizzles and the smell of bacon rises to his nose. She notices that he notices and leaves the room. He throws aside the covers, jumps over a pile of puzzle boxes, landing on the bright yellow Nerf football. Somehow, he avoids stubbing his toes against the dull yellow Tonka truck and wagon as he steps through the plastic cowboys and injuns.

He gets two steps in the hallway and stops. Something is different. Something is wrong. Bacon? On a school day? No, that's not it. Of course, the clutter in his room. She's about to let him eat before making him tidy up.

Down the stairs he goes but stops again upon seeing the clean living room. The empty beer bottles, the spilled food, the cigarette butts, potato chip crumbs, all gone. Newspapers and magazines collected and piled under the coffee table, the rocking chair ottoman no longer flipped over but back up against the wall by his dad's La-Z-Boy recliner. Even the small pillows against the now-straightened sofa cushions sit properly, as if company is coming.

His Mom must have been up early because it's the same in the kitchen. Except for the toaster and cutting board, on which sits an open package of bacon, half a loaf of Wonder bread, and a bucket of margarine stabbed by a knife, the kitchen counters are clear and clean. And what happened to all the empties?

Hissing wisps of smoke dance over the frying pan, redirecting his attention to his growing hunger. The window over the sink is slightly open and through the early morning darkness a cold, fresh breeze pushes the smoke around.

"Mom?"

No answer. Where is she?

Probably in the bathroom. Again. She's in there a lot lately, especially in the mornings. Even so it's not like her to leave food cooking on the stove.

He climbs on the corner chair at the small dining table. His favourite blue plate is set out, along with a knife and fork resting on a folded white paper towel. From this spot, feet dangling, he has a perfect view of the entire kitchen.

What a dull kitchen.

Everything is beige, brown, or dull green. The floor tiles, wallpaper, counters, cupboards and appliances, as if red—his favourite colour—or any bright colours have been banished. The worst are the matching stove and refrigerator. His father calls the colour almond, as if that sounds better. If anything, it sounds worse. Karl once called it wet-snot-green, after hearing Uncle Douglas say it. His dad didn't like that.

At least the pictures he drew at school help hide the ugly colour on the fridge. The latest is of a large ship about to enter the Welland Canal from Lake Ontario at Lock One. Mrs. Takahama, his teacher, wanted to hang it up in the classroom, but Karl made it especially for the kitchen. On purpose, he used the deepest red crayon for the hull, and the brightest blues and yellows for flags, hatches and other parts, all to add as much colour to the kitchen as possible. Luckily, his mom likes it enough to let him keep it on the fridge, unlike the one a while back of Toronto and the big buildings. For some reason, she doesn't care for the Toronto drawings, even though they get higher marks.

"Mom?"

Still no answer. Should he go find her? Maybe she's punishing him for teasing her about wanting to skip school. Of course he likes school and wants to go, and of course he knows Daddy often sleeps in on days after football games, and of course—but hold on—she said 'they,' didn't she?

Karl closes his eyes, thinks back to last night, how dark it was, how slow he had to walk. How, when he finally reached the basement, he found the guestroom light on, the door open. The cool, damp air smelled of cologne and cigarettes, a smell that got stronger when he pushed the door fully open. On the pullout sofa, on his side under the sheets lay Uncle Douglas. It took a bunch of shoulder shakes before he turned up his handsome face.

"Karl? What time is it? Why aren't you in bed?"

"Can we go to the canal tomorrow? You said it might be frozen. I want to see a ship trapped in the ice."

"I'd love to, sport, but I won't be around."

"What? Why not?"

"I have to get back to Toronto early, before rush hour."

"When are you coming back?"

"I can't say for sure."

"I hardly ever see you these days. Last season you were here every Sunday for football. But this year, hardly at all."

"I know. I know."

"Nowadays, whenever you leave, I worry that you'll never come back."

"Don't you ever worry about that, all right? I'll always find a way to see my favourite nephew."

"Promise?"

"Yes, I promise. Now, why don't you get back to bed?"

"There's a big mess upstairs. We should clean it up, together, before Mom gets mad. I don't like it when Mom gets mad at you. I think that's why you stay away longer."

"Sometimes, my young nephew, your mom just likes to get mad at me."

"No she doesn't. It was her idea to get Dad to invite you."

"Her idea? You sure?"

"I remember Dad being surprised. Me too."

"I see."

"So you're wrong about Mom. She's only mad when there's a reason, and the mess upstairs is a big one."

"Just let it go," Uncle Douglas said, before falling back asleep. Moments later, Karl's tiredness returned too. In fact, now he can't remember how be got back to bed.

A crackle and spatter from the frying pan reminds Karl of his hunger, but there's still no sign of his mom. He slips down from the chair. Just as his feet touch the floor she returns and he scoots back up.

"Where were you off to?"

"To see Uncle Douglas."

She walks toward him and pours a glass of orange juice, her head shaking slowly.

"You're not going anywhere except to get dressed and go to school. After you eat. We don't have time for delays."

So Uncle Douglas *is* still here. Karl sips from his drink, more to hide his grin than from thirst. The tangy delicious coolness settles him back in his seat while his mom gets busy at the counter. Somehow, she can turn over the bacon, load the toaster, make tea, start the coffee maker, and butter bread for his father's lunch, while still checking on him, as if knowing what's on his mind. When the toaster pops, her mind seems to be in another world, but then she responds to scrape butter on the toast. Just as the frying pan sizzles away and the kettle rumbles, almost ready to whistle.

This is his chance.

With the stealth he used last night, Karl climbs down from the chair and, hoping the kitchen noises shield his creaky steps, tiptoes down to the basement.

It's dark, damp, chilly. Even through his warm slippers he feels the coldness of the cement floor. Karl crosses his arms and rubs his shoulders while his eyes get used to the darkness. He has a couple of minutes at most before she notices him gone. Now that he's certain Uncle Douglas is there, his mind tries to figure out ways of talking him into talking his mom into letting him skip school and go see the frozen canal.

The air thickens as he approaches the guestroom. His nose twitches due to an unusual smell, a weird mix of familiar odours with a sickly sweetness. His heart beats quicker and inside his stomach, butterflies. It's like an adventure movie. The kettle whistles above him. The sound is muffled yet he still jumps. A warning? Bah, warnings are for chickens.

The guestroom door is shut this time, darkness in the crack underneath. That's no mystery though. Karl now remembers he turned the light off to let his uncle sleep. Karl twists the knob slowly and pushes the door open but can't pass beyond the doorway He's stopped by a thick stink-wall. Now he knows where that awful smell is coming from.

Beating his hands about him does nothing. Squeezing his nose with his thumb and forefinger helps allow him to slow his blinking enough to look at the bed. Among the scrambled white sheets, flannel blanket, and white pillow, his uncle lays on his back. He's wearing no pyjamas. His head is arched back, showing his Adam's apple. His tall body is spread out and covers the length of the bed while his big thing is in the open for the world to see.

"Uncle Douglas?"

No answer. Karl slowly steps forward, keeping his nose plugged. He has seen his uncle passed out before but never like this. Not with his neck and shoulders covered by a puddle of greyish brown liquid, mixed with solid specks of dull orange and dull green like the carrots and peas they had with the Hamburger Helper yester—yuck, yuck, yuck—it's barf.

For a split second, it seems funny, a joke, and Karl tries to laugh, but can't. He's woozy instead. When he opens his mouth to repeat his uncle's name, he wishes he hadn't. Like in some science fiction movie, the stink seems to gather in a whoosh and jump down his throat, reaching deep down to his belly, collecting, growing, and swirling like a tornado. Karl heaves and then sucks air into his mouth to keep it down, tightening his lips to trap the stomach storm. His next breath starts up a rush of stuff inside, flowing up to his lungs, and he heaves. Again he tries to hold it by gritting his teeth, but on the third heave it all gushes out on the floor. Gushes and gushes until there's nothing but dry, empty, painful coughs. It's as awful as last summer when his mom forced him to swallow that Ipecac medicine—he'll never forget that terrible word, Ipecac—after she thought he ate a poisoned pear. Like then, water now fills his eyes and turns to tears when he sees his own brown and green and orange barf on the floor.

At least it's in front of him, not on his pyjamas. Slowly he steps away, but then senses a presence behind him. He turns around. Three feet away, his mother looms over him, staring at him, her mouth open and eyes wide, terrified. Karl points at his uncle, his small hand and index finger shaking.

"I don't think Uncle Douglas is feeling well."

She gasps. As if she's also having trouble breathing and trying not to be sick. That makes Karl feel less ashamed about his accident, though she doesn't seem to have noticed that yet. After a couple of huffs and deep breaths, she kneels down to him, her voice clear.

"Go upstairs, sweetie."

"Is he drunk?"

She nudges Karl toward the stairs and then steps toward Uncle Douglas. Karl knows he should go but wants to know what's going on, what she'll do. Besides, if Uncle Douglas is sick, maybe he can help.

"Mom, is he all right?"

"Honey, please, just go, okay?"

"Do you want me to get Daddy?"

She shakes her head and points her finger toward the stairs. Karl starts to obey, then pauses to listen. She doesn't call out his uncle's name as he expects. By mistake, he lets out a little cough. His mother jerks around to face him. Her wild eyes flash in a scary way. He can't move.

"Karl Philip. Upstairs. Now!"

He bolts up the stairs, runs through the kitchen, but stops on hearing the violent sizzling and crackling from the frying pan. It's burning the bacon. Weirdly, the grease smell settles his tummy, which also makes his tears dry up. He walks up to the pan. A spatter of grease shoots up, arcs, and lands on his arm, making him wince, but not cry. He slides a chair against the stove, pulls himself up on his knees, and then pushes the frying pan to an unused element in the back. He reaches across and twists knobs until every oven light is off and the kitchen, the house, his fright, are all quiet.

A glance toward the basement gives no sign his mom, or Uncle Douglas, are coming up anytime soon. In a way, he's glad about that. Karl brings over his blue plate and helps himself to the unburned bacon strips in the pan. He stands in the middle of the kitchen and thinks about taking the plate downstairs to share with Uncle Douglas and ask his mom to make more. A tiny, sharp, cold gust of wind blows across his face, which somehow reminds him of her expression. So he takes the plate to his bedroom where in silence he munches on the crispy strips, happy at being able to use his hands.

Just as he swallows the last bite, Karl hears his mother's footsteps. He puts the empty plate on the floor, wipes his fingers on his pyjamas, expecting her to come in any second. Instead, she passes by his room and heads straight for the master bedroom. His parents' door closes behind her. He sticks his head out into the hallway where he can faintly hear his mother's frantic voice.

Karl edges closer to their room, close enough to catch some of the words, but far enough to retreat if necessary.

". . . choked . . . yes . . . no . . . disgusting . . . and Karl saw it all . . . awful, awful, John, awful."

There follows a few minutes of silence, except for some sobs, then a bunch of loud whispering, none of which he can make out. A commotion of creaking springs, rustling sheets, and feet sliding into slippers sends him back to his room. More footsteps, heavier ones, his father's, rumble through the hall and thunder down the stairs.

Several minutes later, his mom enters his room. She gives him a big tender hug that she holds for several seconds longer than normal. Her shoulders are shaking. When she lets go, he's glad to see she's changed from that awful bathrobe into jeans and an old grey sweatshirt. Perfume too, not strong, but something that smells sweet and fresh like peaches. It clears the greasy bacon odour, which Karl no longer finds pleasant, now that he's full.

"Karl, oh honey, sweetie, I'm so sorry I snapped at you," she says, wiping away a tear.

"What's going on, Mom?"

"Can you be a good young man and wait here, until we come get you?"

"What about school?"

"I'm afraid you won't be going today."

That's what he wanted earlier but now it's the other way around and he wishes he was at school.

"It's because of Uncle Douglas, isn't it?"

"Yes, but—"

Distant sirens cut off her answer. She puts up a hand for him to keep quiet. When the sirens become louder, she rushes out, closing the door after her, trapping him, like a prisoner. Soon the high pitched wails stop. Strangers' voices, live and over walkie-talkies, fill the house, along with many footsteps, heavy ones like his father's, thudding across the floors below, up and down the basement stairs.

Too bad his window looks out on the backyard, not the street where he could at least watch the flashing lights of police cars or ambulances or fire engines or whatever is out there. All he can see, surrounded by patches of snow and dead grass, are the two snowmen from yesterday, standing useless and lonely, between the leafless maple trees.

Every half hour or so, his mother or father checks on him, sometimes bringing Oreos with milk or potato chips with cream soda. Whenever he needs to use the bathroom, they wait until he's finished, which he hates. Over and over they say how pleased they are with his patience and promise to tell him everything later, as long as he stays in his room, quietly. It's funny to watch in a way because at one time his father will be calm and his mother nervous and the next time it's the other way around.

Still, he gets bored.

Yet whenever he picks up a Tonka truck or his remote controlled Porsche, he puts it down a minute later. Only last week he read through his entire Donald Duck comic book collection, including the special issues with Uncle Scrooge and Huey, Dewey, and Louie, so that's out. He could start the giant Taj Mahal puzzle but then remembers his promise to wait for his uncle to help and continues looking for something to do.

Karl's dozing on top of his covers when he wakes to a light tap at his door. Other than the moon's yellowish grey glow, twinkling around his navy blue curtains, it's dark. Both his mother and father enter, bringing in more light from the hallway and the living room. Karl is so good at telling time that he can read his father's watch upside down. It's eight-seventeen, almost an hour past his bedtime.

His father still has on those silly green cotton sweat pants and the faded yellow golf shirt. Karl's used to seeing him shaved and in a suit; these clothes don't look right. Like how a tuxedo would never look right on Uncle Douglas. A few wrinkles around his father's eyes show, even when he's not smiling. His mother, on the other hand, doesn't look as upset as earlier, though she's not smiling either.

They sit on the edges of his bed, one on each side, his mother by the window. His dad picks up the Tonka Truck and pokes at it until he gets an impatient look from his mom. He puts the toy down and speaks, in his deep and smooth storytelling voice.

"Son, I'm afraid we have something difficult to tell you. About Uncle Douglas. I know how close you two were, how much you loved him. This is why it's so hard to say this."

"Say what?"

"I'm afraid that, last night, Uncle Douglas passed away."

"Passed away?"

His father scratches the side of his head while his mom stares at the stars, or something outside. Karl supposes she's listening, but can't tell for sure.

"What I'm trying to say is that, well, your uncle is no longer with us."

"No longer with us?"

"Yes, like—do you remember when we lost Smokey?"

"Smokey? Smokey ran away. Uncle Douglas isn't a cat."

"No, of course he isn't, wasn't."

"Dad, stop fooling. Where is he? I want to talk to him."

"You can't talk to him, not where he's gone," his mother suddenly says.

Her gloomy voice bothers Karl and it seems her words have startled his father. Karl feels himself getting upset.

"Where's he gone? Tell me."

"Why, to heaven of course," his father says, as if he just came up with of that.

"To a better place," his mother adds, still staring out the window.

To Karl, it sounds like heaven and a better place aren't at all the same thing. His parents look how they do whenever they try to trick him into trying a new food like spinach or broccoli or porridge.

"What place? And when's he coming back?"

His mother puts one hand on Karl's knee and rubs his hair with the other.

"No, Karl, what we are saying is that he's not—"

His father interrupts by shaking his head. Karl, despite being more curious than ever, feels an odd wish for her not to finish either.

"So who won the Super Bowl?" Karl says.

"I thought you didn't care about the game."

"I'd still like to know who won."

His father grins like he did last summer in Niagara Falls when the policeman let him drive away without giving him a ticket.

"Dallas did, son. 24-3."

Karl knows that's Uncle Douglas's team so this is good news. He settles back in his bed to go to sleep. His parents look like they're going to stay until he does. Karl closes his eyes, keeps still.

They leave but forget to close his door tightly. From the hallway he hears his mother let out a heavy sigh, followed by what sounds like a sob. He's tempted to open his eyes.

"Are you all right, Helen?"

"How could I have allowed my son to see that?"

"He'll be fine. No way you could have prevented it."

"I suppose . . ."

"I still can't quite understand what happened though."

"He got drunk, John. His wild ways finally caught up to him."

"That's just it, Helen. If it happened several years ago, several months even, I wouldn't be as surprised."

"What do you mean?"

"I was so looking forward to sharing this."

"Sharing what?"

"Last night, at McCready's, Doug didn't drink much. I drank more than he did. Much more, I admit. I truly believe he was changing his ways. With what he had last night, even you wouldn't have gotten drunk, let alone sick."

"It didn't look like that this morning," she says.

"You mean the mess in the living room?"

There's a pause before Karl hears his father chuckle.

"Actually, that was me. I was pretty toasted. So for him to die that way, and for him to get so sick, it's just strange."

"Perhaps he had some after you came to bed."

"Perhaps, but it doesn't fit with how his mood was at the bar."

"How was his mood at the bar?"

"You know, it's hard to describe. He was quieter, almost contrite; especially after I shared our good news."

"You did what?"

"Sorry, Helen, I know you didn't want me to . . ."

"Never mind. I suppose it hardly matters now."

It's weird. Karl's mom sounds as if she's mad about something that she knew would happen anyway. And what's this good news?

"You should have seen his reaction. He was thrilled, for us, and anxious to help in any way he could."

Another pause before his father continues.

"Which is why I find it hard to believe he'd go on a drinking binge afterward, especially in our house."

"What are you saying, John?"

"I'm not really sure."

"You don't think there'll be an autopsy, do you?"

"An autopsy? Oh no, not at all. I spoke to the coroner. He seems satisfied it was an accident."

"Well, that's a relief."

"Stevenson, Douglas S. Born February 27, 1944, passed away in his sleep January 17, 1972, in St. Catharines, at the age of 27. Brother of Jonathon, uncle to Karl . . ."

Died peacefully, dearly departed, lovingly remembered, sadly missed, beloved so and so, adored such and such, all pleasant, respectful epithets adorning the adjacent death announcements: it only makes their absence in Doug's so conspicuous.

Perhaps, John thinks, setting the newspaper aside and picking up his cup of steaming coffee, with more of the tender care she usually takes in such things, Helen could have stretched accuracy a tad and squeezed in a few of those modifiers. If only to keep the announcement from looking so meagre next to the others. It does sound rather cold.

Then he lets out a reproachful sigh. How unfair to criticize his wife. After all, over the past three days he's done little other than observe Helen labour tirelessly over the funeral arrangements, taking care of details he would have neglected. True, she did so willingly, refusing all his offers to help. Like Jack Biltmore banning John's presence at the office for a full week, she insisted this was his time to mourn, to grieve.

John takes his coffee to the front window and begins pacing. The first snowflakes of today's predicted storm are falling. He swears the tiny bursts of white are expanding right in front of his eyes as they settle down and create a smooth cover on the street, driveways, roofs, trees, and lawns.

How he dreads the upcoming funeral, now just a few hours away. For one thing, who will attend, besides them? What kind of people? They included their phone number and address at the end of the death announcement in one of the Toronto dailies as well as the local paper. No one contacted them, which is strange considering Doug's popularity. Maybe his friends are not the kind to read newspapers. Then again, maybe it's not so much which individuals will appear but rather how he'll act toward them, and they toward him. Will they see through his grieving? He hates that word because, sadly, despite his optimism that Doug's ways had changed, John cannot avoid coming to the troubling conclusion his brother's death is a relief.

The pile of white on top of the hedges protecting the front porch is a good six inches high. He can no longer see the station wagon. John puts on his boots, gloves, trench coat, and steps outside. He clears the car as best he can, more than a little discouraged at how quickly new snow replaces what he's brushed away. Recent tire tracks are becoming invisible on the street. Nevertheless, John gets the big snow shovel from the shed in the back, and clears a swath from the backdoor to the car. He's glad there's no sidewalk to shovel, just one of the many attributes he loves about their home and street. Which is why he wants to stay.

The day after Doug's death, Helen hinted at not feeling comfortable living in a house in which someone died. John's sure part of it comes from her long-term desire for them to move to Port Colborne, where she grew up, where they got engaged. He has no wish to leave St. Catharines, not yet. He likes the Garden City and most of his real estate listings are close by. Also, Karl's school is an easy ten-minute walk. John uprooted often enough in his youth and would prefer not to put his child through that anguish. Helen, having lived in the same house until she married, admits moving would have been upsetting to her as a child.

While Karl's potential reaction to moving is one thing, his reaction to his uncle's death, or perplexing lack of one, is another. Normally a curious boy, Karl isn't asking his usual battery of discerning questions, or questions of any kind, except for the odd factual clarification.

Perhaps, as Helen suggests, their son is in denial. She's right in pointing out this lack of curiosity makes life easier. To John it feels like a copout not to explain. It's risky with a boy becoming wise to Santa Claus. They're better off addressing it sooner rather than later, before Karl's fertile imagination concocts something bizarre.

Refreshed from the shovelling, John wants to change his shirt but only gets as far as the kitchen. A beer would hit the spot, but then he'll want two or three more, which would affect his driving. Too dangerous in this weather. If only she had scheduled the funeral and burial for this morning, it'd be done already. He needs to do something to distract him from the accumulation of the white stuff. Then John remembers the boxes in the LTD.

The other day Helen asked him to take Doug's car to Toronto to look after his things. Armed with a large suitcase and a few boxes in the trunk, he looked forward to getting away for a few hours. But as soon as he was on the QEW, all alone, a rotten, empty feeling took over and stayed with him the entire drive. It intensified the instant he entered the lobby of his brother's hi-rise, near the Science Centre, where he felt like an intruder, or a looter, on edge every moment. If he heard a bark or a police siren or the door and lock of a neighbour, he would jump, afraid someone was about to catch him in the act. It helped that it was a furnished unit and Doug's few belongings packed quickly.

To avoid confusing Karl, John has been parking Doug's car around the street corner until they can dispose of it. He finds it blocked in by snow and has to swipe away a pile before he can open the trunk. He ignores a suitcase containing jeans, work pants, work shirts, fancy evening shirts and tie-dyed t-shirts, and lugs in three boxes, one by one, to the house and into the living room.

The heaviest he opens first. It's stuffed with paperback novels, new age books and magazines, and a stack of psychedelic and blues records by artists John has never heard of. He tries to imagine his brother in that apartment, wearing faded jeans with legs flopped over the sofa arm, watching television over the top of a book. He can't and finds that sad. Sifting through these boxes one day might reveal more about Doug. Not today though. He repacks it and takes it and the others to the basement.

A light is on in the guestroom, spooking John, causing him to stumble and nearly drop one of the boxes. A pungent whiff of ammonia, a mixture of Lysol or Pledge or Mr. Clean or Ajax—whichever was on sale—assaults his senses, as does the muffled melody of the Beatles' *Hey Jude.* He walks past the room, past the freezer and washer-dryer combo, and stacks the three boxes deep in the basement, among other containers packed with old clothes, Christmas ornaments, and Helen's childhood possessions.

John opens the guestroom door and the treble of the tinny transistor irritates his ears. On one side of the stripped bed, Helen is on her knees, in an old pair of jeans and light blue sweatshirt, her hair tied back in a ponytail, scrubbing the floor. She doesn't notice him. A pile of brown rags beside the green pail looks familiar. When he sees the loose brown strands hanging from the scissors, he smiles, glad she's finally come round to cutting up that ghastly old robe.

"Don't you think it's clean enough?" he says, and plops on the bed.

She jumps, turns her head around.

"Oh, John, I didn't hear you."

"You know, if you do this to all the rooms we can sell the house as brand new."

"Funny, what brings you down here?" she says, turning the radio down.

"Doug's things."

"Doug's things? They're here? In our house?"

"Not his clothes. I plan to take them to the Sally Ann tomorrow. But we'll keep the books, records, knick-knacks, ball caps, souvenir pucks, stuff like that. I figured you or Karl might want to help me sort through them someday."

"Not me. Just give it all away, or throw it away."

"What about Karl?"

"John, the less there is to remind us of Doug, I mean, of what happened, the better for all of us, especially our son. That may sound harsh but it'll make it easier for all of us to move on."

Deep down he knows she's right. No, not exactly. Deep down he's not sure she's right, but he respects her logic. Still, from a sense of sibling loyalty, he realizes there will never be, and probably never would have been, any other adult willing to defend his only brother. Regardless of the many issues between them, Doug is family, Doug is blood.

"Out of sight, out of mind, Helen, is that it? Are you trying to scrub his existence away?"

He intended to sound casual, teasing, but failed. Her body stiffens. She lets out a short breath, then a small sigh-like sound John can't peg. A half whimper, half chuckle, her way of saying she feels bad for how she gave the message but not the message itself. For some reason, he finds it difficult to express the same for what he said.

Without warning her eyes glaze over, as if she's about to cry, before they grow bigger and became radiant. The last time he saw that lusty look was two months before, after he returned from a conference in Kitchener, the same weekend she took Karl to Toronto for his birthday. The look excited him then and it excites him now.

She tosses the scouring pad in the pail, gets up on her knees, gently pushes him back on the bed. She unties her hair and climbs on top of him. Her hands caress his face and she kisses him quickly and deeply, cutting short his breath for a moment. She loosens his tie and begins unbuttoning his shirt, one by one, while he moves his hands about her smooth body, over her soon to be growing belly. When she gets to his belt, he sits up and nods toward the ceiling. She puts her hands behind his head and whispers in his ear.

"Don't worry about Karl. He'll be busy with his new suit a while. Besides, he knows he's banished from the basement, indefinitely."

Karl sucks in his belly and strikes a catalogue style pose in front of the full-length mirror next to his closet, beaming with pride at his brand new three-piece suit. It's his first one ever, navy blue with cool silver pin stripes. The vest makes him look bigger, tougher.

While his father was in Toronto for his business trip the other day, he and his mom went on the highway to the big shopping centre and the big department store where she let him choose the suit he wanted. It was a task he performed with what she called earnest intensity, whatever that means. It probably means how he paced back and forth among the racks. While the salesman was nice and didn't care how long he took, his mom was in a hurry. She only let him try on three before forcing him to pick one. Then she chose the plain white shirt and light blue clip-on tie with the tiny silver snowflakes. He didn't like her doing that but now, seeing how it looks in his mirror, Karl has to admit she has good taste, like his father and uncle always said.

Though the shirtsleeves stick out over his hands, his mom promises he'll grow into them and she can fold them back for now. His main issue is the tie: it keeps drooping from the top of his shirt. He's about to try again when his mom enters.

She's wearing the black dress she bought from the same store she bought his suit. It's long and with her smoothly brushed brown hair flowing down, she's as pretty as he's ever seen her. Around her neck hangs a pearl necklace she also bought the other day, on sale. He redoes the pose for her.

"You know, this suit highlights blond streaks in your hair. I never noticed them before."

"It does?"

"Definitely the greenness of your eyes."

She kneels down and helps fold back the sleeves under his jacket. He squirms as she does up the top button. Again she has to show how the tie works before she puts it in his impatient hands. Fumbling, yanking, twisting, he finally clips it on. Another pose, this time tugging his lapels, swaying his shoulders. He likes the fact his mother's smile stays.

"Don't you look smart dear? You like the suit?"

Karl nods eagerly.

"Why not show Daddy?"

He finds his father in the master bedroom, standing in front of the big oak dresser mirror. His white shirt looks different from the one his father was wearing before lunch. His tie is different, a toughie, Karl thinks, as he watches his father's thick fingers fuss with the long grey, silky thing. However, instead of getting mad, his father is humming. Everyone's in a good mood all of a sudden.

When Karl tries to grab his own tie in the same way as his father is doing, it falls to the floor. He glances at it as if it's someone else's litter and then lifts his head. His dad looks important in his black suit, older but just as handsome as in the black and white framed wedding picture in the centre of the dresser. His mom's jewellery box is still open, silver and gold shining from the tiny mirror in the box top.

"Daddy, what's a fun real?"

"You mean a funeral, don't you?"

"Yeah, that."

His father loops the last loop in his tie and yanks it. He notices Karl's tie on the floor, picks it up with one hand and with the other grabs Karl around the waist and lifts him onto the big bed. In one motion, with no fumbling, he slides the clip between collar and neck, snaps it in place.

"Now you're fashionably handsome, ready to go."

Karl tugs at it. It holds. Then he repeats his question.

"Well son, the funeral is our way of showing how much your Uncle Douglas meant to us."

"Oh. Is it better than an oh topsy?"

"An autopsy? That's got nothing to do—where'd you hear that word?"

"Uh, nowhere. Is a funeral like a party?"

"I suppose, in a way."

"Then why's Mom acting weird?"

"What do you mean?"

"Well, one second she's okay, then she's sad, then mad, and sad, and then okay again."

Karl's father reaches into the jewellery box, pulls out a thin and straight and golden object, and slides it over his tie.

"We're all sad Karl. It was a sudden unexpected loss. We miss him and wish he was still with us."

"He's been away many times before, no one made such a big deal about it."

"It's different this time."

"How? What's different, this time?"

His father pauses and Karl thinks he'll get heck for his tone of voice.

"Don't you know?" Karl adds, carefully.

"Yes, Karl, I know. What I don't know is, well, it's just that, oh I wish I knew of a better way to explain it to you."

I wish you did too, Karl thinks, but doesn't want to push his luck by saying it out loud.

"Uncle Douglas was going to take me to see the frozen ships in the frozen canal."

"I'm not sure the canal freezes, Karl."

"Uncle Douglas says it does."

"Nevertheless, it's winter and in winter the canal closes, so there won't be any ships, frozen or otherwise."

"Are you sure? Can we go there later, after?"

"Maybe, son, maybe. We'll see how the day goes."

Karl gets back to his room where he admires himself in the mirror again, fiddles with his tie. It falls off. Karl picks it up and sits on the small plastic chair at his student desk with his back to the window, his feet on his Captain's bed where he keeps his most treasured items like his piggy bank and stamp and coin collections. As well as his most secret ones. He pulls a folded old sweatshirt from a drawer, opens it up to withdraw a framed picture he leans against his pillow.

Karl climbs on the bed and, on his stomach, chin in palms, he stares at the photo of him and Uncle Douglas. It's one of those souvenir pictures where people stick their heads out of barrels, Niagara Falls in the background. It was taken back when Uncle Douglas's hair was long and curly and fell below his shoulders, like a rock star. His eyes are blue like the water just before it tumbles over and he's wearing the smile that got the camera girl to give them an extra copy. According to his mom, Uncle Douglas doesn't like to have his picture taken, though he seemed okay with it that time.

"You are coming back aren't you, Uncle Douglas? Like you promised? I'm scared. This time it seems different."

Karl sighs, tries to clip his tie back on again, fails. He rolls on his back, closes his eyes, and recalls the other night, as he often has over the past three days, each time the faith in his uncle's words shrinking a bit more.

Before he can get far, footsteps and the sound of doors opening and closing break the quiet in the house. It tells him they'll be leaving any moment. He sits up, photo in hand.

"I want to believe you, Uncle Douglas. If you're gone a long time, I can wait. But maybe you can send me a message or something."

"Karl, are you ready?"

"Yeah, Mom, coming."

He puts the photo away with care, grabs his tie and runs downstairs. His mother is waiting for him at the back door. She watches, ready to help, while he puts on his shiny new loafers and hooded parka with the mittens hanging from a string. She groans when he turns around.

"Oh, that silly tie."

She tells him to wait, leaves for the kitchen, and returns a moment later with a safety pin.

After seeing the name, Applewood Funeral Home, in plain block letters on a plain brick building, Karl is surprised to find it so dark inside. The dim light from the chandeliers barely touch the deep brown walls. Walls covered with sad paintings of dark fruits and eerie forests, along with several gloomy black and white photos of old people. Thick, red and black carpets run down two long and narrow hallways. There are flowers everywhere, in vases, on dark brown tables with rug tablecloths. Karl feels trapped, like in some mysterious evil castle. Combined with the chalky, semisweet odour and creepy organ music, Karl realizes this is not a fun place.

His father hangs up their coats and leads them through a wide doorway into a large square room that has no chairs. They are the only people in it. Except, on a long table at the far end of the room, there rests a long rectangular chocolate coloured box. In the box, laying on a puffy, white cloth, a sleeping man who looks like Uncle Douglas.

He looks much better than Uncle Douglas looked last time, in the basement, though silly in that baby blue suit. It looks like one Karl's father owns. Someone has cut his hair too, which makes him and Karl's dad look more like brothers. Flowers surround the box, white and yellow ones, smelling like fruity medicine. Uncle Douglas hates flowers. He certainly would never come to a weird place like this, if not forced to. Also, something about his face looks unreal. It's too smooth, like those spooky wax people they saw together in Niagara Falls.

Karl gasps. Maybe it's not him. Maybe this is a fake, an actor. Then his father moves toward the box. Thinking he's supposed to follow, Karl takes a step, but his mother holds him back. He looks at her but she's too busy staring straight ahead, as if afraid Uncle D—or rather the person in there—is about to move.

His father puts a hand on his heart, mumbles something at the shined up face. Karl once heard, on TV probably—no, maybe it was in a book—anyway, he read or heard someone describe a person as having a blank expression. Seeing his father's face now helps Karl understand what that means. It's hard to tell whether his father is sad, glad, mad or whatever. Whenever the Bills lose a close game, he'll get angry and look the way he looks now, blank.

His mother loosens her hold a moment and Karl thinks she's going up too, and then it'll be his turn. Though part of him wants to see, if only to prove he's right, Karl is glad when she stays put.

But she doesn't stay put for long. Next thing he knows, they are out of that room and into another that's like the inside of a miniature church, and much brighter. All the half-sized pews are empty. They sit quietly in the middle until a minister comes in and begins talking. His voice is boring and Karl doesn't listen to a word. He's relieved when it's over.

Outside, the sky is bright clear, the winter air no longer damp but refreshing. Hard to believe such thick clouds could disappear so fast. The snow stayed; it's white all around, a perfect winter day. Karl thinks about making snow angels but figures his mom won't like it, especially while he's wearing his new suit.

His father scans the parking lot. It's not a long search because there are only three other cars. When he doesn't find what he's looking for his blank face becomes an angry face. He slaps the roof of the station wagon, causing snow to fall at the tires.

"Damn it."

"Honey, don't swear. What's the matter?"

"I thought for sure Violet would be here."

Karl also wonders why his babysitter hasn't joined them. She's like family, she knows Uncle Douglas too. He feels bad he hasn't thought of her till now. Then again, as with Uncle Douglas, he rarely sees her. Still, she should be here. Unless, maybe, like Karl, she doesn't believe it's really Uncle Douglas in there.

"Why would you think that, John?"

"Well, why wouldn't I?"

Karl considers sharing his reason for her not being there but is afraid to start something.

"Don't be so hard on her. Violet hasn't been well lately, even you commented on that."

"I did? No matter now, I suppose. Karl will just have to come along."

"To the graveyard? John, you can't be serious."

"Well, without Violet—"

"You mean you counted on her to take Karl home?"

"Sure, how did you think we'd manage it?"

"I want to go to the graveyard," Karl says, not exactly sure what it is.

"I don't know, John. How about I drop you off and take our son home? We can come back for you later?"

"And go to the canal?" Karl says.

"Yes, we can do that in the meantime," his mother says.

"Out of the question. I don't want to go by myself."

His mom has no answer for that and, within a minute, they're on their way.

Karl's father drops them off while he looks for a cleared spot to park the car. Hand in hand, Karl and his mother plod through the snow, zigzagging among the upright stones, to a row of unfolded grey chairs, all cushioned with snow.

While his mother swats at three of the seats with her gloves, Karl steps to the edge of the big empty rectangular hole. It's like a bathtub in the earth, only deeper and longer. A piece of wood sticks out of the ground, just outside the hole, with a number painted on.

"What's that?" he whispers, pointing at the number.

"When we get the headstone, that's where it'll go. The number helps them keep track."

"Oh."

Karl's about to ask what a headstone is when he spots two strange men behind them in black jeans and leather jackets. They both have stringy, shoulder-length hippy hair and look serious. One is tall with a long dark beard with lots of grey. The shorter one is darker, rougher, though not in a scary way because of his small nose and ears. These men weren't in the Applewood place.

Whoever they are, they act as if they're in the right place but don't sit down or even come closer. Karl stares at them until the older one stares back, making Karl blush and turn away.

His mother nudges Karl to straighten and look forward. The chocolate coloured box from the funeral home is there now, completely shut, hiding whatever is inside, Karl happily notes. The minister talks about ashes and dust as the box lowers down the hole. While his parents pray, Karl glances over at the strangers. They smile and Karl smiles back.

When it's done, Karl's father walks off with the minister. His mother waves at some people putting flowers down by another grave. She drags him along, nearly twenty yards. Up close, Karl recognizes the older couple, the Templetons, who have no children and live down the street. He lost a Frisbee in their yard once and had to trespass to get it back. While no one caught him at the time, it's possible they were spying from a window and are going to tell on him now.

He tries to break away but his mother holds his hand tightly. Just before they reach the couple, he gives a hard tug at her dress. She stops to give him a mild but sharp glare, and then he points to where his father stands. She nods and lets him go.

The two strange men are talking to each other and he wanders in their direction. The older one, who looks even older than Karl's dad, rubs his beard with skinny but strong looking fingers. The shorter one reminds Karl more of his uncle. Not as handsome but the same age. He also has a nice smile, and twinkling eyes. Neither are wearing a hat or gloves. The older one has a silvery bracelet around his wrist.

"Who are you guys?" Karl says.

"I'm Craig, and you must be Karl," the shorter one says, putting out his hand, which Karl shakes.

"How do you know who I am?"

"Your Uncle spoke a lot about you."

"He did?"

"Oh yes, he was very proud of his nephew."

Karl's smile amuses the men. The taller one bends down and introduces himself as Gareth. His breath smells like peppermint and cigarettes and some kind of booze, not beer.

"How do you know my uncle?" Karl says, to Gareth.

"We're old chums."

"Chums. Uncle Douglas always says that word, and you speak like he does. Are you from England too?"

"Not only am I from England, young man, but I'm also from the north, Newcastle."

"The Magpies," Karl says.

"Well, well, well, you know your football," Gareth says.

"Football? You mean soccer, right?"

"Sure."

"My dad's from Newcastle too. He told me about the England soccer teams. He doesn't talk like you and Uncle Douglas. Well, a little maybe, but he talks more normal, and he cheers for Sunderland. Mom says he lost—"

Something wraps itself around one of Karl's mittens and tugs at his arm. By the hard squeeze, he knows it's his mother's hand and that she's not happy.

"I thought you were going straight to your father."

Karl points up at Craig and Gareth with his free hand. She grabs that one as well and pulls it down.

"Don't point, Karl."

"Mom, these are friends of Uncle Douglas."

"I see. Go join your father. I'll be there in a minute."

Karl obeys, but stops after a few steps. When Craig and Gareth introduce themselves, his mother says nothing and refuses to shake their hands. They say how sorry they are for the family loss. She just nods and says thanks, though too quickly. This is not like her, Karl thinks. She'd never let him get away with being rude like that.

"I sense we've upset you, Mrs. Stevenson," Craig says.

"That depends on what you said to my son. Specifically, what did you say to him about my brother-in-law?"

"What do you mean?" Craig says.

"The boy was infatuated with his uncle, thought him a saint. No need to hear about things he's too young to grasp."

Gareth steps forward, smiling, though not in the same friendly way he smiled at Karl.

"With all due respect, Mrs. Stevenson, your son seems every bit the clever boy Doug described. I'd be wary of keeping things from him, things he's liable to find out, or work out, on his own."

The accent seems to surprise his mother as much as it did Karl, as she becomes quiet. Then she clears her throat.

"I take it he won't find anything out from you two."

Her tone shocks Karl but also warns him he'd better get moving. Barely seconds after reaching his destination, his mother joins them and whispers something to his father. When Karl looks back, the two men are out of sight.

"Son, what did those men say to you?" his father says, kneeling down, putting his hands on Karl's shoulders.

"Why? Are they bad men? They seemed nice."

"I didn't say they were bad men. I'd just like to know what you talked about."

"Nothing. They said Uncle Douglas was proud of me."

"In what way?" his mother says.

"Beats me. That's when you showed up. Can we go to the canal now?"

"You still want to go, do you?" his father says.

"Yeah, I want to see a ship stuck in the ice."

"I told you before Karl, the canal isn't frozen."

"Bet you an ice cream it is."

"You're on, son."

"See," Karl says, pointing east.

On the other side of the winter drained and snow laden canal, among a set of low-rise structures, and between two cranes, a ship is in dry dock: the *D. H. John Henry*, hailing from St. Catharines.

"That ship there. It's frozen."

John laughs and is happy to see Helen smile too. It is amusing because, from their son's angle, the locked-in ship indeed appears frozen in place.

No doubt encouraged by their reactions, Karl declares himself the bet winner. Of course, it would be easy to escort him across the bridge, or even across the canal itself through the snow, to prove him wrong. John chooses to concede.

Karl doesn't want his treat right away, preferring instead to spend more time at the canal. To John's surprise, Helen does too. She surprises him further by ignoring the snow and sitting on a bollard, in a leaning "L" shape, body upright with her legs together pointing straight to the canal, palms pressed behind her back.

"This is how I used to sit on these as a kid," she says.

It looks uncomfortable to John but when he says so, he gets a frown in response.

"Anyway, my friends and I would sit like this, chatting away, waiting for the ships to sail by, hoping to see a foreign one with foreign sailors, maybe even catch some coins."

"That sounds like fun," Karl says.

"It sure does," John says.

Clouds pass overhead, driven by a cool wind that blows across Helen's dress, lifting it. She doesn't notice. She's in another world, relaxed, despite a few tears running down her cheek. She doesn't try to fight them as usual; good to see her release some emotion.

"You know, Karl, I must have watched dozens of ships like that so often they became like family."

John nods. The lonely trapped ship captures his interest too. Why is this vessel in dry dock for the winter? There is no activity around the machinery to give a clue, no industrial noise of any kind, just a soft whirr of the wind. A closer look reveals jagged, staggered parts of the hull where pitch black turns to deep red.

"Well, I'll be darned, Helen, it's our ship. They're painting it."

Helen grabs John's hand. "Yes, I noticed." She smiles at him and then addresses Karl.

"As kids, we used to guess how many gallons of paint it took for a single coat, and then how many coats. How many gallons do you think, Karl?"

"I don't know, ten thousand?"

"You're a bright lad, Karl," John says. Try and figure it out some day. It'd be a different kind of puzzle."

"So what happens when the ice melts, Mom?"

Helen pulls Karl closer. John squeezes in on the small space left on the bollard. She brushes their son's hair back with her hand before speaking.

"In spring, when the ice melts and the canal fills up with water again, the *D. H. John Henry*, the freshly painted *D. H. John Henry*, will sail between Lake Ontario and Lake Erie, back and forth on countless trips via the Welland Canal, carrying cargo from one port to another. Since this ship is a laker—"

"Laker? Isn't that a basketball team?"

"Yes, but it's also a type of ship. All kinds of vessels go through the canal but two kinds carry heavy freight: lakers and salties. The up-and-down shape of the hull is sharper with lakers, the decks are flatter. Salties, on the other hand, are ocean ships and need wider hulls to handle the big waves they have to contend with. Lakers like this transport cargo between Great Lakes ports in Canada and the USA."

"I never knew that," John says, impressed. He's aware of his wife's fondness for the canal but never realized it went beyond simply enjoying the sight of the ships.

"What kinds of things do they carry?" Karl says.

"All kinds. Solids, liquids, gasses but for lakers it's primarily grain and industrial material like steel and ore. What's fascinating is how it's all hidden underneath the hatches. The decks are always clear and empty. You can't tell what a ship is transporting unless you already know, ask, or look inside."

Helen seems to be enjoy giving this little lesson and becomes disappointed when their son runs out of questions. They let him wander off, within eyesight but out of earshot. Helen then sits up ands let John squeeze beside her on the bollard.

"I'm glad today's over, Helen. I think it went well, don't you?"

"I didn't like seeing Karl talk to those men."

"Funny, I think I recognized them from the bar the other night. In fact, I'm sure one was the bartender."

"Good grief, John, don't tell me they're from Niagara. I thought they were from Toronto."

"Trust me, Doug's got friends all over Niagara too."

"Well, if those men are from around here, I'd like to—oh, never mind."

There we stood in Arrivals at Aeroquay One, Toronto's modern new airport. All that glass, all that sun, gleaming with such optimistic energy. Amplified by a boisterous crowd of at least a hundred people. So busy, so loud, so diverse. Black, White, Indian, Chinese—you'd never have seen such an array in our WASPY bubble of St. Catharines.

Weary travellers kept emerging every few seconds from behind a pair of frosted glass doors—immigrating families, older couples returning from Florida vacations, singles too, pilots, stewardesses, businessmen—pushing carts filled with bags, greeted by one to a dozen relatives and friends. And my poor husband, till that day so forbearing and confident in handling the bureaucratic formalities of his younger brother's immigration, now fidgeting, biting his nails, needing to excuse himself again. I was the pregnant one and here John was having to go more often than me.

He had just gone out of sight when the doors slid open for a young couple drifting through, arm in arm, like royalty, the other passengers making way. The buzz quietened save for a low whistle at which the young woman demurred in a haughty but practiced manner. Her long, perfectly groomed black hair framed a china doll face in the shape of a curvy diamond. And those eyes. She looked like a movie star. Her rather short skirt showed off a pair of slim, tanned legs.

Yet that exotic allure was no match for her companion's casual beauty. His thin but solid frame expressed a manly ruggedness to match his squared chin. Not a fan of long hair for men, the soft waves in this man's shoulder-length mane converted me. His deep blue eyes confidently laughed as they roamed the airport hall. Unlike the superficial features of the girl, his bore a natural grace that could never be affected. It was arrogant and humble at the same time. He was the most physically perfect man I had ever seen.

When those roaming eyes caught mine, they halted. The cobra stare seemed to penetrate my inner self, commanding like an invader, as if flexing its power but choosing not to exercise it. The man started to approach. I tensed up, shut my eyes, and counted out steamboats—one, two, three—before I felt a sensation down my arm from a warm hand touching above my elbow.

"Mrs. Helen Stevenson, I presume," the voice said. Its tone was neutral but the British accent carried a smidgeon of mockery, or at least irony. I nodded meekly, unable to speak. "I am Doug Stevenson, your brother-in-law."

My face heated up. I stammered something foolish but somehow managed to shake his hand. All John had shown me was an old black-and-white photo from when they were children, a time when Douglas looked more like John. God how different the two were now. No one could have guessed a lean man with such rebellious blond hair would be related to my brown-haired John, who was shorter and stockier, albeit in a more powerful way. The two would have made great teammates in football, John at running back, Douglas at wide receiver. While John was handsome in his own way, off the field there would be no question Douglas would win over the head cheerleader, and most if not all the others. Of course, I was never a cheerleader.

John returned in time to rescue me before I made a complete and utter fool of myself. I watched with fascination as the brothers greeted each other. Their smiles were genuine but their embrace appeared forced.

"I see you two have met."

"Lovely, John. Much prettier than the picture you sent."

"Thank you," I said. Compliments on my looks came often enough that such words rarely affected me. But to hear them in that rich accent did bring out a blush.

"And when's my little nephew on the way?"

I instinctively patted my belly. "Two months. But she could be a niece."

Douglas laughed, as if I had said something impossible. Then a cough interrupted us. In my dizzying discomfort, I'd forgotten about the girl. Up close, her glamour lost much of its splendour. She inserted herself between us to put her arms around Douglas's waist. He introduced her—I didn't catch the name at first—and explained they met while waiting for the plane in London. As we chatted, the girl kept brushing my husband's arms and laughing after almost every comment he made. I could tell by his slight stutter that John liked it. Having never experienced jealousy before, I couldn't say that's what I felt toward this girl; I just knew she was trouble.

"Perhaps we could give Angeline a lift into Toronto," Douglas said, once we had depleted our arsenal of small talk.

Fat chance, I thought, and waited for John to say so in a more diplomatic way. But once it seemed he was pondering a detour I intervened.

"I'm afraid we're going the other way."

"Oh, where do you live?" Angeline said.

"St. Catharines. It's about sixty miles. The other way."

"I know where St. Catharines is."

Her cattiness was lost on the two men so I let it go. She then fished in her alligator purse for a business card, which she held out between John and Douglas like a bone. When the two puppy dogs hesitated, I snatched it from her and walked off, expecting my husband and his brother to follow. John did but Douglas held back to kiss her goodbye, on the lips even. After they had just met that day.

The drive home was quiet, the lake uninspiring, the industrial scenery flat and dull. Douglas kept looking back, no doubt pining over that model—according to what the card claimed—and John, never one for talking while driving, kept his attention on the road.

That left me wondering what had gotten me all worked up. Then we came upon the sprawling Ford plant in Oakville.

"I hear they're hiring," I said, to Douglas.

"Yes," John said, as if I had just solved a puzzle. "I hear it's a terrific place to work. Strong union. Good pay."

"Excuse me, what?" Doug said. "Oh, you know, I'm not sure I'd be up for anything like that."

"Oh?" I said. "What are your plans?"

"Not sure, really. How about you, John? What is it you do for a living again?"

"I sell houses."

"That sounds interesting, and rewarding."

"It is. In fact, I sold the house Helen's parents live in now. That's how we met."

"So you were the commission," Douglas said, to me, but it made John laugh.

I giggled, though it troubled me Douglas did not know what John did for a living. What had they discussed in those dozens of correspondences? If John found it appropriate to send a photo of me then surely they would have shared more about each other.

"When I first came to Canada," John said, "I'd have killed to work at Ford or GM or someplace like that."

"I'm sure," Douglas said, no doubt sensing as I did that he'd just been given a mini-lecture.

A thin haze of smog, along with a sulphurous odour, greeted our approach to the Burlington Bay Skyway. John slowed to pay the toll, while I pointed to the right to the massive Stelco plant fronting the Hamilton skyline.

"Are they hiring too?" Douglas said, before I could explain I was only pointing it out as a tour guide. His ensuing chuckle precluded the tension returning, at least for the rest of the drive.

A long stretch of flat agricultural countryside separated Lake Ontario on the left from the Niagara escarpment on the right. Pleasant but not exciting, perfectly suiting the small talk about the unusually warm weather, driving on the right hand side of the road, highway sign comparisons, and other chitchat until the sign welcoming us to the city of St. Catharines.

Minutes later, we were in our downtown apartment with Douglas's bags filling the hallway. I offered to cook dinner though not sure what food we had. Fortunately, neither Douglas, who had eaten on the plane, nor John, were hungry.

"I'm sure you're exhausted," John said, sounding more as if describing himself.

"Let's find a pub," Douglas said, "the three of us. To celebrate—yes, to celebrate the bloody plane not crashing."

I laughed but John didn't say anything, so I gave him my husband a light shove.

"Going out for a drink with Douglas sounds like fun."

"That's the spirit. Amazing girl, big brother. Now what's a good place?"

John and I weren't ones for bars and had no clue where to go. So we stepped outside and walked about. Apparently, Douglas had a radar for these things and quickly found a place just off St. Paul Street. Amidst the murky smoke and seedy patrons, one could see little and it seemed impossible to find an empty table. John and I exchanged helpless looks.

Douglas broke away from us to slalom through the crowd and somehow succeeded in finding one. He surprised me and horrified John by ordering a full tray of small beer glasses. The waitress didn't think the request odd, though her attention was distracted. After placing the last glass on our table, Douglas stroked her wrist.

"What's your name, sweetheart?"

"It's not Sweetheart."

She pulled away and walked off in a huff. Instantly I liked her. Her nice figure and blonde hair complemented the prettiness of her girl-next-door face.

"I hope all the birds in this town aren't as uptight as that one. I hope they're more like you, Helen."

"Doug, here in Canada we refer to women as women. We treat them with respect, more than you might be used to giving."

"Ah, she liked it, big brother, just you watch."

We were thirsty and the glasses emptied quickly. With only a nod from Douglas, the waitress replaced the empty glasses with half a dozen more while I switched to Canada Dry. The beer livened up our conversation. One could not have recognized us as the same laconic threesome driving back from the airport. The music was loud and forced us to huddle to speak, though even then we had to shout. Thank goodness the band took frequent breaks. During one, our waitress came back with refills, set them down, then lingered, swaying back and forth, empty tray against her belly, until Douglas looked up.

"Excuse me, but where are you from?"

"London."

"England?"

"There's another one?"

"Sure. London, Ontario, my home town."

"What a coincidence."

"I'm Janet."

Douglas shook her offered hand. "And what do you do for fun in this town, Janet?"

"Since you ask, I'm off in an hour. There's a party after work. Maybe you'd like to come along?" Douglas appealed to John with a silent look. Something in John's face alarmed Janet who then said. "Oh, did I interrupt something?"

"My brother and I have not seen each other for ten years," Douglas said.

"Is that so? You guys can come too, if you want."

Her offer was sincere. I was tempted until John shook his head, nodding toward my belly.

"We should go," John said. "Stay if you wish, Doug."

"I do wish."

John pulled out a spare key, which he dropped on the table, along with money to cover the bill.

"I feared it would be like this," John said, while opening a beer back in our apartment, his first words since we were in the bar.

"Like what? He's young, and in a new country."

"Even as a kid he was wild, just like our uncle."

"Then why did you invite him to come here? I mean, all that effort, the delayed honeymoon."

"Don't remind me of the honeymoon. It'll just make me feel worse. I'll make it up to you."

"That's not my point, John, and you know it," I said, now a little frustrated too.

"What was your impression of him?"

The question took me aback because it seemed a test of something.

"He's charming."

"Yes, he is that."

"Cheer up. Bills season begins tomorrow. 1964 could be the year."

This brought a smile to his face. I decided to go to bed to ensure we ended this strange day with a positive thought.

I slept in till noon and rose with the hope John's spirits had improved. Instead, they had deteriorated, evident by the sour look that greeted me on my way to the kitchen. He looked rough, as if he hadn't come to bed. He didn't even have a cup of tea or coffee in front of him. The only thing he'd accomplished was to turn on the television on which three men droned on about the upcoming game. I began to boil water for tea.

"What's the matter?" I said, my back to him. "Where's Douglas?"

"The answer to your second question answers the first."

Seeing my bewildered look, he pointed at brother's unpacked bags, left in the same spot as the night before.

"You mean he never came home? Maybe we should call the pol—"

Then the front door opened and in walked Douglas, bright and cheerful, wearing the same clothes he'd worn on the plane. I couldn't help a smile but John glared at him.

"Morning folks. Boy do I need a shower and a nap—oh, don't look at me like that, big brother."

"Where were you all night?" John said, his eyes violent, his lips trembling.

Douglas muttered something to me, perhaps a greeting or an apology, then went to his room. The shower started as the Star Spangled Banner began playing. I suggested to John he sit by the television and let me bring him some tea and something to eat. He consented but still seemed intent on nursing his anger into a rage. This was a side of John I had never seen before. Not even a thirty-one point offensive explosion by the Bills in the first quarter could mollify my husband.

Douglas rejoined us during the second quarter and quickly succumbed to the atmosphere by aping John's gloom. Opposites physically, their stubborn brooding belied the sibling connection. No apology was likely to come from either man. While I could see

John needing to learn tolerance, I fully supported my husband in this. It was drearily uncomfortable until an idea came to me.

"How about I take Douglas for a little tour."

"Good idea," John said, glancing at his brother who nodded.

It was a pleasant end of summer day, ideal to show off the Garden City. I began at the top, with Port Dalhousie and Lakeside Park. From there, we drove along Martindale Road where Douglas had me slow whenever we caught a glimpse of the Henley Regatta, which he had heard about.

"The best natural course in the world," he said. "Reckon there are any clubs around here?"

"I imagine there would be. Why?"

"I rowed competitively long ago. It'd be nice to take it up again. I miss it."

This reference to England teased my curiosity but I did not want to risk upsetting him with questions too soon. We continued on. Douglas seemed uninterested in the vineyards, orchards, and green countryside, judging by his taciturnity and occasional nodding off.

"Are you from this town?" he said, as if the question had been in his head a while.

"No, but not too far away. A place called Port Colborne on Lake Erie, at the southern end of the canal."

"I'd love to see it."

"It's small, nothing special."

"If it produces women as pretty as you, Helen, it's special. At least in my book."

I made a face that made him chuckle. I couldn't deny his request. It took minutes to see my hometown and drive by my parents' home. Fortunately, they were away. I wasn't sure I wanted to introduce them to Douglas yet. I drove around a bit before turning back toward the Welland Canal.

"Hey," he said. "Let's watch that ship go through."

"Absolutely," I said, pleasantly surprised.

I parked next to a small family eating ice cream cones by their station wagon. The ship was about to enter the lock. As the giant gates opened, I saw it was the *D. H. John Henry*. I rushed toward the canal's edge to sit on a bollard. The sun gleaming on the water obscured my view but its warmth was enjoyable.

"That ship," I said, pausing to let Douglas squeeze in beside me. "It was passing through when John asked me to marry him."

"My brother proposed to you at a canal?"

"You don't understand. I love the canal, the ships, for me this was the perfect place. And this was the perfect ship to witness our happy moment. As you know, Henry is John's middle name so the John Henry part is obvious. But the initials, they stand for, 'Divine Helen,' according to John. Silly, I know, but so sweet."

"I suppose if I'd been the one to come to Canada first then the 'D' could stand for my name and the 'H' for yours."

This struck me as a queer thing for him to say, improper even. I stared at him, unsure whether to read any disrespect in this. His face was impassive.

By now the ship was fully encased in its concrete cage. Water spilled out the northern end until the level in the lock matched that on the other side. The change in elevation was slight when the ship exited downbound.

"This lock isn't as dramatic as the others," I explained. "It's purpose is not to raise or lower the ship but to control the water levels in the system."

"Ah ha," Douglas said. "Now tell me, why was John so put out about last night?"

"Put out?" I said.

"Don't play innocent," he said, his grin too ambiguous to interpret.

"I don't know what you mean."

"I don't think John had much fun last night but you looked like you enjoyed yourself."

"Give your brother time to adjust. He's not as wild as you appear to be."

"And you are?"

He took my hands in his and I felt a tingle in my wrists that compelled me to look away. When he said nothing I looked into those gentle but manly blue eyes. Hypnotizing eyes, just as they were at the airport. But he was a stranger then. This time an uneasy feeling passed through me. Yet I didn't withdraw from his hold.

"Before we do I want you to promise me something."

"What?"

"Call me Doug."

I sighed a chuckle. Silly me. He was a flirt, the type who acted this way with every girl he met, pregnant or not. This was his way of complimenting me, making me feel worthy.

We found John in a terrific mood, bolstered no doubt by Buffalo's 34-17 victory over Kansas City. The three of us watched the late game together and I could see the younger Brit was hooked. He asked a great many questions about 'American' football. John was only too happy to indoctrinate his brother into his autumn passion.

/2\

His small fist smashes down, rattling the dining room table's thin chrome legs, crinkling its vinyl tablecloth, collapsing the mound of puzzle pieces in the box. Karl pulls his hand away and leans his back into the chair, bum on heels, toes wiggling out the opening, staring at the result. It's not right.

The knobbly ends of one piece stick out and look funny. Karl has to admit he can't blame it on a bad jigsaw job. He peels away the piece gently, rubs its frayed edges, tosses it back in the pile.

A warm breeze coming through the window screen brings a sharp scent of freshly cut grass. The midday sun is yellowing the entire backyard, casting no shadows from the house, the trees, picnic table or shed. The swing set, tricycle, soccer ball, and lawn darts all seem lonely, waiting for him to use them. He wishes he could.

But no, he has to remain inside and stay clean in his warm, freshly laundered brown shorts with matching belt and his brand new red and white checked short sleeve shirt with a pocket over the heart. This was so, according to his father, he could greet his mother's return like a young gentleman.

When will that be?

Maybe Violet knows. His babysitter is in one of her daydream moods, stretched out on the sofa, flipping through her magazines, switching between the *Teen* and *Tiger* she brought and his mom's stack of *Chatelaines*. Her straight black hair hangs over the armrest, almost touching the powder blue carpet, while her thin bare feet rest on two cushions. Today, Violet has on jean shorts and a bright pink tank top, the outfit his mom once called trashy. In a joking way, not a mean way. His mom likes Violet a lot, and used to call her the little sister she never had.

He likes Violet too. Also a lot. Except for his parents, he's known her longer than anyone in the world, even longer than Uncle Douglas.

He's missed her. The last time she babysat him was long before Christmas. These days his parents rarely go out and when they do, Violet's unavailable. His other babysitters are nice and all but they aren't as much fun. Either they're too young and childish and treat him like some cute doll, or worse, older folks who are strict. At seventeen, Violet is the perfect age, easy to talk to and willing to talk about fun things. Kid things. Though he'll never admit this to anyone, not even to Uncle Douglas, he finds Violet, even with those dorky glasses, pretty. Seeing her gives him a smooth, strange feeling inside his chest, an oddly wonderful thrill. Once he found out she was coming over today, he didn't mind taking that bath so much.

One of the best things about Violet is that, like him, she hates his parents' music. His mom's pop is too soft and sweet and his dad's classical records either too dull or too heavy. So Violet usually brings over a few of her own albums like the Black Sabbath one playing now. And she plays her music loud, loud enough to drown out other noises, like the annoying neighbour's lawnmower or, in this case, his fist hitting the table.

His left foot starts falling asleep so he slides his legs out and sits normal on the chair, his eyes now barely above the table. He flips over the puzzle box for the umpteenth time to study what it should look like when finished.

A fancy white castle-like building, it stands in the middle of nowhere, all alone except for a reflection of itself in a calm river in front. But the building isn't actually white. In fact, many of the bricks are brown. The scene must be of late afternoon because the sun is starting to set, the sky filled with different colours, from light blue up high to red and even purple below at the horizon. It's easy to tell the difference between the real building and its reflection because the water is darker, dirtier.

At five hundred pieces, it's the biggest puzzle he's ever worked on. He feels guilty having started it without his uncle who gave it to Karl for his seventh birthday. He feels even worse because his uncle often talked about the Taj Mahal as a place he wants to visit. Actually, it's India that Uncle Douglas wants to visit, not the Taj Mahal, but he says the Taj Mahal is the most famous place in that country. Maybe that's where he is now, holding on to the last puzzle piece.

The scrape and click of the record needle, followed by its clunking back into its holder, ends in silence. Instead of playing side two, Violet tunes the radio to a Toronto top forty station before coming over to sit across from Karl. She picks up the frayed piece and does a really nice job of smoothing it out. Then as she drags it to its destination Karl stops her hand with an open palm and takes the piece away, which amuses her.

"You really mean to finish this all by yourself, don't you? How long have you been at it?"

"I don't know. Two months?"

"Two months. You haven't even finished the border."

"So?"

"Who on earth would give a seven-year-old such a tough puzzle?"

"Uncle Douglas."

Her slight frown is softer, but still like his mother's, whenever he mentions Uncle Douglas's name. Did Mom and Dad ask his babysitter not to talk about his uncle?

Violet begins to twirl another puzzle piece between her fingers. He won't need that one for a while but if she fidgets like that too long he'll have to grab it from her. Then she lets out a heavy, sad sigh, tosses the piece back in the pile, and leans back in her chair, running her hands through her hair.

"It's funny," she says.

"What's funny?"

"You know you still haven't said whether you're getting a baby brother or sister."

Her voice is nervous and shaky. Karl grunts but doesn't answer. It doesn't really matter to him.

"Well, which is it?"

"Beats me."

"Little liar, you know."

Karl shrugs again, picks up the puzzle box and puts it to his face, in order to hide his smile. He likes to tease her and she's a good sport. She reaches across and gives him a light shove against his shoulder.

"Hey, maybe it's twins."

He puts the box down, stares at Violet, eyes squinting.

"Twins?"

"Yeah, when someone has two babies at the same time, they're twins. If three, it's triplets, four are quadru—"

"One'll be enough."

"One'll be enough. Boy Karl, you don't seem excited. Won't it be nice to have someone new in the family?"

He blindly picks up a piece of the water and, by accident or by magic, fits it in perfectly. Then another, and another; he's on a roll. Violet excuses herself to put her records away.

He tries not to let on that she's right. The instant his parents told him the news, Karl couldn't wait for his baby brother or sister. It's so dull without Uncle Douglas around. His parents don't talk about him at all. With a new person in the house, things might change and become fun again.

The fourth puzzle piece isn't successful. Violet returns with her black ropy hair now in a ponytail. She looks sad for some reason, and her voice is too, though she is still smiling.

"You know, I was always thrilled whenever an aunt or uncle had a kid. Each one was special. I can only imagine what getting a brother or sister would be like."

"I'd rather see Uncle Douglas."

"Of course, Karl, I know. But as they say, whenever someone in a family dies, a baby is born."

"Violet, do you really believe my uncle is gone forever, like my parents say?"

She stares at him a long moment, her face seeming to say she's already said so. Her brown eyes soften as she takes his hands tenderly in her smooth palms and squeezes.

"You miss him a lot, don't you?"

She says it the same way his parents might, except with Violet it's not just that she cares about his feelings, but that she shares them. Looking into her eyes, a strange thought comes to him, a weird thought from what she just said.

"Is it ever the same person?" he says.

"Is what? What?"

"You just said that when a person dies a baby is born. Is it ever the same person?"

She stares at Karl, as if checking to see if he's pulling her leg. He repeats his question with more force, which makes her chuckle just like the old Violet.

"That's called reincarnation," she says.

"Re-ink? I've heard that word before. Say it again.

"Reincarnation, say it, re-in-car-nay-shun."

"Re-in-car-nay-shun, re-in-car-nay-shun, reincarnation."

"That's it."

"Spell it."

"I-T," she says, with a straight face.

Karl jabs a red crayon at her. She takes it and looks for a piece of paper. He pushes the puzzle box forward. She writes the word in capital letters on the inside of the box. Karl turns it around and mouths the letters. With each attempt, he's more certain he's heard it before. He just can't remember where.

"What does it mean?"

"Oh my, everything's a mystery to you, isn't it? Now I wish I hadn't mentioned it."

"But you did. So tell me."

"I don't know, it's adult stuff."

"But you know it."

"Oh, so you don't think I'm an adult, do you?"

"Come on, please tell me."

She sighs. Karl knows she'll give in and tell him, sooner or later. Her delay is only for show. However, he becomes less certain when she gets up and picks an apple out of the fruit basket. He says nothing while she plucks out the stem and carefully rinses the apple, drying it with a paper towel.

Finally, after a couple of bites, she sits down again and looks him straight in the eyes.

"All right, here goes. Some people think that when you die you eventually come back as a different person."

She takes a few more bites while he ponders this.

"Is that true?"

"I'm not sure. It's just what some people believe."

"Do you believe it?"

She shrugs, as if trying to be casual. To Karl, it seems she's bothered and trying not to show it.

"Honestly, I don't think about things like that and you shouldn't either, at least not until you're older."

She takes the last bit of her apple and throws the core in the garbage. Karl expects her to go back to her reading but instead she returns with a can of 7-Up.

"Violet, why weren't you at Uncle Douglas's funeral?"

Her face turns red but she says nothing, pops open the fizzy drink, and takes a sip.

"After all, you knew him too. You were his friend."

"I wasn't feeling well then, Karl."

"Were you sick? Did you have the flu?"

"Kind of, no, but—"

"What was wrong then?"

"Boy, you're full of questions today, aren't you? Let's talk about something else, otherwise go back to your puzzle and I'll go back to my reading."

"But—"

They hear a car door, a pair of voices. Violet rushes to the window, then to the front door, which she opens and holds for Karl's mother. Karl stays at the table, annoyed at the interruption, especially the feeling he could have gotten more information out of his babysitter, that she knows more than she says.

His mom enters in loose jeans and a sweatshirt. In her arms is a bundle shaped like an oversized football. A blue cloth covers it and he gasps as he recognizes it as his Winnie the Pooh blanket. Only his gasp is covered by his mother's upon seeing Violet who she clearly did not expect to see. For a moment Karl is afraid she'll drop the baby. Then his mom gives Violet a sharp glare. With her recently cut short hair, he can see her red ears and the look is sharper than all the ones he's gotten for forgetting to clean his room or washing his hands put together.

"What the—what are you doing here?"

"Mr. Stevenson said you were in a bind and—"

Violet looks behind the door but no one's there.

"Your father had to go pick up diapers," Karl's mom says, to Karl, ignoring Violet.

Head down, Violet gathers her records and magazines and returns to the door to put on her shoes. Karl wants to ask his mom why she's angry but shock has let the cat get his tongue. Then his mother's expression becomes less harsh, though it still doesn't look happy.

"Oh never mind, Violet. Since you are here, you may as well see the baby too."

Violet stands behind Karl and looks over his shoulder as his mom kneels down to show them the bundle.

"Karl, meet your brother, Samuel. Samuel, this is your big brother, Karl."

Karl pulls away the cloth covering and stares for almost a full minute at the tiny, pink, and peaceful round face. The eyes are scrunched shut and stay that way even after Karl touches his small nose. Karl looks up and his mother's smile is more natural and beautiful than he's ever seen. He twists his neck to see Violet's strange smile. Her lips shake a bit and she seems about to cry.

"Tell me what you think, Karl," his mother says.

"He's sleeping, like Uncle Douglas."

The baby's wailing sounds like a sick ambulance siren, or like those air raid warnings in war movies that go on and on, but at a higher pitch. And this is only the first night, Karl thinks, as he covers his ears with his pillow. It doesn't help.

He sits up, stares out the window. The stars shine over the trees and on the swing set, tempting him to go out and play. He would too, except it's too big a jump to the ground from the second floor. Once he gets bigger, he'll find a way.

Another baby-scream. He knows babies cry, though his mom always brags how easy Karl was. Maybe he should have cried more. No footsteps come this time and Samuel's crying stops as quickly as it started. How does she know?

The silence makes Karl's heart race. He thinks back to what he and Violet talked about earlier in the day, before the baby came. Especially that word. A word he's seen or heard before. Somewhere. Toronto? That sounds about right. It's worth a look.

He waits a good five minutes longer to make sure the house remains silent. Then he slinks out of bed and makes his way downstairs, tiptoeing, like Elmer Fudd twacking the wascally wabbit. Near the dining room, he considers taking the puzzle box. But it's filled with the extra puzzle pieces. Too noisy. He'll have to trust memory. As he walks down the basement steps, he plays the letters through his mind, remembering R's, N's, and T's, as well as lots of vowels.

The guestroom seems smaller without the sofa bed, old dresser, night table, and lamps, all sold months ago in their big yard sale. Now the room is used to store stuff. Stacks of cardboard boxes that used to be deeper in the basement line the walls, including some that belonged to Uncle Douglas.

Belong, not belonged. Hey, why would they keep Uncle Douglas's things? If he's right in guessing Uncle Douglas has gone to India, then it could be whatever didn't fit in his suitcase. If they are right and he's not coming back, why not sell it along with the other stuff? It makes no sense, unless they forgot about it. He can't ask because then they'll know about his snooping.

The first box he opens is a big one full of clothes, little clothes, his old clothes in fact, hand-me-downs for Samuel, eventually. How nice to be the oldest and never have to wear hand-me-downs.

He rifles through several more boxes before finding a heavy one full of books and records. He turns on a light to read the titles and keeps still to listen for noises from upstairs. One by one, he scans covers, and puts books back on the floor in the opposite way to how he found them. The pile has reached about a dozen when he comes upon a thick, white one. The title has a big number twenty, in red, and in letters only a bit smaller, it says: *Twenty Cases Suggestive of Reincarnation.*

Reincarnation.

That's the word and this is the book where he's seen it before. The third word, Suggestive, sounds familiar and he's sure he can figure out what it means. Twenty cases, he can understand that.

Twenty is a lot. If it happened twenty times—then he looks at the author's name: Ian Stevenson, M. D. Stevenson. That's his family's name. No one's ever talked about a relative named Ian though.

He flips to the first page but after a minute of trying to read the long sentences and big words he's disappointed. It's useless. His kids' dictionary won't have many of these words. He can't ask his mom or dad for help either because they won't approve of him looking at such an adult book.

Why would Uncle Douglas possess a book like this unless it's important? He just has to be patient. He'll get older, he'll learn new words until eventually he'll be able to read the whole thing. It's like the big puzzle he's working on upstairs. Once he figures it out, his uncle could return in some way, to fit in the last piece, even if it takes years.

Lake Ontario's calm waves splash against the beach at Lakeside Park while on the soft, uneven sand Karl gives his parents a demonstration of his brother's latest triumph. As the sun shines on his golden curls, a naked Samuel waddles a wobbly triangle from Karl to his father, then to his mother, and back to Karl. Occasionally Samuel stands still, distracted by people scattered on the beach, their colourful swimsuits, beach toys, shouts and shrieks. After three laps, he falls down on his belly, turns his head up at the applause from his parents, and gurgles. Instead of clapping as well, Karl throws his hands up in the air, sighs.

"That's all he can do. He still can't talk."

"Give him time, he's barely a year old," his father says.

Karl huffs in silence before using his fingers to pry apart his brother's lips. Samuel thinks it's a game and resists by tightening his mouth until their mother pulls Karl's hands away and raps them lightly.

"What are you doing? Stop that."

When Karl looks up at her, she turns away, her hand to her mouth, but not quick enough to hide a tiny smile. She's in a good mood today, which is happening more often lately. Not only are her moods better, she's gotten thin and pretty again, letting her hair grow long below her shoulders. In her new orange and yellow bikini, she's as bright as the sun. Karl notices people—all men or teenage boys—stopping to look at her, staring. That bothers him. It's one thing when Uncle Douglas does it. He's family and only teasing. With strangers, it's just rude.

They arrived early to grab their favourite spot by grey, nearly square, flat-topped rocks sitting like crooked molars. They're as big as Karl. Trees behind the rocks act like a curtain, hiding the concrete pier that runs out into the lake. Back when Uncle Douglas would join them, he would sit on one of the rocks to scope out the lay of the land, as he would say.

From there, Karl and his uncle used to walk to the end of the pier where strong winds and waves splash violently against yachts and motorboats in the channel. Two lighthouses across the way were always a magnet. Once he learned to swim, Karl vowed, he was going get across to them. His uncle agreed he'd be good enough but didn't think it was a good idea with all the sailboats entering and exiting the Port Dalhousie marina. They then followed the channel into land, going as far as the old wooden lock, the original opening for the Welland Canal, as his mother reminds them every time they come here, as if it's their first visit. They'd cut across the big parking lot, to the water, and wade back to rejoin his parents. Now he has to do the walk alone.

"Mom, can I go for a walk and a swim?"

"I can't now, honey. I have to stay with Samuel."

"Can I go on my own?"

She looks at his father. He's taking a nap and she probably doesn't want to wake him. Karl points out it's a weekday and not as busy, therefore almost impossible for anyone to get lost.

"All right, but not on the pier. Stick to the beach so I can keep an eye on you."

She points to a group of cottonwood trees sticking out of the sand beyond the bathrooms: his boundary.

Inspired by Billy from *The Family Circus*, Karl mentally charts a crooked, dashed path along the beach. His route isn't as complicated as the cartoon's, but tricky enough to make her eyes work, without forcing her to call after him.

His first obstacle, an older couple sitting on cheap foldout lawn chairs. The woman wears a white dress with flowers and light brown panty hose to her knees while the man has on light green shorts and a short sleeve shirt out of which sprout hundreds of grey hairs. Ugly black socks cover his feet, which are wedged into equally ugly brown plastic sandals. Karl glances back at his father, in fear, but breathes a sigh of relief to see bare feet. While the woman talks about what sounds like nonsense, her husband nods a lot as he leafs through a *Time* magazine.

Karl zigzags through a bunch of scattered towels, blankets, and beach chairs, many empty but many with a man or a woman, alone, sitting up or lying down, sunglasses on their heads, their bodies gooped up with suntan lotion. A few are reading thick paperbacks or doing crosswords in newspapers; most do nothing other than let the sun burn their backs or stomachs. At least two men have on those tiny tight bathing suits Uncle Douglas wore.

Before he knows it, Karl reaches the clump of trees that marks his boundary. He looks back. His mother is in sight but not paying attention to him, busy putting a diaper on Samuel. He doesn't want to risk going further and worrying her. Also, the lifeguard is watching him, like those clerks at the toy store whenever he strays into an aisle by himself.

Above the parking lot loom the old red brick buildings of the town of Port Dalhousie. Directly below, the tiny jail, an old building made of grey stone, shaped like the letter "A". It's no bigger than a small house. Uncle Douglas always joked it was his Port Dalhousie crash pad. At least Karl thinks he was joking. What's no joke is that the merry-go-round isn't operating.

No point going further so Karl returns by wading along the edge of the water and soon comes upon a group of high school kids. Three boys and two girls share beach towels laid side by side, bodies crunched together, touching. Shoes, shorts, and t-shirts surround them, along with two Frisbees, pink and black, and several foam holders with pop cans sticking out. A small transistor radio plays some kind of rock music he likes but has never heard before. The teenagers are laughing and goofing around, shoving each other. To Karl's surprise, no beer or skinny cigarettes.

Two of the boys are huddling, whispering, laughing, staring in the direction Karl is heading. Karl slows to see what it is they're looking at. He can see his dad and Samuel playing with a bucket and shovel while his mom is lying on her stomach, her bikini top undone.

Karl jumps when another girl, a sixth member of the group, lying on her stomach on a separate towel, splashes sand at his feet.

"Hello there, young man," she says.

Her long black hair reminds him of Violet, except this girl is a few years younger and not as pretty. On the other hand, she's not as thin and her skin is much browner. Karl remembers how his pale babysitter avoided the sun. It's almost a year since he last saw Violet on the day Samuel was born. He feels sad. He turns away from the girl only to see the boys staring in his family's direction. He growls softly.

"What's eating you?" the girl says, with a nice voice.

"Make them stop staring at my mother."

Karl points at the two boys who turn toward him, their mouths open, their faces so red it makes the girls and the third boy laugh. One of the blushers scowls, which only increases the laughter. Then the staring boys begin laughing too and Karl can't help joining them. Maybe these kids are okay.

"Karl!"

The teenagers, except for the two guilty boys, turn with Karl to look in his mom's direction. It's his turn to be embarrassed as they watch her retie her bikini top, get up, and motion for Karl to come over. The teenagers' faces show sympathy, as if it wasn't so long ago that things like this happened to them.

"See ya later, alligator," the nice girl says.

Surprisingly, his mother doesn't scold him for talking to strangers when he gets back. Instead she hands him an open can of cream soda with a bobbing straw sticking out. She then points at his brother. Samuel's hands are smeared with sand and chocolate. His mouth is a mess with odd sounds coming out.

"Daiy. Ung. Da. Gng."

"Want me to clean him up in the lake?" Karl says.

"You hear that, Karl? He's trying to say something."

Karl says nothing, sips his drink. Then he frowns.

"That's just baby talk. Probably wants something."

"No, he's fed, and changed. I think he's trying to talk."

"Then what's he trying to say?"

"I think it's obvious he's trying to say, Daddy," she says.

Karl shakes his head, about to say it could be another D name. Except, she said it to his father, who picks up Samuel with both hands, holds him up at the belly, and nuzzles his tummy. Samuel laughs.

"So, what are you trying to say, Sam, my boy?"

"It's Samuel, John. And I think he's trying to say, Daddy."

"Well that's only fair."

"What do you mean, Dad?" Karl says.

"Because your first word was Mommy."

"Really? How old was I?"

"Just over a year."

"So it should be soon for him then, right?"

His parents look at each other but say nothing.

"Ung. Daiy."

"Come on, learn to speak faster," Karl says.

Samuel laughs and crawls toward the plastic pail, picks up the shovel with his left hand, and starts loading sand. Karl takes a seat next to his father who is gazing out at the water, far beyond the lighthouse. In the distance, through the haze and behind several sailboats and a couple of guys paddling a canoe, beyond two ships moving toward the Welland Canal, Karl makes out tall buildings in the skyline of Toronto that appear as squared off puzzle pieces.

The waves are bigger now, the tide almost reaching their towels. Already the water has chased the teenagers away, except for the girl with the black hair. She notices his glance and waves, which makes Karl blush. The water is about to wet Samuel's toes when his father calls out to the younger brother. Samuel stumbles over as Karl watches in wonder, especially at how his father acts, as if he expects it.

"Maybe your brother can't speak yet, Karl, but I think he's starting to understand us."

"How old was Uncle Douglas when he first talked?"

His father pauses to look behind Karl, as if checking whether his mother has heard. But Karl said it softly, on purpose.

"Honestly, I don't remember."

"I bet you it took longer than a year too."

It's a guess but it sounds right to Karl. His father looks at him oddly for a moment, and then lightly squeezes Karl's neck with his strong fingers.

"Say, I think now's a good time to clear out of here and go get us some ice cream."

*

John Stevenson feels terrific, cruising along Lakeport Road with his family, windows rolled down to let in a warm summer breeze as the station wagon rumbles over the grates of the bridge linking the lake and Port Dalhousie to the city of St. Catharines. A clear sky above shines on the marina and the remnants of the first canal on the left, the still waters of the Henley Regatta to the right. An early start for several delightful hours of swimming, sunning, and playing on the beach at Lakeside Park, before it got too crowded, has earned them their ice cream.

His two wonderfully behaved boys sit in the backseat, Karl feeding words to his little brother with purposeful whispers, as he has done for three years now. Samuel's vocabulary was unusually slow developing the first couple of years, but it's fine now, more in spite of Karl's efforts than due to them. To John it seems Samuel is purposely laconic just to annoy his older brother and pay him back for all that pestering.

Helen, now past thirty, is getting more attractive with age, more youthful as if each year unloads another burden. Particularly in moments like this, dreamingly looking out the window, smiling naturally. Samuel's unexpected arrival, so stressful at the time, was the best thing that could have happened after Doug's tragic death. John still misses his brother and thinks of him from time to time, but Samuel's presence has filled the gap. Someone once told him a death in a family often coincides with a birth. A profound notion for John for whom Samuel's birthday will always be a special and personal reminder of his brother.

Of course, he'll never voice that sentiment to his wife. Three and a half years have passed since Doug's death but John's younger brother remains a taboo subject. Just the other Saturday, when he commented on how both Samuel and Doug were left-handed, she became upset. For a good hour, she moped about by herself, hiding behind the excuse of a headache. John knows it's more than that, as if she fears some kind of influence on Samuel from beyond the grave.

Would that be such a bad thing?

Not to John. It shouldn't be to Helen either. She needs to recall how wonderful Doug was with Karl. He never crossed the line between his dubious lifestyle and being a good uncle, not even close. He was a great help to the family, especially to John, in raising their first son. It was Doug who taught Karl to swim, tell time, and even to ride his bike, and plenty of other things for which John's career got in the way.

A left onto Lakeshore and they're heading east toward the canal. Oh, how he enjoys driving around his adopted hometown. Of course, St. Catharines is a city, as Helen will often correct him. The Garden City. But it feels like a town to John, sometimes a village. Traffic is never a problem, even on weekdays during rush hour—the seven-minute rush hour as someone at the office once described it. Within fifteen minutes, you can go from farmland through urban streets and residential areas, passing verdant lawns dipping down into shady ravines or charming creeks, and back to farmland again. Aside from accidents and unusual weather, slowdowns occurred only trying to cross the canal at an unlucky time and getting caught at one of the lift bridges.

At Arthur Street, he stops for a red light. Up ahead, sure enough, the Lakeshore Bridge is being raised, evidenced by the bridge's flashing yellow and red lights and a growing line of vehicles queuing to cross the canal at Lock One. A lane opens on his right and an impatient nod from Helen impels him to take the alternate route. He glances at Karl, who is busy with Samuel, before he turns right. They pass a park in which several boys are kicking around a soccer ball while other kids are throwing a Frisbee, chased by an eager puppy. A left, a right, and then a left brings them to the canal road. The upbound ship is still rising in Lock One, on its way to Lake Erie.

John likes to linger along this section, take it as slow as traffic will allow. He's intrigued by the homes with yards that front the waterway. How surreal it would be to hold a beer in one hand, a spatula in the other, hamburgers and hotdogs barbecuing, while a giant ship passes a mere football's throw away. If Karl had his wish, they would buy one of these houses. Then his son would pitch a tent in summertime and spend every night in the backyard, setting up office to track the ships.

However, these houses rarely come up for sale. When they do, it's even more rare for his office to try for the listing, due to Jack Biltmore's myopic insistence they specialize on new development and look askance at re-sales for houses more than a decade old. It's a policy that will hurt them in the long run.

John can't linger if he wants to beat the ship and the raising of the Lock Two bridge. He looks in the rear view mirror and can see it's just exiting Lock One; he's good. A sharp left turn up a short climb and they cross over the lift bridge. The grating rumble underneath, followed by another curve stirs his passengers. Shortly the familiar white silos of the dairy come into view.

Helen and Karl go to buy the ice cream—double chocolates for the boys, butterscotch ripple for John, strawberry for Helen—while John and Samuel corral two picnic tables close to the car, shaded by a pair of maple trees.

As they enjoy the best ice cream in Niagara, trucks enter and exit the complex through white picket fence gates, from and to the busy country road. Behind the gates, activity is brisk in and around the white structures with their dark green roofs. The flat, varied farmland is dotted with farm buildings and greenhouses. A bucolic scene enhanced by the air, which smells fruity and fresh.

At one table, Karl and Samuel start a jigsaw puzzle, alternately licking their quickly melting cones and trying to fit pieces in, leaning in and leaning out, not spilling a drop.

"Aren't puzzles fun, Samuel?" Karl says.

"They're okay."

"They're best done together, don't you think?"

"This one's nice because I love pictures of mountains."

"Uncle Douglas loved puzzles too, and always did them with me."

"Who?"

"Nothing, never mind."

Karl frowns, as if angry with himself for a mistake. John glances at Helen and it looks as if she hasn't heard the last part of the exchange.

"Isn't it wonderful how those two get along?" John says, with fatherly pride.

"Karl treats his brother well."

"Just like . . . a third parent."

John is about to compare the relationship between the brothers to the one Doug had with Karl. Helen glances at him and smiles, as if in appreciation for his holding his tongue.

"I wonder if that puzzle's a little too difficult for Samuel though. On the box it says it's for children four and up."

"Nonsense, Helen. From my standpoint, the little guy is doing fine. Even if he's not as bright, with his good looks—well, look at that."

John points at Samuel, specifically the way the young boy holds the puzzle piece, between his thumbs under his chin, fingers crossed and elbows on the table. Samuel's gaze is intensely focused on his target, oblivious to his audience. The words come out of John's mouth before he can censor himself.

"Spooky, isn't it? Exactly like Doug, remember? Even as a kid my brother did that."

Helen's face pales as she turns to sneeze. Then John notices Karl's profile. His son is watching her too, but with an impassive, oddly chilling expression, beaming as if he's found a long lost toy. Meanwhile, Samuel continues to work on the puzzle.

When he finishes the last bite of cone, he abandons the puzzle and asks his father to toss the football with him. John is on his feet in an instant and the two go to an open area about twenty yards away. Whenever John glances back, he sees Karl with an intense face as he observes his younger brother, almost clinically.

Karl stands against the backdoor, in his freshly cut-off jeans and brand new medium top North Star running shoes. He's waiting anxiously. Today feels as good as the day, a few years ago, when at last he finished the Taj Mahal puzzle. Which is appropriate as now there is no doubt in his mind his five-year-old brother is the reincarnation of his Uncle Douglas.

It's Samuel's birthday so normally they would be at the beach on such a hot, humid, perfect-for-swimming day. However, they aren't going this year because of the trouble with the teenagers last summer.

It was hot that day too. As usual, they arrived early to get their spot by the rocks by the pier. For an hour the beach was quieter than the previous three years. Then a rush of at least a hundred teenagers invaded the park and beach and marina. Why did they have to choose that day out of all their summer holidays for a mass party? With their cheap beer and Baby Duck, their marijuana and weird music coming out of their cars, the Stevenson family did not have a nice time.

So when Karl's mom suggested not going this year, his dad agreed, saying he could use the time at the office. He promised to return after lunch to take them to the dairy for ice cream, which satisfied Samuel who was the most upset about the change. While Karl will miss the beach too, he has other plans, ambitious plans.

Not until this summer, five years after finding it, Karl finally began to make sense of the reincarnation book. Once the first parts became clear, the rest came easier. Many of the words and sentences are still a challenge but he is confident that, with more patience, and the use of the school library, they will come to him too, eventually.

More importantly, he's gotten ideas on how to observe his brother—his case—and how to record observations like the author did. Karl now diligently records incidents as they happen, recording them as items in rows, capturing details under columns, such as Item, Informant, Verification, and Comments. He got rid of the Verification column because it's always the same as the Informant: himself. His evidence list isn't as long as those in the book, yet, but it's growing. Today could be a big day. With his parents not around, there'll be no interference, and a lower chance his uncle will be shy in coming out.

Staying home is better for Samuel too. Not only because he can discover who he really is, but also to make him feel less scared about kindergarten in September. For weeks his baby brother has worried about that, constantly saying he doesn't want to go. Only when Karl offered to do a trial run did Samuel settle down.

In that sense, Samuel isn't like Uncle Douglas, who isn't shy or scared of anything. There are other differences too, such as Samuel's shorter height and wider body, which is more like their dad. Those details aren't worth recording as much as observations such as both being left-handed. And of course the gestures. Like the freaky puzzle piece fingering thing he started doing at the dairy two years before, as well as how his shoulders shake from side to side when excited, and how he can slit his eyes and smile at the same time. But most of all, the blond hair. Even if it doesn't curl up, it's still blond.

"So what do you do when you reach your brother's school?" his mother says, while she ties Samuel's shoes.

"I wait until he's completely inside before I go on to my school," Karl says, acting peeved.

"And after school?" she says, turning to Samuel.

"I stay inside until I see Karl."

"Good. Of course, you'll have to make believe those parts."

A few more instructions that Karl barely listens to and they're finally out of there. Karl senses her eyes on them all the way down the street as the brothers walk hand in hand. When they turn a corner, past the O'Neil house with the two German Shepherds, Karl removes his hand.

"Aren't you supposed to hold my hand all the way?" Samuel says, being more smart aleck than obedient.

"Did Mom say that?"

"Yes."

"Well, did Dad?"

"No. He wasn't there to say anything."

"Okay then."

They stare at each other a second before Samuel's face cracks into a smile. His eyes narrow and he starts walking ahead. Karl lets him and lags behind. With the air so muggy, he doesn't want to sweat.

Five minutes later, they reach the school, a one-storey dark brown brick structure with a parking lot taking up most of the space in front. Two portables occupy a good chunk of the baseball diamond outfield, which needs mowing. A thin, red-haired girl is walking a collie by the creek beyond right field, the dog sniffing at everything in its path. Farther along, behind the main building, the white metal posts at both ends of the football/soccer field have reddish-brown rust patches that need painting. At the other end, a man pitches golf balls the width of the field.

Without warning, Samuel sprints away from Karl to the near goalpost.

"We should have brought a football," Samuel says.

"Yeah," Karl says.

"Let's go back and get it."

"Another time, Samuel. Come here so I can show you the door you'll have to go in."

"Come get me, try to tackle me."

Samuel is getting big and will be bigger than Karl some day, probably sooner than Karl expects. He has to make sure his little brother knows who's boss while he has the chance. Karl lunges at Samuel who rolls away and avoids the tackle. Samuel picks up an imaginary football, tucks it against his armpit, and starts running. Strong and sturdy as he is, Samuel isn't as quick as Karl who surprises his younger brother by diving and grabbing his ankles and pulling him down, yelling out fumble, causing Samuel to protest. But when Karl goes for the imaginary ball, Samuel does too. After a few seconds of wrestling, they stop to catch their breath.

"We used to goof around together here, just like this," Karl says.

"We? No we didn't. I've never been here."

"Yes, you have."

"I don't remember."

Karl sighs. He's tempted to give Samuel a hint, except that would be unscientific, cheating.

"You will."

"What's that mean? Karl, you often say weird things."

"Never mind. Say, when we get home, you want to try a new puzzle?"

"Keep your puzzles, Karl."

"What?"

"I'm sick of your puzzles."

Karl frowns, more annoyed than offended. This is not going well at all. Okay, Samuel doesn't remember the field. Not yet. Not liking puzzles isn't a big deal either. Maybe Uncle Douglas didn't like them when he was a kid.

"I'll show you another way home, a secret way."

"Where?"

"Just follow me, it's okay, it's just a different way."

"What about the front door?"

"What front door?"

"You know, where I'm supposed to go in."

Karl points to a set of black double doors.

"Those. Don't worry. I'll always take you, remember?"

"Oh, right. So shouldn't we get back home then?"

"We've got loads of time."

"I don't know. I'm getting hungry and I don't want to be late for when Dad comes home."

While Samuel hesitates, Karl walks toward the orchard where the smell of mixed fruit of varying ripeness fills his nostrils. Many peaches and apples have fallen to the ground, some whole, some rotting and worm infested. The treetops touch together to shade the whole area.

"This is a nice spot," Samuel says, after catching up.

Karl jogs to a large tree in the middle, leans against it, and slides down to sit. He watches Samuel who remains standing, nibbling at his fingernails. Then Samuel picks up one of the pears and puts it to his mouth.

"Put that down," Karl yells.

"Why?"

"It may be poisoned."

"Poisoned?"

"Yeah, and then you'll have to take Ipecac. It'll make you throw up."

Samuel studies the fruit and then shakes his head, as if his brother has lost his mind. Karl holds a firm stare. It works. Samuel throws the pear deep into the orchard, impressing Karl with the velocity and distance.

"Come on," Karl says.

Now they are at the small creek, the girl and her collie long gone. A pair of planks span the trickle of muddy water and the boys cross. Samuel kneels to catch a frog but a look from Karl makes him get up. They walk through a fenced-in laneway to come upon a street with houses like the one they live in, only bigger. Karl can see his little brother is lost, but also curious and starting to see it as an adventure.

"Where are we, Karl?"

They hear the click-clop of high heels behind them as the clouds approach from the north, from the lake.

"Why, Karl Stevenson, is that you?"

Both boys turn around. A woman stands over them, an older lady, wearing a black dress and black nylons and an old-fashioned hat, also black. Samuel jumps behind his older brother, which only adds to the creepy feeling that comes over Karl whenever he sees

Violet's mother. But he knows the feeling will pass. She's actually a nice lady, easy going like her daughter. Seeing her in black makes Karl wonder if something has happened to Mr. Baxter.

"Yes, Mrs. Baxter, it's me."

"And so this must be, let me remember . . . Samuel."

Instead of shrinking back further, as Karl expects him to do, Samuel comes forward.

"Yes, Ma'am."

"So, what brings you two young men wandering by?"

"Finding my school," Samuel says.

"He's starting kindergarten in a few weeks."

She smiles at them and then points down the street.

"I see, but isn't the school down that way?"

"Yeah, but since we were out, and it was such a nice day, I thought Violet might like to see him again."

Mrs. Baxter's smile fades and her voice become strange.

"Does your mother know you came to see Violet?"

"Uh, I'm sure I mentioned it to her."

"I see. I'm afraid Violet moved to Thorold some time ago."

"Karl, come by the window and check out the snow."

Karl ignores his brother and continues twisting the television knob, stopping each time he gets a clear picture, first on VHF, then on UHF. Football season is over and the television is free again on Sunday afternoons. Free for what? Religious shows, talk shows, animal documentaries, old movies? All boring. Last year, his Grade Seven teacher told the class no area in the world can boast Niagara's variety of television due to its closeness to Buffalo and Toronto. So what, if there isn't anything to watch?

Even football is better than this. He kind of misses the announcers, fans, and his dad's cheering or jeering the Bills—mostly jeering this past season because they only won two games—or complaining about the referees.

If only they could afford cable. He twists the On/Off knob until it clicks and the black and white image and high-pitched hum collapses into a soundless white point. Upstairs, a discussion is going on, louder than usual, between his parents. Karl can't remember the last time they argued, let alone had a real fight of the kind his friends often described.

Karl joins his brother, knees on the floor, elbows on the window ledge, and chin on the backs of his hands. Together they gape in wonder, hypnotized by millions of tiny floating flakes that slowly descend, a powdery invasion laying siege on a defenceless neighbourhood, smothering streets, sidewalks, lawns, driveways, cars, and flowerbeds.

An upstairs door whisks open and then shuts heavily. Not quite a slam, but loud enough to cause the boys to turn around in unison. Their father is descending the stairs. He's unshaven, wearing a sweatshirt and tracksuit, jingling his keys. His stern expression tells Karl he won the argument but isn't necessarily happy about it. Kind of like how Karl feels when his Monopoly victories make Samuel pout just before the five-year-old sweeps the pieces off the table. His father walks toward the front door and pulls out his coat, Karl's blue parka, and Samuel's red one.

"Put your boots on boys. We're going for a ride."

Instantly Samuel abandons the window, grabs his coat and rushes to obey. Only when he's ready does he ask where they're going.

"You'll see," their father says.

Except for his nervous yet cheerful humming to a classical station the boys barely hear, they drive in silence. The snow tires crunch on crisp tracks of packed white along Scott Street, past gas stations, crowded churches and empty schools and plazas, toward the canal. To Karl, directions in St. Catharines are simple: you're either heading to or away from water, whether it's north and south for Lake Ontario, or east and west for the canal. Diagonal Niagara Street complicates matters as it leads to both lake and canal.

Just before Bunting Road the snow stops coming down and their father turns right. They approach Towers, their favourite department store. Since it's Sunday, it's closed. On they drive past Woolco and several desolate industrial businesses before passing under the giant columns of the Garden City Skyway. A left turn at Queenston Street brings them to an area familiar to Karl. He recognizes the curving of the road and the bridge over train tracks that leads to the large cemetery. His father stops the car and parks against the curb.

"Why are we stopping here?" Karl says, a nervous feeling growing in his stomach, a realization what his parents' argument was about.

His father doesn't answer, motions for them to get out. He takes both sons' hands while they cross the street and then lets go after they enter the grounds. The boys follow their father under an archway to a field of gravestones near a cluster of frosted willow trees. Karl vaguely recalls images from the time they buried his uncle. Not images really, more like shadowy outlines of people, his parents, a minister, and several rows of white covered chairs, empty.

Samuel looks bewildered, sensing he's on the verge of a major disappointment. His mind, no doubt filled with fun stuff like toboggans, snowball fights, making snowmen, and snow angels, isn't ready for such a serious place. They reach a marble plate with his uncle's name on it. Their father kneels, puts his arms around their shoulders and gently pulls them toward him in a huddle, before letting out a heavy sigh. Then Samuel points to the stone.

"Douglas Stevenson? Who's that?"

Karl's father smiles, as if rewarded for the trouble he's gone through taking them here. He puts one hand on Samuel's shoulder and, with the other, pats the marble.

"Who's that, you ask? Douglas Stevenson—Doug—was my brother, your uncle. Tomorrow, it'll be six years since his death. This is where he's buried. Every year, on the Sunday after the Super Bowl, I come here to visit him, to tell him the score. Usually I bring a beer or two but this time I brought you boys. I'd have brought beer but, well, you know how fussy your mom can be at times. Besides, I can't give you boys anything to hold over me."

He pauses to give them a knowing grin. It works, as it makes Karl and his brother relax. There are times his father really impresses Karl.

"Can I tell him the score?" Samuel says.

"I think he'd like that."

Samuel has to think a moment to figure out the answer. When he has it, he first looks at his father, and then Karl, who both nod encouragement.

"Okay, Uncle Doug—"

"—las," Karl said.

"Karl, let him do it his way."

Samuel pauses until sure they've reached the end of their mini-argument.

"Okay, Uncle Douglas, it was Dallas who won the Super Bowl. And they beat the Broncos, 27-10."

"He'll be happy. The Cowboys were his favourite team."

"They were?" Samuel said, and he sounds disappointed.

"He would cheer for the Bills too. Now where was the game played?"

Samuel puts his finger to his lower lip and looks.

"At the Superdome, in New Orleans."

"Good job, son. He'll appreciate that, wherever he is."

Suddenly Karl feels trapped, enclosed in some kind of bizarre bubble, disconnected from his father and brother. As if on cue, Samuel asks about their uncle. Their father takes in a deep breath and lets it out, his signal he's about to tell a story. The three sit with crossed legs, flanking the grave.

"When I was young, I lived in Newcastle, which is in England, a country far away across the Atlantic Ocean."

A police siren sounds in the distance, which distracts Samuel. Their father waits for it to die down.

"Like Karl, I was the first-born with a brother several years younger than me. Together, with our parents, the four of us had a nice life. Simple. Nothing special. Not rich. Not poor. Much like our life here. My dad was a railway conductor, my mom chipped in by sewing for people in various neighbourhoods. Because of the age difference, my brother and I did our own things, had our own friends, but the family always ate together, as all families should.

"One hot summer day, in 1955, while Doug and I were alone in the house waiting for our parents to return from shopping for dinner, a constable, a policeman, came to our door. He told us our parents were in a terrible car accident and didn't survive."

Karl's father stops speaking as Samuel shudders. He is uncomfortable but keeps quiet, so his father continues.

"I had just turned seventeen, Doug was not yet twelve. Of course, it was a big shock and it took a long time to get over it. Because we were so young, they wouldn't let us live by ourselves. We moved from Newcastle to London, where we stayed with an Uncle William, my father's oldest brother.

"Before that we barely knew Uncle William. He lived alone and never married. We had plenty of other aunts and uncles so how he got custody of us remains a mystery to me. Our parents would not have approved but that's how it turned out."

Nearby a family—two parents and three daughters—stand over a larger gravestone. Two of the girls cry while the third lays down a small wreath.

"If Doug and I had nothing else in common, at least we shared a dislike for the man. When not supporting each other after one of Uncle William's drinking binges, we would dream up ways to escape. Being older, that dream was more achievable for me. A year or so later, an opportunity opened up for me to catch a ship to Canada, which I did."

"You left him behind?" Samuel says.

Their father clears his throat. "Yes."

"Sorry Dad, but I don't think I'd ever leave Karl behind. I don't think he'd leave me behind."

Samuel's words affect Karl in an odd way, touching and gloomy at the same time.

"Son, I agree one hundred percent. I felt bad for doing it, but you must understand things were different then. For one thing, Doug and I were not as close as you and Karl are. More importantly, if I hadn't gone when I had the chance, neither of us would have been able to escape. So, yes, I left but I promised Doug I'd send for him when I could. It took a few years, but I kept my promise. However, I'm getting ahead of myself."

Karl can see this answer pleases Samuel who has given up his desire for snow games and wants to hear more. Karl has to admit he does as well.

"In Toronto I survived by taking a series of small jobs like painting, furniture delivery, night watchman, before landing a steady shift at a meat packing plant. That was yucky work, I'll tell you, filthy, smelly. But it paid well and I got to work a lot of overtime. Throughout that period, my younger brother and my promise to him were never far from my mind. In that sense, he inspired me to work hard.

"But there was a limit. Within a year I'd had enough of that plant and, despite the money, I had to get out. It wasn't a life for me so I studied to earn my real estate licence. The great thing about real estate is you can do it anywhere. Since I wasn't too keen on the big city, I moved to St. Catharines."

"Where was Mom?" Samuel says.

"I'll get to that. Anyway, my first couple of years in real estate were tough and I learned some hard but valuable lessons. That all reversed in 1961 with my first boom year. I was finally able to put away money to pay for my brother's documents and airfare to Canada. But I needed more than money. Even though Canada wanted immigrants, there was an enormous amount of paperwork and bureaucracy given our family history. So much it required a level of patience and attention to detail I could never match.

"Then came the best and most profitable real estate deal of my entire career. Of course, you've both heard the story of how your mother and I met when I sold that house in Port Colborne to her parents. So I won't repeat it here."

Thank goodness, Karl thinks, but then feels bad about it, especially when he notices how Samuel continues to listen intently, with great awe and respect.

"Your mother, who is good with details, offered to help. To this day, I sometimes wonder whether Doug and I would have reunited at all if she hadn't gotten involved. Of course, this was only a tiny part of how special she was. Long before Doug's arrival, I asked her to marry me. You know that part.

"Finally, with all the documents signed and stamped, the ticket bought, the day came for your mother and I to see the new Toronto airport and welcome my younger brother to Canada. It wasn't an easy trip for your mother because she was carrying Karl who would be born a couple of months later. What a year that was, 1964, because it was also the year the Buffalo Bills won their first AFL championship?"

"AFL?" Karl and Samuel say, at the same time.

"Oh yes, before 1967 there were two leagues—but I'm getting away from my story. I'll save the football histories for another time."

His father pauses again. To Karl it seems he's now regretting not bringing beer. How strange that, after all this time, after all this silence, suddenly his father is talking openly about Uncle Douglas. And he seems happy doing so.

"Go on, Dad," Samuel says.

"In 1964, your mother and I rented a small downtown apartment above a store on St. Paul Street, which we now shared with Doug. In the cramped space, my brother and I rediscovered our differences. Unlike your tame old father, your uncle was a wild one. It didn't take long to get on each other's nerves. I didn't care for his friends, his smoking, his late nights, and many other things. He got frustrated with my attempts to apply rules. Your mother helped keep the peace but even she and Doug fell out after a while. Once again we lost touch."

"How could you lose touch when you lived in the same place?" Samuel says.

"Easier than you might think. Only a few months after arriving, your uncle moved out of my apartment and, not long after that, out of Niagara altogether."

"Where did he go to live?"

"Toronto," Karl says.

"Yes, Toronto, eventually," his father says, and stares at Karl with a hard to read expression.

"Where was he before Toronto?" Karl says.

"That's not important. What is important is that, in due course, we connected again. We had one thing in common. You see, he was almost as big a football fan as I was. All my friends were hockey fans and, if they watched football, it was the CFL. Also, by then we were both a few years older, more mature, and could tolerate each other's differences better. Karl helped, once he was old enough to talk. When Doug and Karl got to know each other, well, your older brother has probably told you many stories."

Samuel gives his brother an accusing look.

"And we come to the tragic day on which your uncle suddenly passed away."

It begins snowing again. Karl can't help but reflect on how, in those six years, he has spent so much energy on figuring out Uncle Douglas's return. Now his memories, not just from the cemetery but from everything else, are fading. Less and less can he recall the Christmases and birthdays, the countless jigsaw puzzles, sitting on his lap falling asleep while he drank beer and talked with Karl's parents. The Saturday swimming lessons at the YMCA in winter, the beach in Port Dalhousie in summer, all drifting away.

A few tears well up in Karl's eyes. He looks away before his father or brother notice.

"How did he die?" Samuel says.

The question, so natural, so obvious, snaps Karl out of his melancholy. Beyond knowing he died in the guestroom, Karl has never thought to ask. He's been preoccupied with making everything more complex than maybe it should be.

His father, on the other hand, is not surprised at the question. In fact, he seems ready for every question, every response, as if he's working from a script he's been rehearsing a long time.

"It was an accident," his father says.

"What kind of accident?" Samuel says.

"It's too complicated to describe."

"That's a sad story," Samuel says.

Karl exchanges a glance with his father who also seems to be fighting back a tear or two, but with better success.

"Sounds like a neat guy. Must have had lots of friends."

"He was," Karl and his father say, together, and then both chuckle.

"As far as friends go, he had a lot when he was alive though none came to his funeral. It was just us."

"That's even sadder," Samuel says.

"Wait, Dad, that's not true," Karl says.

When his brother and father turn to him, Karl points.

"Over there. I remember. I was talking to two of his friends. Gary and Craig, I think. Mom talked to them too."

Now his father studies Karl with wonder.

"You're right, Karl. I'd forgotten. Funny though, we've never seen or heard from either of them since."

"Maybe we can find them," Samuel says.

"Maybe, though I'm sure they've moved on."

"We can try," Samuel says.

"Sure we can. Listen boys, time we leave these gloomy surroundings and do something fun, something your uncle would have liked to do."

From his pocket, he pulls out a small dark brown vinyl football. It's so small and his hand is so large that his father can almost hide it completely in his palm. When Samuel sees it, his face lights up while Karl feels his own drop. He wants to go, to get home, to go to his room, be by himself. Samuel grabs at the football, which his father yanks away and stuffs back into his coat.

"Not here," he says.

They return to the car and continue along Queenston Road to the canal road where they turn left. Near the Carlton Bridge, even though they're approaching it from the other direction, Samuel recognizes the dairy. It's closed. Still, their father parks in the empty lot and ushers them out. He opens the back where, hidden underneath a blanket, there's a small cooler with room for half a dozen beers. Instead of beers, it contains a Creamsicle for Karl, an ice cream sandwich for his father, and a Fudgsicle for Samuel. After the ice creams, their father once again produces the football. They play catch for a while and then scrimmage, father against sons. Karl isn't sure what bothers him more, that his little brother can throw a consistent spiral, or how much it thrills their father.

V

It turned out Douglas—Doug—was joking about not being up to factory work. It took him barely two weeks to find employment at General Motors on the assembly line, as well as a host of friends. When not on nightshifts, he'd come home for dinner after work and then go to McCready's, a bar in Thorold near Lock Seven. John and I were long in bed by the time he came home those nights. We never met or saw his friends. It's possible Doug consciously insulated us from his other life and I could only imagine the unsavoury people he associated with. We heard nothing more about Janet or that awful girl from the airport. The shine from my first impression of him was wearing off.

That was the least of my concerns. Outside of Sundays, the two men did not get along. John's set ways frustrated Doug while the younger brother's wildness angered the older brother. I couldn't count the number of times Doug would be late for dinner, get a lecture from John, and then storm out to his bar. Then I would try to calm John down in the evening and, on those rare times Doug came home before I went to bed, do the same with my brother-in-law. I doubted my interventions mattered. The antagonism between them never threatened to get violent but simmered under a veil of begrudging tolerance. Only Sundays, when the two shared beers and football, offered a reprieve. It helped that the Bills were having their best season ever.

So much seemed to be going right if it had to do with our football team. Even my newborn son obliged us by waiting until Monday before pushing to get out. His arrival further cramped an already tight living space but we adapted. Doug doted on his nephew and did more than John to take care of him, including changing diapers and giving baths. I believed the experience made him self-conscious of the hours he kept as the amount he drank and smoked at home decreased.

One day John's lawyer friend, Ted, invited John to Boston to see the last game of the season in person, the game that would decide the East Division winner. I was excited for my husband but felt odd about watching the game alone with Doug. John, with his silly superstitions, insisted we continue the tradition without him. Tradition. It had only been one season. True, the Bills hadn't lost whenever Doug and I were together to watch a game, but that was only coincidence. If the team was that good, coincidence wouldn't stand in their way of winning. I'll admit part of me was sore John hadn't found some way to bring us along to Boston; Karl and I could have watched from the hotel room.

My son was particularly difficult that morning, leaving me no chance to clean. Doug was out most of the night so I expected to find the living room a mess when I awoke. Instead, everything was tidied up, the Saturday paper neatly folded underneath an end table, the coffee table empty, save for a pair of cork beer coasters and a freshly wiped ashtray. The pullout sofa on which Doug slept on his late nights had been reassembled with throw pillows symmetrically placed in the middle and both ends. It remained empty, though, as I sat on my rocking chair, slightly out of breath, while my brother-in-law occupied John's armchair.

"I thought that boy would never fall asleep," I said.

"Relax, you haven't missed a thing. There's a big storm in Boston. It's delayed the kick-off."

"Oh, I hope John got there okay."

"I'm sure he did. He's a careful driver."

"Yes, he is," I said, comforted by that thought.

Doug left for the kitchen and returned with two beers and two glasses, set one pair down at the edge of the coffee table closest to me, and took the other to John's recliner.

"I usually wait until the second half," I said.

We watched the grounds crew clear the snow in Fenway Park before the national anthem. The Patriots won the toss, chose to receive, but got nowhere and had to punt.

"Lucky bastard," Doug said. "I'd love to be there."

"I suppose. But you know, in all that snow and cold, the comfort of a living room is looking pretty good to me now."

"Yeah?"

"I wonder if we'll be able to spot John and Ted in the crowd."

Then the Bills quarterback and my favourite player, Jack Kemp, threw a long pass to Elbert Dubenion, who broke a tackle and scored. 7-0 Bills.

"How hollow it feels without John's cheering," I said.

"The important thing is that you're here."

"Don't tell me you subscribe to John's superstitions."

"Helen, Buffalo lost two games all year. I saw those losses. John saw those losses. Only one of us was away for both games. It adds up."

"I'm shocked that you're also superstitious. I'll add it to my microscopic list of sibling similarities."

His smile disappeared so quickly it startled me. Doug finished his glass of beer and refilled it with the rest of the bottle before giving me a serious look.

"Why?" he said.

"Why what?

"Why would it surprise you if I were superstitious?"

"I don't know, I—"

"There's a deeper, spiritual side to me, you know."

The beer was beginning to affect me and I couldn't hold back a giggle. "You mean football superstition is spiritual?"

His response was interrupted by the Patriots who, after a long drive, pushed through for a touchdown. The home team then lined up for a two-point conversion.

"Why the hell are they doing that?" Doug said.

"Boston has to win, a tie gives Buffalo first place. Given these conditions, they may not have another chance."

Doug stared at me, impressed, and that felt nice. We watched anxiously. If the Bills could stop them, they'd be in control of the game. The pass came, the receiver was open, but he slipped in the snow. He slipped and Buffalo held on to the lead.

"Still don't think you're a good luck charm?"

Then he got up to replace our beers. He was taking a while in the kitchen. He looked comically domestic coming out with a tray of crackers, cheese and kielbasa, and a stack of napkins, which he set down in the middle of the coffee table. Another trip brought back fresh beers.

We both moved to the sofa so we could eat without reaching. We settled in to our snack as the Bills settled into their game. The missed conversion had set the tone. Still we watched intently, taking nothing for granted. Not surprisingly, once in a while our hands would touch, usually while I was scanning the audience for John. Difficult with so many heads hidden behind frosty breaths or covered by thick, tight toques.

Through two quarters I finished four beers. Two more than usual, for an entire game. But it was a special occasion. Too often John's team had suffered heartbreak at the hands of the Boston Patriots. Now this victory, the Bills' greatest ever, was at hand. Next week, if they held on, they would play the San Diego Chargers in the AFL championship.

Was I the lucky charm? Maybe not me, but rather Doug, because their winning started with his arrival in Canada. That first victory over Kansas City, the day after he arrived, that was the start. I looked at him and smiled. He smiled back.

Then he put his right arm around me, his left hand on my thigh. Before I could say anything, he pulled my head to his, kissed me, his tongue separating my lips. I could muster no resistance at first. His breath was warm. It subdued me and I found myself kissing him back. He let out an aborted chortle before leaning into me until our bodies were horizontal on the sofa. His hands moved up my legs, under my loose sweatshirt, up my waist. Big hands. Warm hands sending a powerful tingling through my body. It felt so good I wanted to disengage my mind and succumb.

But when his thumb pressed against and then over my bra, I flinched in pain, my nipples still sore from Karl. My good sense returned. I broke free and my arms found the strength to push his shoulders away. He did not fight me. I escaped the sofa and started to run out of the room but, for some reason, stopped to look back.

He was sitting forward, the expression on his face not at all what I expected. His magical eyes were half-closed, he was shamefully looking down. He could be acting, I thought, but then brushed that theory aside, concluding instead he was genuinely remorseful. The drinks and celebratory mood had overcome him, had overcome me, and I saw ourselves as mutually guilty. We exchanged a glance, a visual contract, to keep this from John. Nothing dangerous had occurred. It would never happen again, the contract stated, so it was in the best interest of all parties concerned to forget about it, to never speak of it.

I wasn't sure what to do next. While it was unlikely Buffalo would lose, it was still possible. My fear of John's superstition stopped me from ordering my brother-in-law to leave. Doug returned to John's chair and everything seemed like it hadn't happened. Then he flashed a confident grin at me, as if reading my mind.

"I'll watch the rest elsewhere."

He got up. I didn't stop him. Soon after his departure, Karl woke and started crying, distracting me from brooding over what happened. I settled my son down, watched the game until the final whistle, then took a nap.

It was no nap, rather a deep sleep plagued by dreams of my brother-in-law kissing me, fondling me, telling me I was beautiful, that we were meant for each other, all kinds of tripe. Only my successful spurning of these romantic assaults classified the images as dream rather than nightmare.

The front door opening woke me. I was about to bolt out of bed to greet John, but the sound of a second voice stopped me. Had he brought Ted home with him?

"I'm afraid Helen went to bed some time ago."

Hearing Doug say my name made me panic inside. Now I had the fear my dreams hadn't been dreams at all. When had he returned? Why hadn't I heard him?

"I'd hoped she'd be awake," John said, the disappointment in his voice painful to hear.

"Listen, John, I'm moving out. I've found a place."

I got up and stepped close to the door to hear better.

"Are you serious?" John said. "When?"

"Right away."

"But why would you need to get your own place?"

"I can afford it now."

"But you don't save any of your money. You blow it all in bars and on girls and on who knows what? What'll you do if there's a strike?"

"There won't be a strike."

"It's not a good idea." Shut up, John, I thought, let him go. "Why are you telling me now? Something happen while I was away? Did you two have an argument?"

"Not at all," Douglas said, as coolly and calmly as only he could.

My poor husband, coming home so buoyed by the Bills victory. I'm sure he sensed something off, the way he came to bed. His tossing and turning—no doubt a subtle attempt to waken me—saddened me. But I had to act asleep, unable to tell him what had happened, unsure he'd believe me. Or whether I'd believe myself.

When Doug said he was moving out right away, he wasn't kidding. The next day his things were gone, his existence virtually erased from our apartment. All the while he acted his normal self, as if nothing had happened. My concerns over Karl, who had picked up a fever, kept me preoccupied. John was equally absorbed with business matters and the incident dissipated into history.

We all did get together to watch the Bills claim their first AFL championship against the Chargers. That victory was anti-climactic; the win over Boston being the treasured one. Not once did I feel uncomfortable or fear a repeat of what had happened during the Patriots game. Doug was too drunk to drive but refused to stay over, preferring to take a taxi and come back for his car the next day.

In the morning, John suggested we drop his brother's car off, as we hadn't seen his new home yet. I wasn't thrilled about this but gave in when it was obvious Karl's fever had broken.

Well, what could I say, the place was a dump. It was in a so-so neighbourhood near the twin locks and the border between St. Catharines and Thorold. A dark, once elegant two-storey wood and brick structure with a long patio, the house suffered from years of neglect. Bent eaves and loose wires everywhere. One window had been covered with a thick plastic sheet. The lawn, strewn with car tires and weeds protruding through the snow, looked decrepit.

As we approached, John slowed to point at a "For Sale" sign with his name on it. It made me feel proud but also concerned that he dealt with people who lived in such neighbourhoods.

I drove Doug's car up the gravel driveway while John parked ours on the street. I waited until he and Karl reached me before opening my door. I was nervous as we knocked.

"Oh, hello there," said a female voice, as if she knew us.

And she did. It was the girl from the airport. John seemed taken aback so I stepped forward.

"Andrea, is it?" I said. "We came to return Doug's car."

"Angeline," she said, firmly but not unkindly, unfazed by my intentional mistake. This was a woman I would always detest. "Come in, come in. Dougie, honey, visitors."

The interior was not much better than the exterior. The furniture was rundown, most of it from before the war. Peeling green paint and wallpaper marred several walls, as did the countless holes from removed pictures and fixtures. At least it was tidy, no empties laying about. The ashtrays were clean save for one with a lit and lipstick-circled cigarette resting lazily. There were a couple of new age magazines left open on the coffee table. John and I sat on the soft sofa, which was surprisingly comfortable. But not for Karl who began squirming.

"May I hold your baby?" the girl said.

"Sure," John said, as I was about to shake my head.

He took Karl and handed him over. Angeline held him barely seconds when he began screaming louder than I'd ever heard him. So proud of my little boy and, with great satisfaction, I stood to take him back. Just then Doug came down the stairs.

"What's all the racket?" he said, grabbing Karl before I could. My son rested his head against his uncle's shoulder and was instantly quiet. "What brings you here?"

"Thought we'd drop off the car," John said, "come see where you live now."

"Wish you'd called. This place is a dump."

"I've seen worse," John said, and then in an aside to Angeline, "I'm in real estate."

"So, you live here too now?" I said, breaking her smile.

"Nah, she's just down for a visit." He seemed amused, but also uncharacteristically nervous. "You want a beer, or a coffee, or something?"

John seemed ready to accept but I shook my head. Then Karl, bless his heart, began coughing. He wasn't sick but I pretended his fever was returning. We exited and I took the wheel to get us out of there as quick as possible.

"Doug's good with Karl, isn't he?" John said, in the car.

"You've got to talk to him about that girl. She's bad news. Very bad news."

"She seems nice to me."

"John, I'm telling you . . ."

But I couldn't finish my sentence because I didn't know what to tell him. Doug, I'm sure, sensed my distrust because, whenever we saw him after that, it was always at our place or somewhere neutral; he never mentioned Angeline. Not that we saw a great deal of him through the winter. Apparently, he was spending a lot of time in Toronto. It didn't take a genius to understand what was pulling him there.

One time, with Doug at our house for one of his rare visits, he and Karl were working together on a puzzle. Doug was doing it of course, but Karl was monitoring closely, like a keen student. The television kept John's attention, a hockey game. I didn't care for hockey so I was bored and not in a terrific mood to begin with. It just came out.

"Nice you could break away from Angeline to see your family for once."

Doug just laughed. "That one? She's nothing to me."

"Really?" John said, with interest, belying his silly admiration of the girl.

"Sure, I mean, she's a laugh."

"But you spend your free time in Toronto," I said.

"You think I go to Toronto to see her?"

"Yes," I said.

He seemed affronted, I stood my ground. His smile returned.

"Relax, I'm not getting married or doing anything stupid."

That settled it for John who turned his attention back to the hockey game. Doug turned his to me, giving me several unreadable but nonetheless unsettling looks.

I started having those dreams again in which he touched me and professed his love. They never went further than that, thank goodness, but disturbed me for a week or so. They stopped with John's surprise.

A week in Paris, the honeymoon we'd deferred to attend to his brother's immigration. I never made an issue of it, keeping my disappointment inside all this time, but for John it was a debt to be paid off as soon as he had the chance. I didn't like the idea of leaving Karl behind but it was only for a week. Doug had shown himself capable of taking care of our baby. Once his part in the delayed honeymoon came out, he insisted on vacating his house to live in our apartment while we were gone.

My enthusiasm peaked ten days before our departure. Then I started worrying about what would happen while we were away. I knew Doug was functionally capable of doing it but that Angeline girl haunted my thoughts. Would he dare bring her over? My imagination began eating away at my excitement. It was the night before our departure and I was folding the last of my blouses into my suitcase when my agitation boiled over.

"You still haven't heard from your brother?"

"I've called him, even left a note at his door today."

"John, it's almost midnight, we're leaving tomorrow."

"I'm well aware of that. Don't panic. He'll show."

Even so, I wanted to say, will he stick around for a full week? How will we know? Then the phone rang with an ominous tone. I picked it up and said hello.

"Helen, it's Doug. I'm in trouble. You've got to help."

The voice was pathetic, his usual bravado replaced by desperation; he may even have been crying. I just handed the receiver to John, not hiding my disgust. However, I couldn't help myself and rushed to the bedroom to listen in on the extension.

"Where the hell are you?" John said. "We're packed and just about to go to bed."

"John, I need you in Toronto. Right now. I'm at a police station. I've been charged with murder."

The silence seemed to last forever before John let out a deep sigh and pressed his brother for the whole story.

"All right, well, you remember Angeline?"

"What about her?" John said. "Tell me what happened."

The lack of empathy in my husband's voice heartened me, a small though meaningless victory.

"Okay, so Angeline took me to this bar on Queen Street I hadn't been to before. An okay place, and we were having a nice time when I see eye contact between this guy at the pool table and Angeline. She goes to the toilet, he comes over, tells me Angeline's his girl. I explain that's news to me, that his tense must be wrong. Once he figures I'm being a smartass, he's not happy, though he just walks away. Seconds later, four or five of his buddies darken my light. Angeline's taking a long time so I deem it wise to try and find her. But to do so I have to squeeze past these guys. They shift as if to let me through but sandwich me when I try. Then they hold me up for the self-proclaimed boyfriend to punch me. With no hands available I kick him in the nuts. He doesn't like that and tries to run at me but I manage to get another shot in, which is when the other two began to pound my kidneys and face."

Doug paused. My efforts to picture the scene were blocked by a growing resentment, along with a realization I would die without ever seeing Paris.

"Then I spot a knife in someone's hand. I chop at the wrist holding it until the knife falls on the floor. I pick it up and, well, it finds its way into the gut of the so-called boyfriend. Everything stops. Next thing I know I'm in this police station."

"Where is Angeline?"

"No idea. You have to help me out, John."

"I'll call Ted, the friend I went to Boston with. He's a criminal lawyer. Have you been arraigned?"

John's calmness was impressive. Of course, as he was in the other room, I couldn't see his face. Or his hands, which were probably shaking.

"That's scheduled for tomorrow, I believe," Doug said.

At that point, I put down the phone and began sobbing. John came to find me but when he tried to hug me, I rebuffed him.

"I guess you heard." I nodded. "Then you can guess I'll have to leave right away."

"What about Paris?"

"He's in trouble. Serious trouble. We'll have to go another—"

"Leave him there," I said.

We looked at each other for a long minute in silence.

"You know I can't."

I didn't see John the rest of the weekend. My hours were filled with phone calls. I managed to cancel the plane tickets but we lost our deposit on the hotel. The rest of the time I nursed my anger. I was calm with my husband when he did return—after all, it wasn't his fault, beyond inviting this man to our continent in the first place—but reserved too. We endured many silent arguments.

Douglas stayed in Toronto for his trial and sentencing. He got fifteen years, which was lucky for him. How Ted kept him from being deported, I'll never understand, and maybe I'll never forgive him for that.

Now Douglas had a new home in Kingston. I refused to visit him there and refused to let John tell Karl about his uncle, the convicted criminal. My brother-in-law's ways, contrary to his glamorous looks and easy manner, clashed with ours and always would. That he would involve himself with women like Angeline was enough for me to ban his influence from our family. On this matter time, rather than dissipating such feelings, cemented them.

/3\

From the north, several hundred metres away, an upbound ship, painted Canadian flag red and white, passes between the upright spans of the Homer Bridge toward the third lock of the Welland Canal, where gates open for the ship's arrival. More by the familiar arrangement of letters than by actually reading them, Karl recognizes the ship as that old laker, the *D. H. John Henry.*

On the far side, a football field or so across the way, skeletal trees lay bare the farmland beyond, their red and orange and brown autumn shrivelled leaves on the ground, primer for fresh coats of winter snow only weeks away. Likely the last passage of this particular vessel before spring.

Normally, upon spotting any ship, Karl would join the tourists and other canal aficionados on the top tier of the observation platform. Today he remains at the bottom of the lock on a dirt and gravel landing at the edge of the waterway, waiting for his high school chum, Tom Waryk.

Karl zips up the light windbreaker to his neck. Half an hour earlier the nylon shield, pulled over a thin sweatshirt, was ideal for riding in the mildly damp air. Now the sweat earned from two hours cycling aimlessly about the city leaves him with a chill, aggravated by an occasional drizzle. His sixteenth birthday is not living up to expectations.

The day began well, sleeping in till noon, waking to his favourite two-plate brunch of bacon, pancakes, and a thick omelette. After a long, hot shower, he joined his father and brother to watch the football game, idly killing time until his rendezvous.

At halftime, with the Bills leading the Jets 17-10, his father vacated his brown La-Z-Boy to lower the television volume while Samuel dimmed the lights in an orchestrated sequence. His mother entered the living room carrying a tray with a covered cake pan that she gingerly set down in the middle of the coffee table. She lifted the cover to reveal a dark chocolate cake, football shaped, stitched by sixteen white recessed candles, tiny flames bursting out.

"Wow, that's so cool," Samuel said.

"Happy Birthday Karl," his mother said, the wish then echoed by his father and brother.

Always with the football theme, Karl thought in that moment, while temporarily blinded by the flashbulb from his mother's instant camera. He's getting tired of his father's seasonal obsession dominating every aspect of every Sunday and Monday every fall. Now that Samuel is football crazed too, it will only get worse. The NFL season is the shortest of all the major sports but, to Karl, it seems the longest.

Nevertheless, he had to admit Samuel was right. It was a cool birthday cake, yet another example of his mother's impressively creative baking skills. He blew out the candles and his mother handed him a long knife. As he was about to plunge the blade in the middle, she stopped him to guide his hand to a pre-cut slit on the right. He cut away one piece to uncover an envelope. She helped him cut away three more pieces so he could pull it out. Inside he found money, green money, U.S. bills, and counted out fifty dollars. But there was more. Football tickets, Bills tickets.

"Wow. Thanks Mom. Thanks Dad."

He meant it too, regretting his anti-football sentiment of a moment earlier, but uncertain what to do next. A hug would be appropriate but also awkward, as his father didn't seem to be expecting one.

The moment passed when his mother lifted the three pieces and handed them out on small plates, along with small forks. Now his father leaned forward as Karl inspected the tickets. End zone seats, it looked like, for the Steelers game. The Steelers, defending Super Bowl champions. No doubt these tickets were hard to get. Karl set them down, smiled at his father, and ate his cake. With the third bite, an unsettling feeling overcame him. Not from the cake; that was delicious. No, something else wasn't right, something nagged at him. Weren't the Bills playing in Cincinnati the following week?

Oh no. On the pre-game show the announcers talked about next weekend's Bengals game being a good test before hosting the Steelers, which meant . . . he set down his plate and checked the date on the tickets—November 23—and stared at it a full minute, but the date stayed the same.

A cold shiver cued an internal panic of helplessness, mixed with a fleeting flash of resentment, though to whom or what, Karl had no idea. He glanced at his mother but she was oblivious to the connection. Karl sighed, re-stuffed the tickets and cash, and handed the envelope back to his father.

"I can't go, Dad."

The envelope fell on the floor.

"Karl, don't joke like that," his mother said.

"I'm not joking."

"Do you know how hard it was for your father to get those tickets?"

Reluctantly, Karl glanced over at his dad who looked like he thought this was still a joke. But Karl had no punch line for him.

"All right, Karl, tell me why you can't go."

"Because I'll be in Pittsburgh that weekend, with Tom."

"Oh my god, I completely forgot," his mother said.

His father's smile vanished, his face reddened and his eyes narrowed.

"Who the hell is Tom?" he said, after several seconds.

"He's Karl's friend, from school, the one whose mother lives in Pittsburgh."

"Father," Karl said.

His mouth slightly open, Karl's father stared at his son.

"It's his father who lives in Pitts—"

"Father, mother, who cares? This is your first football game, with *your* father. I remember how excited I was to see my first soccer game with *my* father. Nothing, and I mean nothing, would have stopped me from going."

"Sorry Dad, I promised Tom. All this was planned long ago and he'll be disappointed and—"

"Great, just great. Tell me why you can't just visit your friend another weekend?"

A voice inside urged him to ask his father why he can't just get tickets for another game, but the words never came out. Instead, Karl grabbed his jacket and left, leaving his cake uneaten, to ride aimlessly until meeting up with his friend.

Tom transferred to Karl's high school the previous December but it wasn't until last spring, on a class trip to Ottawa, upon discovering they shared a birthday, that their friendship took hold. Karl recalls the bus ride fondly. For six hours they discussed life, death and other significant topics, without resorting to gossip, weather, sports, or gawking at out of province licence plates.

Prior to the trip, Karl saw Tom at school and pegged him as a loner, but one whose isolation was out of choice. His demeanour was aloofly cool, as if having few friends gave him status. This did somehow make him attractive to the opposite sex. With more than a little envy, Karl would witness girls huddling in their cliques stop their chatter as Tom walked by. Their giggling wasn't mocking and Tom's indifference to them only spiced their interest with mystery.

Unfortunately, Karl never got any benefit from it. While they were buddies, they rarely socialized outside of school because Tom lived in Thorold, too far away. Karl never met any of Tom's girlfriends, not even the ones he claimed to have had sex with from their school.

Then out of the blue a few weeks ago, Tom came up with a brilliant suggestion to celebrate their mutual birthdays in America. Karl was game but hesitant to ask his parents. One day he did catch his mom at the perfect time in the right mood. She not only consented, but also promised to clear it with his dad. Then the daydreams began, scenarios of him and Tom with girls, American girls, double dating. The way Tom speaks of Pittsburgh implies his friend knows tons of people there.

A rhythmic humming disturbs the silent water. Karl looks up as the giant ship passes in front of him, angled to enter the gates; up close cracks in the paint are evident. The low westerly position of the sun tells him it will be dark in an hour or two and the cracks will no longer be visible. It also means it's way past the time they said they would meet. Did Tom forget?

The altercation with his father, combined with Tom's lateness, are allowing doubts to creep in. Karl's sure his mom can smooth it over with his dad and they'll still let him go to Pittsburgh. But what if his friend is having similar problems with his folks who, at that moment, might be changing their minds?

The chill, tolerable till now, is getting to him, even though the drizzle has stopped. Karl will wait until dark if he has to and risk a cold. A day or two off from school wouldn't be a bad thing. With his sleeve, Karl wipes water off a bollard and sits down.

The ship manoeuvres into the narrow slot, expertly avoiding the sidewalls until finally all the way in the lock, clear of the gates. Now it dwarfs the surroundings. Unseen to Karl, the crewmen are tossing hawsers to men on the quay who will wrap them around bollards to stabilize the vessel. The yellow crane-like arm will lower and sound a clunk before rising again. The gates will close and seal the ship tight. All Karl can see is the inverted side of the riveted brown gate and its catwalk.

Behind him, something crinkles, a stray leaf or chip bag. Karl turns as Tom rides up in a fancy-looking red Schwinn. A cigarette dangles from his mouth and some ash drops on his torn jeans, which he wipes away. His mop of shoulder length black hair flops from side to side, concealing much of his face, brushing against his dark brown leather jacket. A pair of light-coloured glasses hold up his bangs enough to allow vision. Tom squeezes his brakes inches in front of Karl, squealing his tires, stopping at the concrete edge of the quay. He spits his cigarette butt into the canal, then wipes his hair back behind his ears with both hands.

"Happy birthday, buddy."

"Happy birthday, buddy."

Karl rises to shake hands. From a jacket pocket, Tom pulls out a pack of du Mauriers, fans through the white tips until he finds a joint. Lighting it takes a while as the swirling wind keeps blowing out his matches, no matter how tightly he cups his hands.

"How come you're late? What's her name?"

Tom snorts as he releases several puffs of smoke.

"I'm still waiting for you to hook me up with someone," Karl says.

"Nah, what for? They're all sluts."

"All of them?"

"No, not all of them."

Tom doesn't elaborate. They exchange tokes in silence, gazing toward the lock where the bridge of Karl's ship juts out, bobbing slightly. Soon the hull appears and the vessel reaches full height. Ordinary and functional as it is, it looks majestic high up, seemingly perched in the air, until it moves on beyond the far gates and out of sight.

"You really dig these ships," Tom says.

"Yeah."

"They're always the same ones though. Going up, then going down, and then going up and down and up and down, until they fall apart, of course."

"So, everything set for the trip?"

Tom flicks the roach away, takes a regular cigarette from the same pack. He doesn't offer Karl one, having already witnessed how cigarettes hurt Karl's lungs and make him dizzy.

"Sure, we're still good for our adventure in America."

Karl nods but then tells Tom about what happened at home with the football tickets. Tom finishes his smoke peacefully, drops the butt on the ground, and crushes it under his Doc Martens.

"We can do it another weekend."

"No, I am going to Pittsburgh the weekend we chose."

"You sure? Football tickets are hard to give up."

"Positive."

A white maintenance truck rolls down the ramp, slows down as the driver glances in their direction, then drives the other way.

"There has been a slight change to the plan," Tom says.

"What do you mean?"

Tom's stare gives Karl a sense of foreboding, a clue that he won't like what he is about to hear.

"My father won't be able to drive us."

"Then how are we getting there?"

"Greyhound."

"By bus?"

"By bus."

"How long will that take?"

Tom shrugs ambiguously, either as if he doesn't know but it makes little difference, or as if he knows but won't say, knowing Karl won't like the answer.

"I'm not sure my parents will go for that," Karl says.

"Why not? You're sixteen now. I do it all the time."

"My parents aren't like yours, Tom."

"Lucky you."

"Lucky me? What does that mean?"

"Nothing. Listen, don't say anything to them until you have to. Leave it till the last minute, then dare them to stop you from going."

"I don't know."

"You have to come, if only to let me make up for Ottawa."

Karl grins, but then frowns. Tom isn't referring to the bus ride itself, but rather to what happened in Ottawa. Or, from Karl's standpoint, what didn't happen.

They were in the hotel lobby when they found out they would be assigned different rooms on different floors. After check-in Karl never saw his friend. Not at the Parliament Buildings, Sparks Street Mall, Rideau Canal, Art Gallery, or any of the museums. No one did for that matter, until it was time to board the bus for home. Rumour had it he escaped every day to meet up with a local girl and that he only slept at the hotel one of the three nights.

On the six-hour ride home, Tom described parties he'd gone to, the girls, booze, and drugs. It sounded fantastic and Karl listened with wonder. With jealousy and resentment too, when he realized how close he was to being part of it, instead of being bored by the life-sized models of tundra people and woolly mammoths at the Museum of Man.

"You'll miss your bus if your friend doesn't show soon."

"Don't worry, Tom'll show," Karl says.

But what if he doesn't, John wonders. They've waited in the nearly empty parking lot at Karl's high school for twenty minutes.

His son's calmness surprises John because Karl is always prompt himself and, like his father, quickly irritated by others' tardiness. For all he and Helen know, this Tom Waryk is a smartass punk playing a joke on their son.

The information Helen extracted out of Karl about his friend is limited. Recently the Waryks separated. Before then, the family moved around a lot, primarily in eastern Ontario, and only settled in Niagara in the last year. Soon after, Tom's parents divorced, around the same time the father accepted a vice-presidency position at a steel company in Pittsburgh. The mother got full custody of the only child, Tom, with specific visitation rules for his father that included trips to Pittsburgh. The arrangements sounded clear. Perhaps too clear. Perhaps the Waryk domestic situation is murkier than what Karl thinks.

If Tom doesn't show, it would complicate matters in the Stevenson household too. After Karl's somewhat ungracious rejection of the football tickets, John worked out a terrific solution: take Samuel. Even better, Karl was all for the idea. Deep down—not so deep, if he's honest with himself—John would rather go with the son whose enthusiasm for football matches his own. Yet there is an obligation to take the oldest son first. So if Karl's friend doesn't show and Karl doesn't go to Pittsburgh, he may have to disappoint Samuel; otherwise, if he takes Samuel and leaves Karl behind, his principles will loom over him and detract from his enjoyment of the game.

John glances at his watch. They're about ten minutes from downtown and the bus to Buffalo leaves in twenty. Ten to drive there, park, buy the tickets—no, Tom already has the tickets, or so he supposedly told Karl.

"You know, son, if he doesn't show—"

"Dad, he'll show. But don't worry, if I'm wrong, I won't ask Samuel to give up his ticket."

"I wasn't going to—"

"Sorry, Dad. That just slipped out."

John nods, a little hurt, but glad to see his son getting edgy, a sign he's having doubts. A little cynicism is never a bad thing, even if it takes a circuitous route to evolve.

For instance, Karl didn't find it strange that Tom turned down John's offer to pick him up at his house but can't explain why the kid would go all the way home from his north end school to Thorold and return, an hour on the city bus each way. Admittedly, curiosity was behind John's offer to drive them to the bus station. Now, in picking Tom up at school instead of his house, he won't have a chance to meet the boy's mother, or to see where and how the Waryks live.

"Dad, there he is," Karl says.

Up the street, twenty yards away, a taxi pulls up. Two boys around Karl's age get out and huddle together for a few seconds, as if trading hockey cards. One of them has short, blond hair, and wears a light bomber jacket, shirt tucked in. John hopes that's Tom, not the scruffy, dark-haired one with the glasses. Karl unrolls the window, letting in a blast of cool air, sticks his head out, and yells for his friend to hurry. The scruffy one waves acknowledgement and says a few words to the blond kid before he ambles over.

Up close, he's taller than Karl, and lankier, with long, thick pitch-black hair that could use a decent shampoo. His ruddy pale face looks paler against the dark stubble. John feels a dread in his gut. Would Helen have agreed to let their first-born go away for a weekend with this character?

After a quick introduction, John puts Tom's duffel bag in the trunk while the boy gets in the back seat. John is afraid Karl will join him there, demoting his father to chauffeur. He lets out a silent sigh of relief when Karl remains shotgun.

Karl and his friend are quiet as John drives south along Vine Street and then turns onto Niagara to cross the highway and head downtown. At Church, several buses clog the left lane. Recently, the bus terminal relocated from Market Square; no doubt they're still adapting, which he ought to have taken into account.

There is no other option now so, patiently, he follows the trail of diesel exhaust onto Academy Street, only to find the customer parking spots at the Greyhound terminal taken. The four diagonal coach bays are empty with no lines of waiting passengers. Though there is still a minute to spare, he fears the boys' bus might have left early. He ignores the strange looks from inside, pulls into the coach bay closest to the building entrance to let them out. Karl waves and even manages a grateful smile. John drives another block to park at the beer store.

Fingering the keys in the ignition, John isn't sure what to do. Should he let the boys be or should he make sure they board the bus? Helen will never forgive him if she finds out he hasn't seen them off. Besides, if they miss the bus, they'll need a ride home, won't they?

John enters the crowded building in time to hear a chorus groan from restless passengers that drowns out an announcement. From the reaction he assumes the bus from Toronto, destined for Buffalo, will be delayed at least fifteen minutes. John spots Tom and his son near the back, in the middle of a row of moulded sea green plastic seats, sitting between a pair of men John's age, one white, one black. They look like down-and-outers but seem to be minding their own business. The boys legs straddle their luggage, an empty seat between them. Karl is not one for crowded spaces but looks indifferent to his surroundings, probably excited by a weekend in a different city, in a different country. John pushes through several passengers and their bags, as well as someone mopping the floor, to take the empty seat between the boys.

"Forget something, Dad?"

"Nope."

An awkward pause follows, as if his son expects him to explain his presence. But what is there to explain?

"Look at that line-up for tickets," John says. "Good thing you guys got yours beforehand."

"Dad, we're okay. The bus is just late. You don't have to stick around."

"As a matter of fact, I do, Karl. While I have no wish to crowd you boys, I promised your mothers I'd wait until you were on the bus."

Karl rolls his eyes but Tom looks at John with a grin.

"You spoke to my mother, Mr. Stevenson?"

Tom's voice is deep, much richer and better controlled than Karl's, which still occasionally squeaks. Instinctively, John senses the scruffy lad will look after his son, and that he'll do a good job of it. And, unlike Karl, whose body language tells John he's not wanted there, this Tom doesn't seem to mind the adult presence, even seems to welcome it.

"Well, no, Tom, I didn't actually speak to your mother but I figured I'd presume to extend the promise for her too."

Karl seems agonized by every word in this conversation but Tom nods, as if what John just said makes sense.

"It must be hard, having both parents so far apart."

"Da-ad."

"Relax Karl, I don't mind. Actually, Mr. Stevenson, I'm used to it. To be honest, the farther the better."

"Oh? Why would you say that?"

Karl walks to the candy machine and stands there, coins in hand, scanning every row. Tom stays put and pulls out his cigarettes, offering one to John. If Helen was there, John thinks, she would do something drastic, like aborting the trip and dragging her son home. John declines with a subtle shake of the head. A minute later, Karl returns with a Three Musketeers chocolate bar. Tom smiles at John.

"Don't worry Mr. Stevenson. Your son doesn't smoke."

Tom's assured tone comforts John who now realizes it could be good for his son to face temptations in life, and the implication he's tried smoking and doesn't like it is as much a positive indication of his son's sensibility, as it is a relief.

"How often do you visit your father?" John says.

"As often as I can. Pittsburgh gets a bad rap but it's a great town as Karl will soon find out. Unfortunately, I only get there every couple of months or so."

"Does your father have a nice place there?"

"Yeah it's okay. Look, Mr. Stevenson, you and your wife, Mrs. Stevenson, I mean, you don't need to worry about Karl while he's with me, with us. Our house is in a nice neighbourhood, a safe neighbourhood I should add. We're just going to hang around, see some sights, you know. There's plenty of food and cable and a VCR, so he'll be well taken care of. Besides, he's too good a kid to get into trouble. Seriously."

A rustle of movement in the building precedes a new announcement, this time of the arrival of the Toronto bus, which is received with several mocking cheers.

"Dad, thanks a million for the lift. We'll be okay from here."

John nods. He'd like to give his son a hug but Tom stands between them now making any such attempt clumsy. Then Karl's friend surprises John with a hearty handshake.

"Yes, Mr. Stevenson, thank you very much."

Tom steps aside, opening up the opportunity for a hug, but it still doesn't feel right. Instead, John reaches into his coat, pulls out an envelope and thrusts it toward his son. Karl takes it and opens it but shows little reaction beyond a grateful smile upon seeing the fifty dollars from his birthday cake.

"Have fun. Maybe you can pick up a souvenir for your mother and brother."

It's long after midnight when the Greyhound pulls into the grimy bus station in downtown Pittsburgh. The building is at least ten times larger than the one back home, with ten times the vehicles, people, and confusion, even at this hour. Mixed in with the strong diesel smell is an unpleasant odour of unwashed human bodies, stale cigarettes, and urine. It's a rather unimpressive start.

While Tom watches as the driver removes luggage from underneath the coach, Karl scans the crowded terminal for an American version of his father, one who is wealthier, and cooler. He imagines a tall man in a tan trench coat, opened up to reveal a blue or grey suit and a white shirt, unbuttoned at the top, tie loosened, and wearing a welcoming smile.

By the time they exit onto Liberty Avenue, no such man has appeared, no greeter of any kind, only taxis and lingering bus passengers. A few bums. The streets are desolate and dark save for the odd streetlight and neon bar sign. Even with his friend nearby, Karl feels oddly alone and can't wait to get somewhere else.

"Have you seen your dad, yet?" Karl says, still searching.

Tom chuckles in between lighting a cigarette. Then he pauses, as if expecting Karl to solve a riddle.

"My young friend, we have Pittsburgh to ourselves."

"What?"

"Surprise."

"You mean he's not showing up?"

"Bingo."

"When did that happen?"

Tom shrugs but offers no explanation. Karl is about to ask if Mr. Waryk is meeting them at the house, but then it sinks in what's going on.

"We're still going to your father's house, right?" Karl says, unable to contain the alarm in his voice.

"If I wanted us stranded, we'd have gone to NYC."

Tom leads Karl to the front of a row of taxis where he gives a large, unsmiling, but friendly-looking black man an address in an area called Brighton Heights. The cabbie is wearing a Steelers jacket and a Penguins cap that looks too small for his thick, hairless head. The first black adult Karl has noticed up close. At school barely a handful of students aren't white: several East Indians, a brother and sister from Jamaica, and a kid from Trinidad & Tobago. Karl doesn't know any of them. Other than skin colour, there is nothing different about those kids, most of whom don't even have accents, but it always seems to Karl there should be. With this man he has the same feeling though the man doesn't smell or act strangely, except to hum off-key to a soft Diana Ross tune on the radio. The cab itself smells stale and old, but it's probably no different from the ones back home.

As the vehicle ascends a long hill, Karl experiences a mild queasiness, similar to anticipating a rollercoaster drop. Could it be homesickness? More likely exhaustion, caused by the eight hours of broken sleep on the upright bus seats.

Every few moments, the cabbie glances in the rear view mirror, as if sizing them up on whether they will rob him or skip out on paying. It eases Karl's growing anxiety to know that if Tom is up to something like that, he has fifty dollars from his father to fix it. When they stop on a secluded street, Tom pays the cabbie, adding a tip that makes the man smile widely. The whiteness of his teeth startle Karl.

Save for crickets, the night is soundless. The moon glances on a pair of tall and thick oak trees barely holding on to their last leaves, creating an eerily erratic glow that's enhanced by the stark absence of street lights.

Tom's Pittsburgh home is a rectangular brick and stone bungalow that doesn't look bigger than Karl's home, though it is detached and on a wider lot. A deeper lot too. For what Karl saw was only the front of the house; the side is much longer.

Inside, the modern, chrome and leather furniture is elegant and impressive though formal. Cold. Ceiling pot lights illuminate an extensive collection of sculptures, pictures, and knick-knacks, mostly African or South American, displayed in glass cases, as in a museum. He counts five bedrooms on the main floor, and as many bathrooms. Presumably, the basement is finished too, but Tom doesn't show him that.

Actually, Tom doesn't show him anything. Instead, he throws his bag in his bedroom and instructs Karl to choose any of the others, except the master bedroom. The one Karl takes has a canopied queen bed and en-suite bathroom.

Karl unpacks his toiletries and clothes before rejoining Tom who is lounging in the large living room, his body spread out on a leather sectional couch that can comfortably fit a dozen people. The main window reveals a hill upon which floodlights shine on an observatory.

"I didn't know your father was this well off," Karl says.

Tom grunts, walks to the kitchen, and opens the fridge.

"He does okay. It's just money—whoa—mother lode."

Tom returns with two opened bottles of Heineken and manages to toss one upright to Karl who manages to catch it without spilling. Tom flings himself on a recliner, takes a few sips, sits back, and lets out a big, happy sigh.

Still troubled by Tom's father's absence, Karl fears that once he takes a sip from the beer he'll be fully complicit in this parental deceit. Maybe he ought to call his mom and hint to her what's going on, and have her reaction help him decide. Tom is watching him with growing impatience.

"What's the matter? Need a glass or something?"

"Does your dad even know we're here?"

Tom raises his eyebrows, but says nothing.

"So, where is he then?"

"To see my mom. I suspect she's trying to dump me on him again."

"Wouldn't he expect to see you there?"

"Probably, but my mom has a better chance if I'm not around. That's why she told me to scram and find something to do on the weekend."

"So, then, she knows we're here."

"Nope, too risky. She'd tell him."

Tom takes a large swig of beer and almost chokes as he begins chuckling, revealing an unmistakably sinister tone behind his glee.

Without being aware of having started, Karl finds himself drinking his beer.

"I told my mom I was staying with you," Tom says.

"You did what?"

"Relax, I didn't give her any information like your full name or phone number. She didn't ask either."

"I take it your dad's not staying with your mother."

"Are you kidding? No, he's got some slut to stay with, in Hamilton, or Harloton as my mom likes to call it, though she's not much better. Harlot, what's that?"

"It's an old term for—"

"I know what it means, Karl. It's just, who uses words like that?"

Before Karl can respond, a pair of cabinet doors slide open. The largest television screen he's ever seen brightens the room. Karl spots a remote control in Tom's hand but no wire connecting it to the set, just a tiny, flickering red light. Tom ignores Karl's technological fascination and keeps pressing buttons, skipping through endless channels until stopping at one showing Pittsburgh Penguins highlights.

An hour and a couple of beers later, without warning, in the middle of a feature on Rick Kehoe and the incoming flood of ex-Leafs playing for the Pens now, such as Randy Carlyle, Paul Gardner, and Errol Thompson, Tom shuts off the television. He lights a joint, and puts on a record by an English band Karl has never heard of, Joy Division.

The haunting music is stark yet melodic, even danceable. Tom explains how, earlier that year, the day before the band was to go on tour in North America, the singer, Ian Curtis, hung himself. When side one finishes, Tom flips the record over but stares at Karl until their eyes meet before setting the needle down.

"Why were you like that with your father?"

"What are you talking about?"

"At the bus station in St. Catharines. You were rude to him, as if embarrassed, not just by his presence, but by his existence. If my father took the trouble to drop me off, and wait with me . . . you know, your dad's a good man."

Karl is speechless, not sure if Tom is serious, drunk, or both. His motor skills are fine, as he can work the expensive record player capably, so Karl wonders if he, not Tom, is the drunken one. When the needle comes down and a song called *She's Lost Control* starts playing, Karl relaxes.

"But what about your dad, Tom? Isn't he fighting for custody? That means he wants you to live with him. That must count for something, no?"

"Ha! You don't get it. You weren't listening. Neither of them wants me. They're arguing over who gets stuck with me. My mom's trying to throw me back here. My dad's gone to fight it but, me being here in Pittsburgh, she's first and goal on the one-yard line."

Clattering plates startle Karl but the familiar aroma of bacon and coffee is what wakes and briefly fools him into thinking he's at home. The large bed, silk sheets, and an odd egg-shaped LED clock on the night table, with its orange digits, a pair of ones, a colon, and a pair of fives, tell him otherwise.

Karl finds Tom in the kitchen facing the stove, tea towel over one shoulder, his hands managing two frying pans while his eyes monitor a sleek six-slice toaster. A radio plays a well-known tune. Karl laughs when he recognizes Supertramp's *Breakfast in America.* The sun, partially veiled by a thin stylish silver window curtain, brightens the kitchen and adjoining dining room.

In daylight, the house seems even larger; it has to be at least twice the size of Karl's home. Everything in the kitchen is double in size, and triple in luxury. The refrigerator, stove, toaster, cupboards, the shiny speckled black counter and, on the counter a thin, cylindrical space age device he is unable to identify. An island longer than the Stevenson dining room table when expanded is surrounded by six leather-cushioned, chrome-legged chairs that separate the kitchen from a formal dining room. On the island, two oversize dinner plates with an orange and blue geometric pattern, cutlery, and napkins are laid out, diner style.

Karl sits down, facing Tom's back. His friend has put on a pair of jeans and a t-shirt and Karl wishes he'd changed out of his flannel pyjamas. The chef looks at Karl but makes no comment as he sets down two glasses of apple juice.

"Thanks."

"There's coffee too."

"I can't believe you know how to cook."

Tom ignores this as he serves plates loaded with bacon and pancakes and eggs. He fills a large Steeler-crested mug with coffee before taking a seat across from Karl. But he has to get up again for syrup from the fridge. Karl notes, with a mix of pleasure and trepidation, it's loaded with Heineken.

They eat quickly, quietly. When finished, Tom refuses Karl's attempts to help, pointing to the dishwasher in which he places almost everything. Karl has never seen one operate before. He listens to it slosh and shake and clunk for a few minutes before going back to his room for a shower and to change. He comes back in jeans and a clean, maroon polo shirt. Tom is standing by the back door, now in navy blue Adidas track pants and a red sweatshirt, shaking his head.

"That was a waste of a shower."

"Why? Where're we going?"

"You didn't bring any clothes for biking?"

"No, I didn't think, I thought your dad would . . ."

Tom shakes his head, then beckons Karl to the garage. A red '63 Corvette, protected by a transparent plastic sheet takes up most of the space. On a wall opposite a workbench and metal cabinet, two bicycles, supported by kickstands, look ready to ride. One is white, the other blue, both Schwinn King Stings, the same model as the red one Tom rides in St. Catharines.

"I'll manage with what I have on," Karl says.

"No need."

Tom rustles through a cardboard box. He discovers a partially torn, grey Property of Pittsburgh Steelers shirt and a tattered mesh jersey, in Steeler yellow and black, but logo-less. Tom sniffs both items before flinging them at Karl who puts them on slowly.

"What would my dad say if he saw me wearing these?"

Tom laughs.

"I think he'd disown me. Do me a favour, Tom, refuse if I ask you to take a picture of me."

"Sure thing."

Further digging unearths a pair of dull red track pants, grossly out of style, but more practical than his clean jeans.

The temperature is mild for late November. Several lefts and rights along leaf-strewn side streets, the names of which he'll never remember, disorient Karl within five minutes. Until they reach Brighton Road, a long, steep street with several big curves; Karl recognizes it from the uphill cab ride last night. The return trip is going to be torture.

The wind hits his face and pierces through the mesh, giving Karl a pleasurable chill as the boys whip past houses and stores in what surely must have been a distinct village or town once. The streets aren't as littered as Karl expects for an American city. On his left, an immense cemetery. A huge, endless hilly expanse of lawns and stones they don't see the end of for twenty blocks or so. There the road flattens and the reduced gravity forces him to pedal harder. The effort is welcome as it warms him up. Soon the urban skyline comes into view, and then the Allegheny River.

At the National Aviary, Karl misinterprets Tom's hand movement as a signal to stop at the large park. His friend speeds on and is soon out of sight. Slightly panicked, Karl guesses at a turn and rides toward the tall buildings, figuring that's where Tom was leading him. At every street and alley he slows to look left and right, swearing at himself for not making Tom disclose their destination, though that would have been of little use, as he forgot to bring the city map his mom gave him.

At Sixth Street, Tom waits, arms crossed with an ambiguous smile indicating he's either pissed off or amused. Side by side, they cross the Allegheny River over the Roberto Clemente Bridge into downtown. Tom says nothing, except when he feels the need to clarify directions and upcoming changes. While he knows the geography cold, Tom would be a poor guide for anyone interested in the city's history.

From Fort Duquesne Boulevard, they enter Point Park at the confluence of the Ohio, Allegheny, and Monongahela rivers. Tom stops for a cigarette, correctly guessing Karl will want to take pictures. While Karl does so, Tom walks off to strike up a conversation with a father and son fishing. Karl considers taking a picture of his friend but figures Tom might not like it, especially if not asked first.

They exit the park and ride along Fort Pitt Boulevard, cross to the south side of the Monongahela and over the Smithfield Street

Bridge. At Station Square, they lock their bikes, take the funicular to the top of Mount Washington, and walk to a fenced outlook.

The view is terrific. The three rivers split out and away below him, northwest, northeast, southeast. The panoramic contrast between the modern steel and glass skyscrapers and the rolling hills of the river valley on the left is particularly appealing. Beyond the horizon, it seems the world drops off.

"Pittsburgh, for tourists," Tom says.

Karl isn't sure if the comment is rhetorical or targeted at him. Taking so many pictures does make him feel self-conscious, silly even, but he doesn't care, and snaps away.

"Sure are lots of bridges, so much steel."

But Tom's attention is fixed on something in the distance, an area to their left, up the Ohio River. Karl can make out a strip of green, an island splitting the river. A murky cloud hangs overtop the island. Bounded by dark green trees and flat patches of light green farmland, the rural vista is surreally charming.

Tom suddenly gets antsy and want to go, but cannot wait for the funicular. They descend rapidly on foot, retrieve the bikes, and retrace their route across the Clemente Bridge, but turn left and toward Three Rivers Stadium. Tom allows Karl to take photos and then leads him to Beaver Avenue on which they ride parallel to the Ohio River. Office buildings give way to warehouses, sidewalks to railroad tracks. The industrial area is desolate except for a few parked cars. It's difficult to tell if the buildings are empty due to abandonment or merely shut down for the weekend. Tom rides slower now and Karl wonders if they're lost. At the end of Beaver Avenue, Tom stops abruptly and Karl almost runs into him. Across the street stands an unattractive modern building with a façade like that of a college.

Farther down a side street the main structure reveals itself: an ominous, older institutional edifice of pinkish brick, topped by spirals of barbed wire. At the rear, people fish the Ohio River. Karl guesses the heavily treed, unpopulated island in the middle of the river is the same one he observed atop Mount Washington.

"I guess this is *not* Pittsburgh for tourists," Karl says.

Tom chuckles and slaps Karl on the back. Then he goes quiet and stares solemnly at the facility, as if trying to peer through its oppressive walls.

"Tom, why'd we come here?"

"Death row."

Even though still warm and sweating from the bike ride, the words chill Karl due to how Tom says them, half-whispered, each syllable dramatically stretched out. It sends a burst of adrenaline coursing through him, along with a foreboding of danger Karl finds surprisingly welcome. Tom pulls out his cigarettes and, after lighting one, studies the package.

"Wonder what this would be worth inside," he says, pointing to the barbed wire on the roof.

A windowless and unmarked van drives by, catching them by surprise. They watch until it disappears into an inconspicuous entrance. Tom gives Karl a knowing look.

"It could just be laundry," Karl says.

"Nah, it's from court, or a parole board, or another jail."

"On a Saturday? And wouldn't the vehicle have bars on the back then?"

"Oh Karl, don't be so common."

Karl has no idea what that means but becomes wary of asking more questions. Something has come over Tom who now seems in a trance.

"Death row must be frightening," Karl says, after a silence of several minutes.

Tom blinks twice and snaps out of it.

"Actually it'd be more frustrating than frightening."

"Frustrating?"

"That's right. Imagine being told you'll be put to death and then end up having to wait, often for years. If they're going to kill you then why don't they get on with it?"

Karl stares at his friend who is staring at the building.

"Think about it. Here you are, convicted of some illegal act, murder, the worst thing you can do according to society. You've just earned the harshest punishment. Then you get subjected to this bureaucracy, jerked around by legalities, last minute appeals, politics, or plain laziness and incompetence. To me, the mental anguish from that is far worse than any physical one. If I were the original victim, or victims, that would vindicate me."

Karl isn't sure if Tom expects him to respond. All he can do is nod noncommittally. But Tom isn't looking at him.

"About ten years ago Pennsylvania got rid of the death penalty, and then reinstated it, only for it to be challenged again. Two years ago, it came back again, for good. But guess how many they've executed since then?"

Tom makes a circle with his thumb and index finger, then gets up and walks to his bike.

"So you're in favour of capital punishment," Karl says.

"I never said that."

"Then what are you saying?"

"Tell me, Karl, are you in favour of the death penalty?"

"No way."

"So if someone you loved, your parents, your brother, was killed you wouldn't want the murderer to suffer?"

"Suffer, sure, but not necessarily killed."

"Exactly."

"Exactly what?"

Tom's gaze turns back to the prison. He lights another cigarette, takes a few drags.

"On death row, you'll never get out of prison. With life imprisonment, you get released, eventually, if you can outlive your sentence. I suppose the difference is what you have to look forward to."

"So, Tom, which is better?"

"Depends whether you're the prisoner or the victim."

Karl studies his friend, trying to make sense of what he's trying to say, but not succeeding. He's about to change the subject when another thought intrudes.

"So those prisoners stuck inside, waiting to die, never knowing when it's going to happen. How is that different from everyone else? We have no clue either, do we? We can die from an accident at any time. The difference really just comes down to level of comfort."

Tom stares at Karl a long moment.

"You've never spoken truer or wiser words, my friend. Not much else to it, is there?"

"Well, of course, there's freedom."

"Freedom, bah."

*

John exits Route 219 but only manages to get a hundred yards before having to brake behind a pickup unabashedly emblazoned with dozens of red, white, and blue Buffalo Bills stickers. He's self-consciously aware of his unadorned car and the lack of team colours in their clothes. At least Samuel, with his blue sweatshirt and black track pants, blends in. John, on the other hand, exhibiting unforgiveable oversight, has chosen to wear cords and a grey flannel shirt. Still, he and his young passenger can match the other fans in loyalty and spirit. And Samuel's spirit seems endless.

Unlike Karl, Samuel is talkative, more than willing to open up about his life, his likes and dislikes, his friends. It's no surprise charismatic charm and good looks make Samuel popular at school. John struggles to keep up with the Mikes and Mitches, the Kevins and Kellys, Adams and the Annas, and the other dozen or so names mentioned in their house at dinner time.

It also comes as no surprise Samuel's favourite subject is gym, at which he excels. Ever since his second son learned to walk, John harboured hopes of him becoming an athlete, a football star with a scholarship to Syracuse or another top school. Samuel is not nearly the brain Karl was in elementary school. No academic. Which makes it odd that his favourite teacher is a Mrs. Purdy who teaches English, of all things.

It doesn't take long to work through traffic, all of which is heading to the same place. And as they're several hours early, John has no trouble finding a spot to park on a massive grassy lot. Like a caged tiger, Samuel bursts out of the car and trots toward the stadium. John coughs slightly and his son halts, looks back as John swings open the hatch door.

"What's your rush?"

"The stadium's over there."

John puts his hands on his hips and keeps quiet until his son comes back. He puts one arm around Samuel and, with the other, makes a grand sweeping motion across the red, white, and blue filled horizon. Buses, cars, trucks, vans, campers—many with large canopies and tents—a virtual fair of fans barbecuing, drinking, talking, playing cards, throwing footballs of all sizes and material, vinyl miniature, foamy Nerf, and good old pigskin. Most, including plenty of dogs, sport Bills paraphernalia: shirts, jerseys, sweaters, ball caps, visors, socks, shorts, leggings, blankets, umbrellas, windbreakers. Patriotic snowflakes: no two alike.

"Son, we're going to have our own tailgate party."

John removes two lawn chairs and a small foldout table, sets them out and motions for Samuel to sit. Then John pulls out a red stainless steel cooler and places it on the ground between them, closes the hatch. He sits down, grabs a can of beer for himself, a can of Sprite for Samuel, and a large bag of salt and vinegar potato chips. Samuel rips open the chip bag, spilling some on the ground. Before he can pick them up, his father crushes them.

"Don't eat those, there's plenty."

"This is great, Dad."

"You bet. Just don't tell your mom about the chips, or the beer for that matter."

"I won't tell, as long as I can have some beer."

"Nice try."

"Then I'll tell Mom."

"I doubt it."

"How do you know?"

"Because I suspect you'll want to return for a game sometime in the future."

Samuel groans good-naturedly. They munch on the chips and observe a stream of vehicles arrive, unload, encamp with practiced precision until the parking lot is full. Soon the air is saturated with the aroma of burgers, sausages, pork chops. Plumes of smoke fill the sky and remind John of English coal towns. Now he wishes he brought the Hibachi as Helen suggested. Samuel, growing Samuel, can't subsist on snacks alone. And the food inside the stadium will be expensive.

A small football—red, white, and blue naturally—bounces waywardly, end over end, toward them and wobbles to a stop at Samuel's feet. He wipes his fingers on his pants and inspects it.

Some kids call for it. Samuel adjusts his grip, and throws a perfect spiral. The kids, several of them three or four years older than Samuel, ask him to join them in a game of flag football. John nods permission and Samuel quickly fits in, putting a smile on John's face that lasts the entire time he watches his eight-year-old son play.

It's difficult to tell Samuel is the youngest because he's nearly as big as they are, and faster. He can catch and throw better than all but the two biggest kids, who treat him as an equal. They don't hold back from yelling at him whenever he hits them instead of pulling the flag, though Samuel is not afraid to yell back too. Forty minutes later, just as their game is about to get intense, the other kids are called back by their parents. Samuel returns to his proud father, out of breath.

"That was fun."

"You play pretty well."

"I know. That's what those kids said."

"Did they?"

"Yeah, they called me a cocky SOB too."

"They what?"

"It's okay. I know the words are bad but they said it in a nice way, like it was a compliment."

John frowns to himself. A subtle lecture seems in order but he lets it go, too proud to risk spoiling the moment. He instead opens another beer while Samuel returns to his pop and chips.

It's just past noon, less than an hour to kick-off. The tailgaters are packing up their gear before heading to the stadium. Among the parade of streaming fans, one man wears what was once an ordinary black bomber jacket, its lapels now coloured in stripes of red, white and blue, with the Bills crest stitched on the back and on top of the shoulders.

"Hey Dad, can I get a jacket like that?"

"I doubt you can buy one. I think someone made it."

"What about a jersey. I'd love a Bills home jersey, but an away one would be good too. With Joe Ferguson's name and number twelve—no, no, Joe Cribbs, number twenty."

"Hold on there. Those are expensive."

"How about a ball cap? Or a scarf? At least a program."

"Of course, we'll get a program. We'll see about the rest."

At the gate, it takes longer than expected to get through the turnstiles. It's a challenge to keep track of his son while staying on the lookout for program sellers and checking their ticket numbers against the section signs. After a bathroom stop, they get a program, find their section, but have to wait with other fans in the dark passage until the anthem ends.

"Can we get my cap now?" Samuel says.

"Later, son. Let's locate our seats first. We don't want to miss the opening kick-off."

Their seats are in the middle of a long, cramped row next to a corner section. Even with Samuel's adolescent size, they need to huddle to squeeze in between the chubby, heavy jacketed men and women around them, who do little to make way. Compared to the openness of the tailgate experience, John feels claustrophobic and a tad homesick.

"Dad, you think Mom and Karl will watch us on TV?"

"Your mom, maybe. I'm sure Karl's out seeing the sites in and around Pittsburgh. Maybe his friend's dad will take him to see Fallingwater."

Karl's head hurts. As does his stomach, throat, sinus. No greeting from clattering plates or aromatic kitchen smells this time. The clock and its orange digits tell him either he's slept in to one o'clock in the afternoon or time stopped after his tenth or eleventh beer.

He gets up slowly, but not slowly enough, as his head throbs with each movement. When he reaches the living room, sees and whiffs the scattered beer bottles scattered, his insides rebel against him and launch him, stumbling, to the bathroom.

Several minutes of praying to the Porcelain God weaken him, yet also make him feel better, more stable. Should he wake his friend and ask about the day's plans? Karl's not sure he wants to do anything but vegetate so he decides to leave Tom alone.

He collects the bottles and moves them to the kitchen. He checks the fridge and grabs the carton of orange juice out of habit. Several cans of Coke tempt him more and he puts the juice back. He drinks half a can and, after a few belches, feels as if he's starting to come around.

Karl finds the remote control under a cushion, turns on the television and sees the Steelers have taken a touchdown lead. He has another sip, belches, and imagines his father saying . . .

*

". . . shit, what kind of a call—"

"What'd you say, Dad?"

"Nothing."

"We're losing, Dad, it doesn't look good, does it?"

"No, no, it's okay. It's early. We'll get it back."

"Lots of people have ball caps just like the one in the program picture. According to this, I think they're on sale."

"That's nice . . . Hey, hey, here we go—touchdown!"

"Yay."

"What a pass; what a catch. Did you see that, son?"

"Yeah, 7-7, should we go now, maybe?"

"Go now?"

"To get my cap."

"Patience Samuel. Let's wait till halftime."

"It's almost the end of the quarter. There'll be a break right?"

"Just a short one to change ends. Only time for . . .

. . . another commercial break. This game is really dragging along. Better to be watching it on television, Karl thinks, easier to get refills. How is his dad managing that in the cold? It helps that the Bills are playing well and . . .

". . . wow, another touchdown, 14 - 7."

"See, aren't you glad we decided to wait for halftime? We might have missed that one."

"I guess so. Now that we have the lead, do you think we're going to win?"

"Yes, son, I have a good feeling about this one."

"Because the Bills are playing good, aren't they?"

"Yes, against the defending champions too. We've got quite a defence this season."

"You think we can win the Super Bowl?"

"It could happen."

"Can we go to the Super Bowl then?"

"It's almost impossible to get tickets."
"Don't they have contests?"
"Sure, we can enter contests."
"That'll be fun—looks like they're going to get a field goal."
"Thirty-five yards. It's no gimme."
"What's a gimme, Dad?"
"Just watch. There it goes . . ."

. . . and just before halftime, a Steelers field goal, a small setback in what is a good game so far, from a Bills fan's standpoint.

Karl finds it amusing how the Pittsburgh announcers make subtle implications the officials are favouring the home team with generous ball spots and lenient pass interference interpretations. Are the Buffalo announcers that biased too? No, they're worse. Karl has to ask himself, does it matter? Is he still a Bills fan? It's probably in his blood and he'll always cheer for the Bills.

Today, of course, there isn't much else to do other than watch football. Still no sign of life from Tom's bedroom and it seems possible his friend might sleep the entire day. Tom seems to have no trouble sleeping, having done so for ninety percent of the bus ride to Pittsburgh.

Karl's hangover is fading and hunger is kicking in. He realizes he's on his own for food. He wonders how much the timing of his hunger is conditioned from so many football Sundays at home. Maybe watching the game here isn't so smart because he suddenly misses his mom coming into the living room with trays of potato chips, crackers, cookies, and some kind of Pillsbury treat, like cinnamon rolls, croissants, or iced biscuits.

What would she be doing at that moment, all alone? Has she ever been alone without any of them around? Karl can't think of an example. She'd appreciate a phone call but it's long distance. If he calls collect and Tom finds out, he'll feel childish. Besides, he's going back tomorrow. Doing it now wouldn't be . . .

". . . good timing. Now we won't miss any of the second—hey, Samuel, where'd you get that cap? And that scarf?"

"You like them? The scarf is warm. Now I'm a real Bills fan on the outside too."

"But how did you get them? You don't have money."

"Oh, that. While you were paying for the hot dogs a man was giving them out. I'd have gotten you a cap too but it was one per person. Because he liked me though, he gave me the scarf too. You can have that, if you want."

"What man? I didn't see any man."

"He wasn't there long."

"Was he wearing a uniform?"

"I dunno, I guess."

"Where is he, now?"

"Dad, the Bills have the ball again. Whoa, look at him going, going, yes, touchdown!"

"Fantastic. But Samuel, the man that gave you the hat and scarf."

"Dad, we just scored. It's 21-10."

"Yes, yes, wonderful. But the man. Where is he?"

"I don't see him anymore, he must have left . . ."

. . . nothing for Karl to eat. The pizza box is gone. A slice or two of Hawaiian would be perfect right now. Even a breadstick. And another Coke.

But wait, Tom took the box to his bedroom. Might be a good idea to check on him anyway. If he's still sleeping, maybe Karl can make that call home, just for everyone's peace of mind. Karl lifts himself off the couch with an unexpected sluggishness brought on by a sudden hesitation. As if the little task is drenched with dread. True, it could be invading his friend's privacy to peek in his room, but is it that big a deal? Would it bug Karl if Samuel did the same at home? Well, yes.

Just as Karl drops back down to reconsider, a new surge of hunger propels him up and on his feet, pushing through his doubt and impelling his legs to Tom's room. He knocks lightly but there's no answer. Karl turns the knob and enters.

The room is dark, the curtains drawn, and Karl barely makes out his friend lying on the bed, motionless. The sight paralyzes

Karl with familiarity. Déjà vu. Not only the image but also a dank cigarette and alcohol smell making Karl feel himself wanting to vomit, just as he did as a little boy when he came upon his uncle in this position. A memory he keeps suppressed to fool his mom into thinking he's forgotten. But he hasn't. It's still there and now fills him with a deep gloom.

Fortunately the hangover has healed enough to give him the strength to keep his food down. But it can do nothing to prevent his head spinning as it tries to recall that memory in greater detail. All those years of suppression have taken away what he felt at the time. It's frustrating. Karl steps back to leave his friend alone.

He tries the refrigerator again, moves some items until he spots a large Tupperware container. It contains a delicious looking serving of meatloaf, though it's impossible to tell how old it is. He picks away a piece with a fork, inspects it. Looks okay. He puts the container in the microwave, presses some buttons and . . .

". . . here we go, fourth quarter, we're on the two yard line."

"Dad, I'm having the best time of my life."

"I'm so glad to hear that, Sam. I've always dreamed of taking my sons to a game."

"Looks like we're gonna score again, aren't we?"

"We have momentum. One more TD for insurance . . . and there it is, yes, nice little toss."

"No way we're going to lose now, Dad."

"Well, I never like to be sure until the last play."

"Bet Karl wishes he was here now, what a blast . . ."

. . . they must be having, Karl thinks, popping open another can of Coke to wash down the leftover meatloaf. What a rip the football game was the same weekend. Yet Karl can't regret choosing Pittsburgh. Tom is the first friend, the first person really, he can talk to, openly. There's a deep level of honesty between them, kind of like what he had with his uncle.

Then again, it's odd to be this free, to have no parents around, to be able to drink beer, eat whenever, do whatever, however you want. In a way it feels somewhat empty, too easy, like winning a game by default.

Tom doesn't seem to care about his advantages. Most kids would kill for his freedom and wealth. Then again, after experiencing it first hand, Karl would opt for his modest life, his parents, his brother. No matter the arguments they got in, it was never as terrible as what Tom described? Did his parents really care so little for him? Or vice versa?

Karl only notices now that Tom's dad's house is devoid of family photos. No portraits, no candid humorous vacation shots, not one school picture of his friend. It seems creepy. It brings back his earlier feeling of homesickness, and a good dose of guilt. But what for? For leaving his mom alone? Perhaps, but he'll have to share that guilt with his brother and father.

His father. That's it. Tom is right. Karl was awful at the bus station and now he cringes recalling the scene.

Tom's silence begins to worry Karl. Maybe he's sick and needs Karl to check on him. But another thought overrides this one: that not once during the weekend have they talked about girls or parties or even Tom's friends in Pittsburgh. He hasn't even had a chance to buy anything with his fifty dollars. Much as Karl enjoys the cable TV, free beer, and deep discussions, he feels cheated.

A meaningless field goal by Pittsburgh makes the score, 28-13. The Steelers are done for. Just waiting it out until the . . .

". . . final whistle. Let's go."

"What a win, Dad, what a game."

"You bet . . . all right Samuel, let's walk slowly . . . let those people in front of you . . . no rush."

"Can I get another hot dog? There's no line-ups."

"The stands are closed. That's why there's no line-up."

"Oh."

"But tell me again where the man was."

"What man?"

"The one giving out the hats and scarves."

"He's gone."

"Where was he standing though?"

"It all looks different now. It might have been there. Or there. I'm not sure. Can we go to McDonald's when we get back?"

"All right."

The telephone rings, just once. Tom's muffled voice can be faintly heard from the living room, but only after Karl turns the television volume down—how he loves that remote control.

There follows a stretch of silence, then Tom's voice, even fainter, as if he's meekly taking orders. Minutes later the bedroom door opens. Tom emerges in a plain black t-shirt and his torn jeans, dishevelled hair and no glasses, one dark eye visible. The morbid expression turns into an ominous grin when Karl tells him the result of the game.

"You don't like the Steelers?" Karl says.

"Absolutely hate them. Of course, my father loves them. Speaking of which, that was him on the phone. He's pissed."

"At the Steelers losing?"

"Yeah, that too."

Tom laughs mockingly, poorly concealing his anxiety; the call looks to have rattled him.

"Listen, bud, you have to go home right away. There's a bus leaving in less than two hours from downtown."

"You're kidding, right?"

"Afraid not."

"Alone?"

"Yep, apparently my mom won. Or rather, my dad lost, twice, if you count the Steelers. Either way, I'm staying. You have to be out of here before he gets home. So shower up, if you need one, and I'll call you a taxi."

"What's the rush? Why can't he drive me to the bus station when he gets here? I don't mind catching a later bus."

Tom chuckles but looks embarrassed.

"The jig is up for you too. It's your mom who's insisting you leave now. She'll meet you at the bus station. Besides, you don't want to be here when my old man gets home."

"I guess we're both in big trouble then."

"Been good knowing you," Tom says.

*

John chooses to keep stateside all the way to Niagara Falls so as to cross at Lewiston, figuring the Peace Bridge will be busier with the mass exit of Canadian fans from the Bills game who are anxious to get the border ritual over with as soon as possible.

A good choice until the Garden City Skyway, where traffic halts due to an accident closing the giant bridge over the Welland Canal. Most vehicles divert north to York Street for Queenston Road, so John goes south. Bad choice. The Glendale bridge is up and they'll have to wait until a ship passes through. Samuel is oblivious to the delay, still abuzz from their adventure.

"Dad, wasn't that the best game ever?"

"One of them."

"You mean you've been to a better game?"

"Sure have. Back in the AFL days. You remember me explaining how there were two leagues and the New England Patriots used to be the Boston Patriots, and so on."

"Oh yeah."

"Well, the best game I've seen live was the final regular season game of 1964, December 20."

"Tell me about it."

"Thought you'd never ask."

Samuel smiles.

"Our Bills and the hated Patriots were the top teams in the East. The winner would get to the championship game. What made it more dramatic was that it was a repeat of the previous year's scenario. We lost that one, at home, our first loss of the '63 season, after nine straight wins. That disaster could only be fixed by beating them at their field this time."

"So the game wasn't here?"

"No, in Boston. Remember Samuel, you asked about the best game I've seen, not the best one at Rich Stadium."

"Right. So did Buffalo win?"

"Let me tell the story now."

"Sorry."

"My friend, Ted Pavlovich—you know our lawyer—he and I drove to Boston the day before. Unwisely, we didn't reserve a room ahead so it took a couple of hours to find a motel more than twenty miles away. Even that far out, we were deep in enemy territory. We went for dinner and a few beers at a local bar, a real dive. Right away they pegged us as Bills fans, despite our efforts to keep a low profile."

"Did you stay?"

"Of course. We were hungry."

"Did you get into a fight?"

"No fights. They were great sports. We ate our food in peace and one of them bought us a round of beers. Our only hostile encounter was with the weather as a huge snowstorm made us late for the game. We would have missed the kick-off if they hadn't delayed it for half an hour to clear the field."

At Samuel's beckoning, John relates the story from so long ago that remains fresh in his mind. The low-scoring struggle in the snow after the two early touchdowns and the missed two-point conversion attempt when the Boston player slipped in the snow.

"And you were there," Samuel says, enraptured.

"And I was there."

"Mom too?" Samuel says, once they cross the bridge.

"No, Karl was just born. She stayed home to watch the game with your uncle."

"Oh yeah, that's the year your brother came to Canada, right?"

"Wonderful, Sam, you've been listening."

"So it was a lucky year for you. I guess you celebrated with them when you got home then."

"Well, not quite, it was late . . ."

John can still recall the unsettling sensation of coming home in the middle of the night, disappointed to find Helen asleep, Karl quiet in his crib, and Doug heading to his bar, but not before his brother's unexpected announcement he was moving out.

"It's not late now, Dad. We'll celebrate with Mom at home."

John points at the Golden Arches.

"Son, this is our celebration."

The news of Doug's impending parole for good behaviour hit me like a wrecker's ball five years later.

During his long absence—and in my view because of his absence—our lives blossomed. Karl was proving himself to be a clever child and the latter half of the 1960s turned out to be a bountiful period for John in real estate. As the new decade approached, we moved out of our cramped apartment to a brand new three-bedroom house in the north end of St. Catharines. Life was good in the Stevenson family for a good five years before the refrain of:

"When can I see Uncle Douglas again?"

For weeks after his uncle's release—I will always regret allowing John to take Karl to Kingston for that—our son pestered us with this request. Once a day. Like a vitamin. As if he was above nagging or understood too well the power of subtlety. We'd have gotten used to it except we could never predict at what time of day it would occur.

"Your uncle's busy, he has responsibilities," John would say. "It's not easy for him to leave Toronto."

"Why can't we go and see him?"

"It's not that simple." Then my son would pout, causing John to add: "We'll try Karl, we'll try."

I grew to dread that pout on that little face, which only echoed John's after each of these exchanges. It was hard on my husband to refuse when he agreed with our son. He also felt seeing our son could help Douglas. Perhaps I had grown weary of fighting it, for the time came when I gave in. Once I overcame this hurdle, and my personal feelings, I began to see things differently. It wasn't fair for Karl not to know his uncle. With my parents gone, Douglas was the only extended family the boy had. The only family John had in Canada too. I shared this with John who was happy to hear it.

"Helen, you won't regret giving Doug a chance. Trust me, he's a changed man." I remained noncommittal and fortunately John could sense when he was pushing it. "So you're saying you're okay if he comes for a visit."

"I don't know about a visit here, at our house. Maybe a neutral place first. And as long as you and your brother continue to refer to the penitentiary as a hospital."

"Karl will find out the truth someday."

"Not if we're diligent."

John accepted my conditions. We decided on a picnic at the Niagara Gorge and to meet at the new observation platform at Lock Three. Douglas was waiting in the parking lot, leaning his long back against a late model Ford LTD, the sun beaming on its deep blue body, reflecting off his sunglasses. It felt much like the airport only this time I was the anxious one, not John.

I watched warily as my brother-in-law picked up Karl and hoisted him up to where their eyes could meet, then shuddered when Karl squealed with delight. Douglas approached me and put out his murderer's hand.

"Nice to see you again Helen." His voice was different. The accent, like John's, was becoming more Canadian.

"Douglas," I said.

"Douglas. Okay, we're starting over, aren't we?"

"Nice car," John said.

"Got it this week. Used. Why don't we take it for a spin to the Falls?"

"What about the ships?" I said.

"I asked someone," Douglas said. "None are scheduled to pass through for at least two hours."

John glanced at me and I nodded as Douglas let my son down.

"You wanna ride shotgun?" he said, to Karl who began jumping with joy.

"Hold on," I said. "He's too small."

I guided a grumbling little boy to the backseat next to me while John and Douglas moved picnic gear from our trunk to his.

Traffic was heavy and turned the twenty-minute drive into one that took nearly forty. That wasn't as frustrating as Karl playing with the automatic window opener on this hot day. We were lucky when Doug spotted a narrow parking spot just large enough to squeeze his car in.

Karl took his uncle's hand and the two walked off to where the crowds were. What pleased and surprised me was that it didn't bother me, Karl choosing to go with his uncle. I wasn't jealous at all. In fact, it was nice to walk freely with John, not in a state of constant alertness in case my son bolted. The bond between uncle and nephew had a natural affinity that seemed their own special thing, independent of, but not threatening to, my relationship with my son. I looked at John. If anyone would be jealous, it would be him at how Karl seemed to favour the younger brother. But he too seemed to appreciate what was happening; judging by how he pressed my hand in that loving manner of his from when we first dated.

John and I drew away to a position against the rail to make it easy for Doug and Karl to get closer. We had experienced the wonder of the Falls often enough; this was new to them. The thunder of the water as it cascaded over the escarpment, punishing rocks in its way, falling into the pool below, casting a cool mist over the receptive crowd. We all laughed when Karl laughed each time he got sprayed.

Eventually the endless flow of people became too much and I could sense Karl getting claustrophobic. I worked my way through to tap Doug on his shoulder. They were about to retreat when Karl pointed his finger down at the water.

"There's a boat," Karl said.

"That's the *Maid of the Mist*," I said.

"Can we go on it?"

"When you're older, and bigger."

"Uncle Douglas, will you take me now?"

"Listen to your mother," he said.

This indeed was a new Douglas. Still the handsome, confident man externally, drawing admiring looks from women around him. But the part that spoke and acted had changed completely. I couldn't say if it was rehabilitation or some magical connection with his nephew, only that I liked it. I liked it a great deal, which was shocking because I had wanted to hate it.

The drive to Niagara Gorge went quicker, its relative sparseness a respite from the overcrowded, overly loud Falls. We surveyed the site, looking among trees, barbecue pits, families with running kids, until we spotted an ideal area in the middle. Karl and I went to claim it while John and Doug brought the chairs, a Styrofoam cooler, reading material, toys and games. As Doug set up chairs, John took me aside.

"You won't believe what just happened."

"What?" I said, an absurd fear that that awful Angeline was going to show up.

"No, no," John said, "you'll like this. When I told him to bring the cooler with the beer he refused. 'Not while I'm driving,' he said. Can you believe it?"

"That is unlike him."

"He's really changed."

"Maybe, John, maybe. Then again, maybe he's just on good behaviour for now."

"Oh Helen."

John's reaction made me feel bad for my cynicism. For I too shared his optimism, just not aloud.

"Of course, this means you'll be dry too."

"Oh, right," he said.

Karl ignored his toys and went to play by a tree. As I sorted the sandwiches, Doug told us about his new life in Toronto. His job at a grocery warehouse didn't pay as well as the one at General Motors, and the apartment he rented in a new section of high rises cost more than the house he shared in St. Catharines. The cost of living was higher yet oddly he was better off, happier. The restrictions of his parole dictated a less flamboyant, therefore less expensive lifestyle, I pointed out. Doug concurred. John came just short of being maudlin in saying how proud he was of his brother while I hinted this was a good example of prison rehabilitation. Doug credited the help of friends he made "on the inside," as he put it. No further mention was made of his incarceration and I didn't dare bring up Angeline of whom we'd never hear anything again, thankfully.

While we talked, I did not fail to notice a cluster of girls smitten with John's brother. I couldn't help feeling impressed and heartened that Doug kept his attention on us. The girls kept their distance, probably unsure whether I was with Doug or not. What was irritating was John's longing glances toward the parking lot. Eventually I got tired of it and told him to get the beer cooler.

"None for me," Doug said, when John offered him one. "I'll wait till I'm back in Toronto."

"Can we go down the trail to see the rapids?" Karl said, just then joining us.

"It's warm and getting late," John said, now hesitating to open his beer. "Maybe we'll skip it this time."

"What trail?" Doug said.

Karl and I pointed toward a small opening, a hundred yards away, where a gap in the fence led to steps down the steep cliff.

"That path goes down to the Niagara River."

"I'll take him," Doug said. "I'd like to see it.

Without waiting for a response, Karl took his uncle's hand, but Doug didn't move until I gave my consent. Barely seconds after they left, the two girls conspicuously rose and followed them. I didn't let it bother me, instead taking the opportunity to lay back on the blanket and look into the tree above and enjoy its leaves filtering the light of the sun, allowing me to remove my sunglasses. John happily opened his bottle and a novel.

An hour later the two hikers returned just as John finished his beer. Everyone agreed it was a good time to go. We stored the picnic items in the trunk and, after I'd settled Karl in the backseat, I turned to Doug.

"Why not come back to our house for a coffee?"

Doug smiled in that gregarious way I remembered from years earlier. This time the smile was touched with humility.

"I'd love to, thanks."

So began the reunification of our extended family as that first evening together went as well as one could hope. From then on Doug was a regular visitor. I was determined to make an effort to trust him, which wasn't always easy.

One gorgeous summer Sunday several weeks later, I was making tea when the kettle stopped its whistling. The house was deathly quiet. I poured a cup and took a sip from the hot beverage A gust of wind whished through the dining room window into the living room and crinkled the newspaper in John's hand.

"Where have they gone?" I said, trying to hide the alarm in my voice.

"The orchard, I bet," John said. When I said nothing, he put his paper down. "Let's go for a walk."

A laneway between two houses led to a school. Children were playing a game of touch on the football field. Beyond the far goal post there was a small orchard, its rows of trees sprouting mature peaches, apples, pears. Doug and Karl stood facing each other, our son's back to us. I sensed our arrival could be an unwelcome intrusion.

We barely took three steps toward them before we saw Doug lift up Karl with urgency and start running at us, my crying boy over his shoulder.

"Oh my God," I said. "What's happened?"

"No time," Doug said. "I know what to do."

His confident manner arrested my instinct to force Doug to stop and explain. John and I struggled to keep pace with his brother, despite the extra weight he was carrying. He had already sat Karl by the kitchen table and was on his way to his car when we came in. My son was moaning and feeling his stomach but otherwise looked fine. I rubbed his forehead and belly until Doug came back with a first aid kit. He rustled around for a small bottle and then a spoon in the cutlery drawer.

"What's that?" John said.

"Ipecac. It'll make him throw up. Karl ate one of the fruits from the trees."

"Oh dear," I said, recalling a recent article about vandals spraying wild fruit trees with poison, which had killed several dogs and squirrels.

My brother-in-law opened a small bottle and poured less than a teaspoon of the liquid in it. He came over to Karl but Karl pushed his hand away. I then gave it a try but he resisted my arm too. I held my ground.

"Karl Philip, now."

This time he let me put it down him. He made a face at first but then relaxed, even smiled for a moment and began to lie down. Doug rushed over, shoved me aside, and lifted Karl up.

"Keep him up, he might choke on his—"

The emetic began to take effect. I followed them to the bathroom where my son's vomit and tears were horrible to watch, but for the best. The Ipecac seemed to work, because he looked better afterward, though plenty mad at all of us.

"I'll leave this with you," Doug said, putting the bottle in the top cupboard, as he closed up his first aid kit.

"I'm surprised you have something like this," John said.

"I'm surprised you don't," Doug said, curtly.

The implication we were unprepared parents offended me, but only briefly. Karl's anger, on the other hand, lasted weeks. We never knew if he'd been poisoned or not and maybe we'd made him throw up for nothing, but it wasn't worth taking the chance.

After that, Doug came down almost every weekend to spend time with us. He declared doing so helped stave off his former temptations. I didn't quite believe him. I was sure he indulged in drinking and partying as much as his parole conditions would allow in Toronto, but happy to remain ignorant as long as he kept that part of his life from us.

It became a standing date on weekends for the four of us to spend at least half a day at the beach at Lakeside Park. Women fawned over Doug, and he paid them attention too, but was never disrespectful to us, or to them. At least not so much as we noticed. He showed more interest in his nephew and it was adorable how the two would go for their little walks to the merry-go-round, followed by a long swim, leaving John and myself some peace and quiet.

That peace and quiet was nice but, in a way, John and I became a little envious of our son and wanted time with Doug for ourselves. Adult time. We were fortunate to find a trustworthy babysitter in a high school student named Violet Baxter. She lived only a short walk away, on the other side of the orchard, and was usually available on short notice.

That was helpful during the World Rowing Championships, being held that year at the Henley Regatta. A nostalgic wave swept over my brother-in-law who stayed in Niagara for the entire event. Not with us but at a friend's house in Thorold. John managed to get away one Wednesday so the three of us could attend some races with his brother. Never had I witnessed something so worldly in our small city; it was that exciting. Doug, though, was in a wistful mood much of the time, perhaps melancholic about what might have been for him. When I asked about it, he shrugged me off, but then offered to take us out to dinner, implying he would open up there. By this time the long day had tired Karl out. I needed to get him home and to bed so I was going take our car while Doug would drive John back after the races. I was doubtful about accepting the dinner invitation until John suggested we call Violet. I did.

"Why can't I go?" Karl said, once we were back home and he saw her there, realizing what was happening.

Violet smiled as she gathered her black hair and threw it back; she was already used to Karl's ways. I really liked this girl, glad to have found someone I felt comfortable leaving alone with my son. Best of all, Karl adored her and, aside from his Uncle Douglas—he refused to say Doug—didn't care much for anyone else.

"Karl, your uncle is taking your parents out to dinner. It's going to be a late night. You have to go to bed soon."

"But I want to see Uncle Douglas."

"You saw him all day," I said. "In fact, you've seen him every weekend for the past month, and in a couple of weeks you'll see him again."

"We didn't go for our walk and swim at the beach."

"I can't believe you're not tired, after all the sun and excitement."

"So how was the rowing, Mrs. Stevenson?"

"Marvellous. What an event for the city."

"I know. I saw some qualification heats the first day and it all just seems so, sophisticated."

I laughed. "Maybe now people will spell St. Catharines properly." Violet laughed and then I felt a tug at my pant leg.

"When are Dad and Uncle Douglas coming back?"

"Soon enough. Be patient."

"Come on, Karl," Violet said. "We'll have fun, just the two of us. Maybe we'll do a puzzle before you go to bed. Why don't you go find a good one?"

Karl left the room just as the back door opened. He darted back to lead his uncle by the hand and guide him to a chair. I introduced Doug to Violet.

At first it amused me to see Violet's predictable reaction to my brother-in-law, her blushing, demure infatuation. But my amusement gave way to concern the longer this went on. Violet kept gazing to the point it became disturbing, more so because he seemed to encourage it.

"So Doug," I said, intentionally interrupting at one point, "how were the rest of the races?"

"Pardon? Oh, great finals, and what a lovely course."

"How did we do?"

"Pretty much an eastern European sweep."

"Mrs. Stevenson tells me you used to row, um, Mr.—"

"Doug, call me Doug. And yes, it's true. Both John and I did. Who knows, I might have been racing myself, if I'd stayed with it."

"Why didn't you?" Violet said.

"John, you ready to go?" I yelled to the stairs, drowning out Doug's response.

I heard a muffled reply and got up, but sat back down as John came into the room. He said hello to Violet who barely acknowledged him.

"Let's go," I said, and stood up.

I spotted Violet's outline in the window observing us as we drove away. While reliable and good with Karl, she was still a naive high school girl, the type who spent her earnings on teen magazines and whatever makeup her parents could tolerate. This fascination with a striking man like Doug was understandable but even the slightest possibility of a teenage crush had to be averted.

It worked out on its own. For once autumn rolled around, Doug spent less time in St. Catharines though remaining a fixture on Sunday afternoons. He wouldn't stay overnight but would go back to Toronto that evening. His time with us at Christmas was brief and we spent New Year's without him.

However, there was one event my husband's brother wasn't going to miss.

"This Super Bowl thing is fantastic," Doug said, taking a pull from his beer and then rubbing Karl's head.

John smiled. "Fifth one. Every year it gets better."

"But my first."

An awkward moment, this rare reference to his time in jail. I announced I would order pizza and returned from the call with a fresh round of beers.

"Too bad our Bills aren't in it. But sometimes it's nice to be neutral. Less tense."

"You mean your Bills," Doug said, drawing a confused look from his brother. "I haven't told you but I've become a Cowboys fan. Hope I'm still welcome."

John's face dropped at this blasphemy. Doug pointed to the television. Dallas had just scored a go-ahead touchdown against the Baltimore Colts. John watched the end of the play and the replays, then turned back to face his brother.

"Once you pick a team you should stick to it."

"Like the Bills," Karl said.

"See, my son understands team loyalty."

"Admit it, John, Buffalo's awful these days. Why not cheer for a winner? Especially one that can win you bets."

"But Dallas? They can't score. They won the conference game 5-0. That's a hockey score, not football."

"They still won, didn't they?"

The commercials ended and Dallas kicked off. When the play stopped again, John sighed.

"Buffalo sure did stink this year. At least you're not cheering for Boston, I mean, New England."

"Ah, yes, I remember that season. That was fun."

I instinctually looked up to see if Doug meant more by that remark. But he was acting as if I wasn't in the room. That bothered me more than the reminder of that difficult day six years before.

The incident remained a clear memory to me—I even suffered the occasional dream—but I was starting to doubt it actually happened as I remembered. What was dream? What was memory? I couldn't always be sure.

Just before halftime, the pizza came. I put the box in the middle of the coffee table and fetched plates and napkins. I replenished everyone's beer, and Karl's juice, then sat next to my brother-in-law.

"So Doug, how will you spend your weekends once football's over?"

Karl stopped eating to look up at his uncle, then at me.

"Haven't thought much about it. You and John are great but sometimes I think I overstay my welcome."

"Nonsense," John said.

"John's right, but that's not what concerns me. There's someone who's gotten used to you being around."

"And that guest room doesn't shut down for the winter either," John said.

"I see," Doug said.

The topic evaporated once the second half began. The Colts kicked the winning field goal with five seconds left in the game. Doug didn't seem in a mood for discussion and surprised us by not staying the night.

When his uncle didn't visit for several weeks, Karl didn't complain. Then there was a visit, followed by others, but they were sporadic and usually on short notice. It appeared Karl adjusted to the lack of regularity in seeing his uncle and we were relieved, albeit confused. Whenever we brought the subject up, Karl would shrug his shoulders in a secretive way, leaving us more confused. To a discrete inquiry whether he was mad at his uncle, Karl was annoyed at first, but then laughed, as if he thought we were joking. We didn't deny it and stopped wondering.

The following spring John's boss offered us the use of his cottage in Muskoka for a weekend. Normally we would never consider going without Karl. But he was six going on twelve and we felt enough confidence in him, and in Violet, to trust her with him for a couple of days.

It was our first time leaving our son for more than a day and it took time to ensure all preparations and precautions were in place. Consequently, we departed an hour later than intended. I relaxed once we reached the highway until, across the meridian a familiar looking vehicle drove by us, the driver's face turned away.

"Did you see that car, John? It looked like Doug's."

"Nonsense. Why would he be here?"

"It's strange."

"He doesn't drive the only blue LTD in the province."

I stewed for another minute, trying to convince myself it was a coincidence. I was not successful. I suggested we go back, just to make sure, but John wouldn't hear of anything getting in the way of a wonderful weekend.

/4\

"Petting time's over."

Danielle adds a gentle but determined shove that makes Karl chuckle. Less in amusement than to conceal annoyance at the romance-neutering reproach in her tone. He slides his hands away from her soft breasts, down her smooth belly, hips, until clear. At a barely perceptible volume, Phil Collins' *In the Air Tonight* plays on the 8-Track. He turns it up, leans back on the driver side door, careful not to let his elbow brush the horn, recalling the water amplified blast he caused when they arrived at the canal.

The moon is only partly visible above the dark horizon, enough to cast an eerie glow over the still water. Soft but cool early summer breezes pass through their rolled-down windows, blowing against her blonde bangs, clearing the last traces of the joint they smoked minutes before. As Danielle adjusts her tube top, Karl becomes absorbed by her face, by its slightly plump oval shape, crescent eyes and prominent lashes, and by a tiny and perky nose, which he can barely refrain from licking. She isn't beautiful, like a supermodel or movie star, but definitely prettier than cute.

He shifts close again and, using both hands, caresses her thick wavy curls past the ears down to her shoulders. When he pulls her closer, she yields, to his surprise. But when his hands move to tug down her top, Danielle scowls, pushes him again, harder.

"I mean it, Karl, we have to stop now."

"But we haven't even started, really."

"Then it'll be easier to stop, won't it? Besides, there's a ship approaching. People might see."

Quietly, they watch the ship glide into the lock, signalling the end of their date is near. It's now a tradition for Karl and Danielle to end their evenings at the canal, lingering until a ship passes by. Several some nights, since the school year ended, unless Danielle has to work the next day.

The ship is firmly in and as the gates close, Karl puts his arm around her. She tenses at first, but relaxes when he merely pulls her head against his shoulder. When she puts her hand on his thigh, a pleasant but uncomfortable sensation returns inside his shorts, forcing him to shift and concentrate on the indifferent waterway, on what looks like a wall of black steel gliding silently by. Karl knows it's actually red by the white letters that identify the upbound laker as the dutiful *D. H. John Henry*, ready to enter the right side gates of Lock Four, the first of the three back-to-back twin locks that scale the escarpment. Never did he imagine such a mundane fact would be helpful in taming his horniness.

"Your family's sweet," Danielle says, just as he regains control and is about to go for a kiss.

"Yeah, sure," he says, looking past her.

"Especially your mom. I hear lots about the trouble other girls have with their boyfriends' mothers. But Helen is so easy to talk to, more like a friend than . . ."

Danielle's words drift off when Karl kisses her.

The vessel reaches its maximum height. Faint voices from the crews can be heard, followed by a hollow, short siren as it creeps forward until out of sight, temporarily hidden by the adjacent lock. He pulls her tighter to him but she resists.

"Karl, just be patient, okay?"

"We've been together almost a year now," he says, still pulling, but with less vigour.

"Try nine months."

"Nine months, a year, same difference. Either way, we know each other well enough by now."

"Maybe so, but there's no point in rushing. I'm not even seventeen yet."

"Wasn't a problem for you two years ago in Ottawa."

With surprising quickness, her head ducks under his arm and retreats, slamming her back hard against the door. Karl's afraid it'll open and she'll fall out. He lunges to help but that only provokes another, harder shove before she tightly crosses her arms.

"Take me home. Now."

"Dani, I'm sorry—."

"Now, Karl, now. Please."

He reaches for her shoulder. She jerks to the side. Her baleful gaze, her lividly red face, spotted with tears becomes, if possible, even more alluring. What a beautiful expression, but one he knows he doesn't want to see. Suddenly she squares to him, her index finger jabbing at his chest.

"Don't you ever, ever, ever bring that up again. It's behind me, behind us. I confided in you because we agreed on no secrets between us. Don't make me regret it."

He gently cups her cheeks and kisses her nose, without licking it. She doesn't react so he kisses her pursed, dry lips. She kisses back, without passion, probably out of politeness. Or habit. Not wanting to push his luck, Karl releases her.

"The thing is, Danielle, you did tell me. In a way, I wish you hadn't. Then maybe I'd be more patient."

"I hoped you'd be mature about it. I certainly didn't tell you to have it thrown back at me and make me feel guilty."

"I know. I know. But look at it from my perspective. It's hard knowing that someone else . . . and then to have to wait and . . ."

"You're doing it again."

"Doing what?"

"Throwing it back at me, using it to pressure me."

Karl's unable to hold back a small sigh of frustration.

"And again, your face. Listen Karl, like I told you, what happened has nothing to do with us. Nothing whatsoever. It's ancient history, never to resurface. Please just trust me."

A tense silence. At least for him. She seems satisfied to have rested her case but plenty of arguments, contradictions, answers, explanations, and words run through his mind, all checked by his pride, or perhaps his fear. He starts the car.

He drives ten kilometres under the speed limit, holding onto a faint hope she'll say something reassuring. He comes to a complete stop at stop signs, slows for green lights. Only one cooperates by turning yellow. Danielle keeps her arms crossed, her body rigid all the way to her home.

The Fosters live on a dark crescent, lighted by just two streetlights, one at the entrance and one in the middle of a curbed grassy circular island. Many of the lawns surrounding the island, including hers, sprout mature trees, maples, elms, and various evergreens. As he approaches her house, a two-storey brick structure nestled in one corner, he notices lights on, the left garage door open. He drives around the circle to park against a curb a few houses away, the station wagon concealed by a massive blue spruce.

His beating heart calms when she doesn't object. And then, after she undoes her seatbelt, and he undoes his, she doesn't rush out: another positive sign. It seems worth the risk and he puts his hand out to grab hers. She tries a smile, less reproachful than sympathetic, but it comes out grim. She slides next to him and grabs his hand to put his arm around her shoulder, nuzzling her face under his head where she kisses his neck. A subtle, pleasant whiff of her strawberry scented perfume tempers his anxiety.

"Dani, I promise I won't bring it up again," he says, exuding more confidence than he feels.

A quick hug. She exits without acknowledging his vow with a nod or even a cynical grunt. Uncertain whether his save attempt is successful but afraid to know one way or the other, Karl does not watch her go into the house as usual. Instead, he drives off, not too fast, not too slow, in case she might think he is trying to be a martyr.

He retraces his route back to the canal, back to the exact spot they just vacated. No cars, no ships, only darkness and dead silence, save for the breathy hush of the still water. How he would enjoy another joint, but they smoked his last one. Idiot. Why couldn't he keep his thoughts to himself?

That she's not a virgin doesn't bother him, even though he is. In fact, he took her confession the week before as a sign of readiness; otherwise why bring it up? She corrected that misconception instantly, and cleverly, by explaining that her experience emphasized the importance of waiting for the right time. Whatever that means. She wants to act as if her past incident never happened, claiming that's how she sees it. As if losing one's virginity can be annulled like a marriage.

That was it. No names, circumstances, no details, except that it occurred two years before, implying it had to do with her family's move to St. Catharines from the capital region.

Since her revelation, he's racked his brains trying to fill in the missing pieces. What could prompt her family to pack up and leave Ottawa? A scandal? A crime? Incest? She has siblings but they moved out long before the Fosters arrived. Besides, Danielle speaks of them with love and pride.

It couldn't be rape. He asked and she explicitly ruled out that conclusion to ease his mind. Nevertheless, the event, whatever it is, hurt her in some way. They've been together long enough for him to see that. So why not tell him? Why not give him a chance to understand and show compassion? He could hold her and—

By accident, his elbow jerks forward and hits the horn. The echoing blast startles several birds that, like the sound, disappear into the air. He laughs, perhaps a delayed reaction to the pot, or for his next thought: maybe she killed the guy and was lining up Karl as her next victim.

He laughs again, at himself, with contempt, and starts the car. Instead of taking the canal road and following the waterway home, Karl turns left at Queenston Street. Soon he comes to the huge cemetery where his uncle is buried and parks in front of the closed gate, but stays in the car.

Karl remembers his father taking him and Samuel there after the Super Bowl, a tradition that only lasted a couple of years, for Karl. Intrigued at first at hearing about his uncle, each year his father would tell the same story like a charming but unessential Christmas tale. Samuel still participates but Karl suspects it's more to make their father happy than out of genuine interest. Samuel never knew Uncle Douglas.

It's after one in the morning when he pulls into his driveway. Except for the porch and hall lights his mother left on, the house is dark. No one is waiting up for him.

These days he only has to say he's out with Danielle and his parents will give him the car keys and not care how late he comes home. After that Pittsburgh fiasco a couple of years back, coming home a day early and alone, it took a long time for them to trust him again with friends they didn't know.

He missed Tom for a while but, in retrospect, it may have turned out best that he never returned to St. Catharines. His parents would have kept them apart and never trusted him. Worse, maybe he would never have met Danielle.

Ah, Danielle.

He takes a beer from the back of the fridge, where it's more likely colder and, more importantly, its absence will be less likely noticed. Karl is halfway down the basement steps and almost chokes on his first sip when he becomes aware of what he's doing, or rather where he's doing it. If his mom catches him, she'll be furious. Not for the beer but for breaking the dry basement rule, a condition she insisted on before letting him move his bedroom downstairs.

How adamant she was in resisting his dad converting the guestroom into a bedroom for Karl. A maternal response to this early sign of her first son's inevitable independence is what Karl and his father put it down to at first. However, the more she argued, the more he suspected she had a morbid aversion to anyone sleeping in that room, the place where Uncle Douglas died. She couldn't win, as it was three against one. Samuel wanted Karl's larger bedroom, his father wanted Samuel's bedroom for a home office. Her complaints about Karl's father's long hours away at work left her with little leverage.

He switches on the light and right away his attention is drawn to the Taj Mahal puzzle hanging above his headboard. His dad had it laminated and framed in appreciation for Karl's vacating his bedroom. He nostalgically recalls finally finishing the jigsaw puzzle before Samuel's second birthday, including the tinge of sadness at finding all the pieces there.

Danielle's contribution to his newfound privacy hangs on the back of the door, so he can look at it while lying in bed. Initially he had a Farrah Fawcett poster there, until Danielle unceremoniously tore it off. It was funny when she did it though he was angry at her presumption. Until he saw the replacement: a large framed photograph of Istanbul and the Bosphorus at night in which the moon is rising over the Asian side, between two mosques. A dark blue sky, with darker blue water, surrounds old Constantinople. Pointed minarets threaten to pierce the pale and full yellow sphere hovering above. He and Danielle often daydream about travelling to Europe and Asia on their honeymoon.

He takes a drink from the beer, nearly finishes it. The bottom of the bottle tastes bitter and, correspondingly, sends him into a sullen mood. Fourteen. His girlfriend had sex at fourteen. The sweet, innocent girl he knows could not have done that, could not have been the same person then, could she?

When he was that age, he thought a lot about sex, but knew little and experienced nothing beyond fantasy. Frankly, it scared him. Could she be lying about her experience? How he wishes that was the case. But why? To put off his advances? To torment him? If so, she's doing a terrific job.

His muscles, as if obeying a Ouija board command to think of something else, rummage through one of the cardboard boxes still unpacked from his vertical move. He pulls out the Taj Mahal box. It contains a Niagara Falls picture of him and his uncle, which he'll show to Dani some day. She'd have liked Uncle Douglas. It'll be interesting to see which part of the picture she responds to more, his uncle or himself at four years old. Then he spots a white book.

He puts the other items back, stuffs the box under his bed, and begins flipping through the pages. He stops at a small marker a third of the way through. It's from the local library, a picture of colourful teddy bears and balloons on it, so he must have gotten that far in reading it.

How much time did he spend scrutinizing this book as a kid, with such intensity, looking for clues to support his silly theory? Deep in the volume are two neatly folded sheets of binder paper with the charts Karl compiled when he was ten or eleven. What a little scientist. If only he could be this regimented in his Physics and Chemistry classes these days.

Despite giving up those childish ideas of the connection between his brother and his uncle, there is a mystery there. His uncle owned the book for some reason. He wasn't a man for scholarly books, as far as Karl can remember.

For all he knows, his ideas about Samuel aren't silly. There's been enough weirdness in the family over the years to make such a theory plausible. It could be a lark in any case, something for his mind to fret over other than Dani. And, looking at the Taj Mahal puzzle, he knows where to begin.

Karl leaves the house through the back door to enter into a blue skied, twenty-seven degree, breezy summer day. All around him unseen birds chirp away, their songs complemented by a sweet, sappy smell from the nearby orchard.

Save for the odd bungalow, most of the houses on his street are semis, built from a varying selection of functional but homely designs. Trimmed dark green lawns and hedges, as well as a variety of shrubs, small evergreens, and manicured gnome-guarded flower gardens produce an elegance the house designs could not.

He kicks a small stone across a manhole in front of him. It bounces funny and takes a sharp turn in the direction he's headed. He'll adopt it for his stroll. On the next street the houses are larger and detached, a random pattern of shapes and sizes, bungalows, two-stories, back splits. Wider lots and gaps between the houses and trees allow more daylight and a brighter, cheerful greenness. A mailman in long shorts nods hello as Karl gets closer to his old elementary school, the one Samuel still attends. The wind blowing from the orchard in the back intensifies the sweet smell, triggering memories.

Number thirty-nine, across from the school, was where Karl enjoyed his first kiss, with Beverly Johnson, who at nine was a year younger than Karl, same as Danielle. He and Beverly were playing checkers when she won and came over and gave him a big, wet smooch, on the lips, and then several more. He was too stunned to react. So she did it again. He liked it and kissed back, knowing her parents were in the backyard, liable to catch them at any time.

Three houses down from Beverly's lived the twins, Billy and Wally Taylor, two dorky boys whose popularity existed only due to their in-ground swimming pool. Having suffered his own period of peer mockery in elementary school, Karl felt sorry for them and became their friend. Of course, Karl would swim any chance he got and, without the pool, he might not have treated them so well. They had terrific water polo games and cannonball contests but what Karl enjoyed most was the schemes they concocted to try and persuade a neighbour's au pair to change into her bathing suit and join them. She'd be on the front porch in tight safari shorts, reading a Harold Robbins novel translated into French, and would look up from time to time and smile at them in such a way that always killed their nerve.

That failure led to his first, and only, slap in the face, though it was a close call last night with Danielle. Acting on a dare from the twins, still brimming with confidence from the kiss, he suggested to the very same Beverly Johnson that she go skinny dipping with them. That slap ended his existence in her eyes. The memory of it makes him cringe; just a few weeks ago he saw Beverly at the Pen Centre and stepped into a lingerie store to keep out of her sight.

Long conditioned habit directs Karl and his stone to cross to the other side to avoid Marty Kalashuk's house. A couple of years after the Taylor boys moved, Karl became friends with Marty. They did everything together, playing catch, flying kites, bowling, mini-golf, biking, teasing girls, other than Beverly. For some reason, Marty always wanted to target her but Karl always vetoed it. Then, possibly to spite Karl, Beverly and Marty began to hang around, even going to movies together, testing the friendship between the boys. One day, a game of marbles ended in a heated argument that escalated into a fist fight. A soft, chubby kid, Marty caught Karl by surprise and smacked him pretty good, giving him two black eyes and a stomach ache that lasted three days.

Spurred by this victory, Marty devolved into a bully with Karl his prime target. Nature supported his quest as Marty grew in height, transforming flab to muscle. He'd be at least six feet tall now, over two hundred pounds, while Karl is a few inches shorter and at least fifty pounds lighter. Still, Karl may be destined to have the last laugh, or the next laugh. Marty's pipsqueak brother, Mitch, is one of Samuel's friends. Samuel is much bigger now at ten than Marty was at twelve.

Several houses clear of the danger zone, Karl and his stone cross back, and pause at a side street where, even now in summer, he can visualize playing street hockey. Every day in winter after school, twice a day during Christmas holidays, with Frankie, Phil, Albert, the two Michaels, all those neighbourhood kids. After Grade Eleven, he lost touch with every single one. A consequence of transferring to a school at the other end of town. On the other hand, he would not have met Danielle if he hadn't transferred. He stops at his destination, kicks the stone one more time. It rolls ten feet before it falls down a sewer grate.

Karl raps the glass pane below the screen and steps back. The house is just as he remembers it, a detached brick bungalow, beige and tan, with a wide concrete driveway and blue Impala in the carport. Except now it doesn't seem so big, with the pine tree's branches clipped and the shrubs in front trimmed. When he was a kid, the freshly cut lawn seemed as big as a football field. Now it looks puny.

The main door is open behind the screen, revealing a familiar hallway. The hat stand, shoe rack, green tiles and worn purple welcome mat are the same. The image triggers a strange memory mix, part fact, part déjà vu; is this what the reincarnated kids in his uncle's book experience?

An elderly, energetic woman, with kind, grandmotherly eyes, appears. Her angular face is patched with sweat and dirt, her forehead covered by a bandana. She has on a pair of mud-stained blue jeans and a pink and white checked blouse.

"Yes?"

"Hello, Mrs. Baxter."

She studies her visitor with uncertainty. He's about to identify himself when her face broadens in a warm smile of recognition.

"Karl Stevenson. Come in. Come in."

She ushers him to the main room and excuses herself. Unlike the exterior and the hallway, the living room has transformed completely. Lush tan leather love seats have replaced the tacky yellow-green flower patterned chesterfield. Modern, silver-legged glass coffee and end tables contribute to a newfound brightness from the wide-open curtains. They used to be drawn shut due to Mr. Baxter's migraines. A fancy light-coloured Turkish rug covers most of the hardwood floor where a burgundy carpet used to be. He sits on one of the love seats and she returns a moment later with two clinking glasses of fresh lemonade and ice cubes.

"My goodness, how you've grown. The last time I laid eyes on you was, let me see, when I ran into you and your younger brother, wasn't it? A few years ago. He's a cutie."

Karl nods while he sips, trying not to squint at the tangy, sugarless taste.

"I remember it well, it was just after Axel passed away."

"I didn't know that. About Mr. Baxter. I'm sorry."

She shakes her head, implying her remark wasn't intended to garner sympathy.

"My parents say hello," Karl says, a bit awkwardly.

Mrs. Baxter chuckles good-naturedly, with a trace of gentle mockery, as if doubting him. Her reaction makes him recall how she was dressed in black when she gave a similarly odd reaction to Samuel and him. The way she watches him, patient and curious like a teacher trying to make a point, he feels his face redden and his curiosity rise.

"Tell me about your little brother."

"Okay. What would you like to know?"

"For one thing, who does he look like? When I ran into you before, I couldn't tell you were brothers, but features can change over time."

Karl senses there's more behind her question, as if she has an 'aha' awaiting the right opening. He's tempted to act like the cops on television and tell her he's the one here to ask the questions. Only he could never be that impolite.

"Actually, I dropped by to see Violet."

"I see. I think I told you last time she moved out."

"Oh, right. Thorold, wasn't it? Can I have the address?"

"Not anymore. Thorold, that is. She's closer, near GM, and of course you may have the address. But you'll have to wait until evening. She's working days. She's a nurse now, at the General Hospital."

Mrs. Baxter embellishes this with a proud smile before writing on the back of a used envelope she then hands to him.

It's too beautiful a day to hang about the house so Karl takes the laneway to the orchard adjoining Samuel's school. He hasn't been there in years. Memory flashes return of him and his uncle, playing catch, kicking a soccer ball, throwing a Frisbee, or just talking. Some even include Violet but he cannot recall his parents being there on any of those occasions.

He finds his old favourite tree, a sprawling willow with branches dipping into the creek. He sets down his knapsack and sits against the trunk, how he did before, and retrieves his uncle's book. Again he's taken aback by the name of the author, though it must be a coincidence. He began reading it last night to keep from thinking about Danielle but now it's become fascinating.

Of the twenty cases, three stood out to his younger self, attested to by dog-eared pages. The logic behind his interest in the Lorenz children in Brazil, and William George in Alaska makes sense in that these cases occurred within the same families and the allegedly reincarnated individuals predicted their own return.

In the Lorenz family the mother, Ida, actually gave birth to two children who reported reincarnations years apart. The first was Marta who allegedly came back as Ida's friend, Sinha, a girl from an isolated rural area who frequently visited Ida's village. That's how the two became friends. Sinha fell in love with a man who, after her father's disapproval, committed suicide. It was the second love her father had ended and this one put her into a deep melancholy. It led her to engineer her own death by exposing herself to tuberculosis. A day before she died in October, 1917, Sinha announced to Ida she would return as Ida's daughter. Ten months later, Marta Lorenz was born. The child acted and spoke as if she lived Sinha's life, recalling specific people and places known to Ida's sad friend.

Marta's case points out a common theme with many of the others: unhappy lives, especially childhood lives, often for the children reporting the past life, but especially for the past lives they reported.

Emilia Lorenz was Ida's second born and first daughter. Emilia had a difficult childhood because she felt like a male imprisoned in a female body. Several years before her death, she told people, but not her parents, that if she reincarnated it would be as a man. Like Sinha, she sought her own death but was more direct in bringing it about, if not as efficient. It took several failed attempts with arsenic before a successful one with cyanide.

Months later, during a séance, Ida received a message from Emilia, regretting her death, declaring a desire to come back to the family. Paolo Lorenz's birth, a year and a half after Emilia's death, was unexpected, and he became Ida's thirteenth child. In his early years, Paolo played with dolls, wore girls' clothes, and frequently made comments linking him to Emilia. But the trait that most associated him with his dead sister was a particularly advanced talent for sewing, for which there was no reasonable explanation.

Most intriguing to Karl, then and now, is the case in Alaska of William George of the Tlingit Indians, a tribe that believes in reincarnation. William George, Sr. predicted his own return in his sixties, going as far as to specify it would be as the child of his favourite son, Reginald. He identified birthmarks for his son and daughter-in-law to look for and gave them a gold watch to keep for his return. On a fishing trip, William George disappeared, his body never recovered. Everyone assumed it floated out to sea with the tide.

Mrs. Reginald George became pregnant shortly after. Upon seeing identical but smaller birthmarks on her son, the parents named him William George, Jr. Pneumonia inhibited the child's speech development and it took him several years to speak. As with other cases, William, Jr. recognized objects and places. He also addressed people with the familiarity his grandfather would have. Some began to call him grandfather. The most telling indication came with the recognition of his watch, which he fiercely claimed as his own. By the time he was eleven, Samuel's age now, William, Jr., like almost all of the other cases, had lost identification with his predecessor and moved on to become his own person.

This was another aspect common to many of the cases. Even if Karl was right about Samuel and his uncle, all traces would have disappeared by now. He'll never know. That had to be why he gave up. Karl can't help being impressed at the perceptiveness of his younger self.

He closes the book and yawns. The sun is no longer directly above and he wonders what time it is. He's hungry but none of the fallen fruit littering the ground tempts him.

Once, with his uncle, Karl picked up a pear and took a few bites. It was juicy and tasted okay, but his uncle became alarmed and rushed Karl home where his mother forced him to take a spoonful of awful syrup called Ipecac. It made him vomit terribly. Apparently, at the time, there were reported incidents of a vandal spraying toxic pesticide in the trees. Whether poisoned or not, they never found out, but he knows he'll never eat wild fruit again.

He returns home to find a message from Danielle, asking him to call her right away, at work. He doesn't like to call her there because her boss sounds like a tyrant. His trepidation is greater now because he's fearful Dani has something terrible to say to him. He eats a sandwich first but curiosity overcomes him halfway through. He's pleased it's Dani who answers, and thrilled to hear her in a good mood.

"So I got my shift switched so I can make up for it. We can catch an early movie, maybe *Terms of Endearment*."

"What?"

"I'm kidding. How about *48 Hours*, and then afterward, well, it is a holiday tomorrow."

Karl hesitates, feeling for the piece of paper in his back pocket with Violet's address.

"I expected you to be working so I made other plans."

"Oh?"

She says it casually but he senses misgiving in her voice, an implied question. It's no big deal where he's going, but the last thing he wants is for Danielle to accompany him and then tell his mother about it.

"All right, I didn't want to mention it, but I planned to do some shopping too, if you know what I mean, since somebody's birthday's coming up . . ."

A little lie. Not even a lie, a minor deception, no more. The troubling part is how well it works. She giggles and plays along, complimenting his priorities. When he hangs up, Karl holds on to the handset, tempted to call her back.

"Hey Karl, hang that up."

Karl hasn't noticed the fast-anh-anh-anh-anh, let alone Samuel coming into the kitchen. His brother grabs the handset and slams it down.

"Hey," Karl says.

"You coming to the mall tonight, with me and Mom? Dad's going to meet us there and take us out for dinner."

With Mrs. Baxter's comments still fresh in his mind, Karl can't resist studying his younger brother. Their hair colour is different, Karl's brown and getting browner, Samuel's blond and staying that way. Viking blond, though it's hard to tell since he keeps it crew cut short and hidden under that grubby Bills cap. Karl considers himself decent looking but he has to admit Samuel is becoming quite handsome, notably due to his squared face.

"Mom said to invite Danielle too," Samuel adds.

"She's work—damn it—that means Mom's taking the wagon."

Samuel nods and Karl swears again. His excuse to Danielle was only a half lie. He really needs to get a birthday gift for her before Friday. The stores are closed on Thursday for Canada Day so tonight is his last chance.

"Listen, little brother, I need a huge favour."

"It'll cost you."

"Yeah, yeah, whatever."

Karl reaches deep into his pocket and pulls out all his cash—sixty-three dollars, plus a few quarters. He holds back a ten dollar bill and hands the rest to his brother.

"Spend every penny if you have to. Just pick out something nice, some jewellery. There's five bucks in it for you, ten if you do a good job."

Samuel counts the money, twice, then winks at Karl.

"Say, if she's working, then where are you going? You're not fooling around on her are you? I am buying this for Dani, right?"

Karl looks up and rolls his eyes.

"Yeah, what was I thinking? Why would a sweetie like Dani be worried about a mook like you?"

Violet's home is tiny, the shape of a Monopoly house, painted off white, and similar in colour and style to others in a neighbourhood of uncurbed streets named for famous long dead poets. Two windows of the same height face the street, one twice as wide as the other, both trimmed deep green. An awning covers the front door and the larger window, underneath which stands an inviting park bench and several cigarette butts on the ground. There's no car in the narrow driveway but there are lights on inside. Next door, two crows peck away at dirt around a birch tree, oblivious to a three-coloured cat staring at them. A myriad of stars above are diluted by streetlights. Karl's stomach rumbles as mosquitoes go at his legs, as they've done since the bus stop. He wishes he hadn't stopped at Harvey's, or at least just stuck with a single burger, not a double, and skipped the extra onions and pickles.

Karl knocks. Instantly the door opens. A man appears, wearing green work pants, steel toe boots, a grey muscle shirt, and an inquisitive expression. He wipes his dirty blonde moustache, which is spotted with grey whiskers and matches his shoulder length hair. He's got to be at least forty.

"You're Karl," the man says, with a brief no-tooth smile that makes Karl suspect he wears false teeth.

Karl nods, and then the man nods and goes back in the house. The thought of Violet, who'd be twenty-seven now, having a husband or boyfriend, never entered his mind, let alone someone this old.

Violet waves from the hallway to beckon him in. She's in her hospital scrubs, her black hair tied back. No eyeglasses though, possibly contact lenses. Violet looks heavier than he remembers, which is good. She's one of those girls who look more attractive with a little extra meat. Like Danielle, it makes them sensuous but also approachable.

She gives him a wonderful hug and a kiss on his cheek. Through his mesh shirt, he can feel her breasts, as the man who answered the door stands behind her, his thick fingers bunched around the neck of a bottle of Molson Golden. The man grunts and says something about being in the backyard, to Karl's relief.

"Don't mind Roy. He's had a rough day."

"I've had an easy day, I could use a beer too," Karl says, as Violet turns down the television volume.

"Is that so? Are you old enough?"

"You'd give me one whether I was or not."

She laughs.

"Maybe. Sure, why not? Do you want one?"

Karl shakes his head. She leaves to shower and change after directing him to the living room.

"Make yourself comfortable."

Many of the items around him are hand me downs from her mother's house. The crimson loveseat and unmatched sofa with the tacky yellow-green flower pattern, the veneer coffee and end tables, the mushroom lampshades on the brass lamps. He doesn't recognize the reupholstered recliner. Roy's chair, no doubt. It's in good shape, but under the grey cloth, some springs appear ready to snap. Two impressionist prints depicting a European countryside hang on the walls; they seem out of place in this blue collar home.

Despite the humble furnishings, the place is clean, dusted, the rug vacuumed. A fresh aroma wafts through the room to combat a faint odour of cigarettes, though he sees no ashtrays.

Behind a glass cabinet, an expensive component stereo system, almost as nice as Tom's in Pittsburgh, glimmers. The door to the cabinet is slightly open, the turntable spinning, playing Led Zeppelin. An extremely long headphone cable leads away through a partially opened screen door to the patio where Roy sits, smoking and drinking. The colour television is bigger and better than the one at his house. On top of the television, a tiny, square, gold plated mantle clock ticks away. Just like the one they gave to his uncle as a Christmas gift one year.

Violet returns carrying two lemonades in the same style of plastic tumbler her mother used. She's wearing a pink bathrobe with a purple towel wrapped around her hair. She unravels the towel and her long, black, shiny, beautiful hair tumbles out. Her mischievous smile as she bunches and dries batches of hair brings Karl back to childhood. Except now he feels a stirring he calms by taking a sip. He's relieved when she sits on the recliner, legs folded together under her. Karl sits in the love seat at a safe distance, but close enough to take in the fruity scent from her shampoo.

"I'm sorry to hear about your father," Karl says.

"Oh, thanks. That was a couple of years ago."

"So, you became a nurse."

Violet smiles, much the way her mother did earlier in the day. She tells him she recently graduated from Niagara College and found a local posting. With overtime, she makes good money now and, as long as Roy avoids strikes and layoffs at GM, as long as they refrain from indulging in too many luxuries like the stereo and the television, she might achieve her ambition to move to a fancier house in a finer neighbourhood in a year or two.

"Get a house with an in-ground pool. I'll come over."

"Do you swim much still?"

"Not as much as I'd like. Too busy. Maybe in the fall, I'll get back to it."

"I remember you bragging about how you would swim the Welland Canal some day."

"Did I say that to you? I always thought it was a secret shared with my uncle."

"Right. I'm not sure how I heard that."

A short lull follows, during which she excuses herself to check on Roy. He'd forgotten about those swimming boasts and feels silly knowing he'd shared them with Violet. Who else did he tell?

"Karl, I am very happy to see you, so don't take this the wrong way, but why now?"

"There's something I wanted to ask you about."

Karl reaches into his knapsack and pulls out his uncle's reincarnation book. Her gasp betrays her recognition, and it's followed by an expression of horror and disgust.

"Get that thing out of here, please."

Bewildered, but seeing she won't be satisfied until he obliges, he stuffs it back in his knapsack, ties the string, and puts the bag by the door. He comes back to finds her biting her nails.

"Sorry, Violet. But I don't understand."

She's about to respond when, from the hallway leading to the bedrooms, a young girl emerges in polka dot pyjamas. Seeing her calms Violet who then introduces the girl as her daughter, Kristen. She's about Samuel's age, with a scrawny but perkily lovely face, and tousled light brown hair.

Violet motions for Kristen to sit next to Karl. The girl thinks about it but shakes her head bashfully and leans against Violet's chair, tucking her head against her mother's armpit to whisper a request for a glass of water. Violet takes her to the kitchen.

Roy comes in for a beer and to flip the album. He hovers by Karl for an uncomfortable drawn out moment. He wishes Violet would hurry back before Roy starts talking or, worse, before his own unease at the silence makes him say something. The music begins again and Roy leaves. Just as Violet returns, without her daughter, but with a grim face, the kind a nurse might use with a troublesome patient.

"How old are you now Karl?"

"Almost eighteen."

"So you're seventeen. The same age I was when—Karl, I'm sorry, I'm not sure I should say anything."

"Of course you should. Why did the book spook you? Does it have to do with my uncle?"

Violet stares. It's remarkable how she is like her mother, just not as poised. She lets out a sigh, checks that Kristen's bedroom door is closed, that Roy is outside, then joins Karl on the love seat, putting one hand on his shoulder. Her manner troubles him, which ensures this time there's no discomfort.

"You don't know much about your uncle, do you?" she says, speaking quietly, but not whispering.

"That's why I came to see you. I don't know anyone who knows him, knew him. My mom acts if he never existed while my dad repeats the same things. I brought the book because I thought you might know something about it."

She frowns at the mention of the book.

"Okay Karl. First off, for the most part, your uncle was a good man, a real charmer, and—"

"Violet, I know that stuff already."

"All right," she says, and seems relieved he wants her to get to the point. "Remember the rowing championships at Henley, in 1970?"

"Actually, no."

"I'm surprised, since it was such a big event for the city. They even took you to some of the races."

Karl shakes his head.

"I was to look after you while your parents went out for dinner with your uncle one night. I had no idea he would be so handsome, so charming. Like a movie star, dynamic and likeable, yet his charisma had a down to earth commonness, a deadly combination for any woman."

Karl shifts nervously in his seat, not liking where this is heading. His pulse begins to race, a nervous stir emerges in his throat, exactly what he felt the moment before Danielle blindsided him with her Ottawa revelation.

"It was innocent at first, at least from my standpoint. I was young but I'd experienced crushes before, on both ends. Your mom knew what was up right away. In no uncertain terms, she warned me Doug was bad news."

"Doug?"

She nods knowingly before going on.

"Your mom told me I should avoid him, but stopped short of forbidding me to have contact with him. I considered her reaction excessive and put it down to her being over-careful. Bad mistake. Her concern was justified and, a few months later . . ."

"What? What, a few months later?"

The double burger makes its presence felt, again.

"Do you remember your uncle's funeral?"

"Some of it."

"I was to pick you up while they went to the cemetery."

"Maybe, I—"

"Only I couldn't. Your father was so upset with me, but I could hardly tell him I was in Buffalo, could I? Or why."

Buffalo. Well, it's not unusual for him and his friends to go over the river for cheap drinks and lax ID checks. But that's usually Niagara Falls, plenty of bars on Pine Street, no need to go as far as Buffalo. Other than for Sabres or Bills games, or shopping, who went to Buffalo? There was that girl Dani told him about who had to go there for an—

Seconds later he's in the bathroom retching away. It's like the Ipecac, but worse, as if it's a double dose due to all the food he ate before. No, a triple dose: what she's telling him puts everything he ever believed in jeopardy, casts doubt on it all. He feels closed in, a droning hum buzzing in his ears, in fact all his senses blocked.

The remain blocked until he makes out Violet's soft voice, the same caring voice from childhood. However, now it comes out pitiless, even cruel.

"Sorry, Karl. You had to come over and show me that damn book. You may be sick now but it can't be as much as I was then."

When nothing more will come out, he washes his face and returns to an empty living room. Violet rejoins him and offers a tall plastic glass filled with water. He takes a drink and allows her to guide him back to the sofa where she sits next to him. They keep silent a while until Karl nods toward Kristen's door.

"Is she his, my—did you go through with the abortion?"

"Yes, I did. Kristen came later, though not much later. She's not Roy's either. After your uncle died, it didn't take long for me to get pregnant again. This time no doctor would take care of it because I had no one to help pay for it. Such a slut."

"I'm sorry," Karl says, meekly.

"Forget about it. It's in the past."

"But what does that have to do with the book? Don't tell me you think my uncle reincarnated as my brother."

"What? Oh my God, what a horrible idea."

"Just tell me the connection. Then I'll drop it, promise."

"Karl, sometimes in life there are things you want, no, you should, keep forever in the past, even to the point where you trick your own mind into forgetting, even purging those memories."

Violet's words disturb Karl in a frustratingly elusive way, like an itchy mosquito bite in the middle of the back.

"It's in the past. I'm doing great. I've got Roy—he's all right once you know him. He's got a good job at GM and all—and there's Kristen. What do I need to look back for?"

/5\

Standing tall on his pedals, chin over the handlebars, Karl jockeys his Targa ten-speed south through the Garden City streets toward Secord Woods. He ignores countless stoplights, inciting honks and glares, ruing every delay, every lost, irretrievable moment with his girlfriend. At last he reaches the street leading to Danielle's where he coasts to regain his breath. He only gets so far when he has to stop upon seeing the last thing he wants to see: the Fosters' bland two-tone New Yorker still in the driveway, both front doors wide open and her parents arguing across the vinyl roof.

He retreats unseen to a neighbour's empty driveway where he conceals himself behind a tall oak tree. He feels silly standing there in his tight black Lycra bike shorts and bright multi-coloured shirt. He intended to find a secluded spot at a nearby park to change but in his rush forgot. He can't risk it now, the neighbour might return anytime. So he parts the fan-like branches to observe—a part of him fascinated by the spectacle of Danielle's parents fighting—and hope it gets resolved quickly.

Her mother utters a monosyllabic reply and adds a huff. Then, instead of getting in the car, she slams the door and walks back in the house, followed seconds later by her speechless husband.

What's he supposed to do?

When he and Danielle began dating, her parents took well to him but after a few weeks the old-fashioned English professor and his equally old-fashioned homemaker wife felt the relationship was getting too serious for their sixteen-year-old daughter. Last Christmas Eve, Danielle asked him over for dinner. Everything was fine until dessert. Then, not long after his last bite of orange sherbet, her father got Karl his coat and shoes ready, and, for all intents and purposes, wished him a good life. They eased up later but imagine their reaction if they see him riding up with a change of clothes and mickey of Crown Royal, ready to spend the evening in their house, alone with their daughter.

A faint light glows through cream-coloured sheers from one of the upstairs rooms, but no shadows, no movement. The fabric shifts and Danielle's pretty face peeks out, her hair tied back in a ponytail. Even with his vision obstructed by tree branches, he can see the distress in her eyes as they search the street for her Romeo. Her forlorn expression confirms her parents' plans have changed, ruining theirs.

He steps out to wave but she's receded, probably given up, assuming he has too. Down the street is a plaza with a payphone. Frantically, he taps his pockets and realizes he has no pockets and that he's brought no change, no money at all.

Karl rides to Glendale Avenue and turns left toward the Welland Canal, making a right at the canal road. Two ships, an upbound laker and a downbound saltie, are encased in Lock Five, the middle of the three twin flight locks. At the top of the escarpment more ships wait. A nautical bottleneck like that used to delight him and make him jump up as much as he could with a seatbelt on, lobbying his dad or mom to stop. Doing so now would make him think about Danielle and he'd wind up frustrated, depressed, or both.

He continues up the escarpment. At the top of the long hill, Karl rides west toward Thorold, the small town that proclaims itself a city. City? It has barely more than a tenth the population of St. Catharines, which itself is not a big city. Yet, it insists on a chartered independence.

Still daylight, the seedy downtown of plain, flat-roofed two-storey structures is filling up with riff raff in various stages of drunkenness. He speeds up Clairmont to get past this part until he reaches Pine Street. A right turn and he's now riding past a plaza, then a factory, then a tree-lined stretch of older residences, back toward St. Catharines.

At St. David's Road, the city boundary, Pine Street ends and he takes a couple of turns before finding Bradley Street and an elevated reddish structure. It's old, double stone with ivy growing on its side, a former lockmaster's residence. Below it, on his right, beyond a patch of grass, a soft steady roar of moving water. Karl has never been here before but is certain this is part of the second canal, built in the mid 1800s. He heard about it from Danielle who told him it would make for a great meeting place. It's a long shot but what the hell.

Karl jumps the curb and rides along a trail parallel to the abandoned canal. A fence separates him from the water but soon he reaches an opening where he can cross. A pair of thin birch trees, one recently split by lightning, makes a good spot to leave his bike. He takes his knapsack and follows a dirt path along the old canal route, his nose adjusting to a mild smell of sewage. At points, water drops sharply in perfectly aligned waterfalls, combing over manmade ledges, where wooden gates would have controlled the flow when ships passed this way. How small those vessels had to be to navigate these thin, grey, finely cut stone passages that seem barely wide enough for a decent swimming pool.

Farther on a patch of ground near a maple tree looks inviting. He kicks away dead leaves and twigs, rifles through his knapsack for his sweatshirt, which he spreads on the hard ground. He sits down, his back against the tree. The sun, already in its downward motion, flickers and glitters through the leaves in golden, orange, and red flashes. The sky is royal blue and clear. A whitish blue crescent moon rises between two diagonal cloud streaks to end a mixed up day.

A day that started with his brother's heavy pounding on his bedroom door that morning, followed by his entrance, without invitation. Samuel casually plopped his body on the bed, the weight of his football gear jarring Karl out of his lingering sleep.

"Get up, big brother. It's almost eleven. You have to drive me to my game, then bring the car back for Mom."

"I thought Dad was taking you?"

"He can't. He has an appointment and said he might not even be done in time to get me."

Then Samuel dangled a pearl necklace in front of him, as if he was a cat. Karl grabbed at it, but Samuel pulled it away and stuck out his hand.

"Ten bucks, remember?"

"How much did you spend from what I gave you?"

"All of it."

Karl stared at Samuel before nodding. However, he only had a single blue bill in his pocket, which his brother took for the necklace, but only after getting a written I.O.U. for the other five dollars. While Samuel pocketed the note, Karl inspected the jewellery closely, not sure what to look for, but enjoying the sensuous texture of the little white globes. The necklace felt expensive. It looked expensive too and, even though it was likely his imagination, smelled expensive. Samuel had done well, very well, much better than Karl would have done on his own. It was unnerving that his nine-year-old brother had such a worldly sense for stuff like this.

"So, where were you last night?" Samuel said.

"None o' your beeswax," Karl said.

"Suit yourself," Samuel said, eyes rolling.

"Why? What's up?"

"It's just that, while Mom and I were waiting for Dad in the mall, we ran into Danielle. She was surprised you weren't with us."

"Oh, shit."

"Right. And you know Mom. Her sixth sense started to act up and she and Danielle began talking about you."

"What'd they say?"

"How would I know? It was my chance to escape and get that thing."

A twig snaps, interrupts Karl's thoughts. Then another, followed by light footsteps scuffing dirt and leaves.

"Karl? Are you there?"

He turns and sees pink toenails poking out of white flip-flops. Then the smooth tanned legs that end at the fringes of denim cut-offs. Danielle looks casual, yet seductive.

"I spotted you behind our tree. When I got outside, you were gone. I hoped you'd remember this place."

He makes room for her to squeeze beside him on his sweatshirt. Her legs touch his. He can feel her warm, smooth hips through his bike shorts. They kiss a while but he pulls away at the moment his hands would normally adventure. She apologizes for her parents. This gives him a chance to grope about inside his knapsack. Her eyes widen when he pulls out the necklace.

"Happy Birthday, Danielle."

"But my birthday's not till tomorrow," she says, at the same time putting out her hands for the gift.

Instead of handing it over, he motions for her to turn around. She not only obeys but also undoes several buttons, revealing more cleavage than he hoped for. She caresses the tiny pearls as they drop between her breasts, fingering them while Karl clasps the chain. She then turns around and catches Karl off guard with a lunge that knocks him back. They kiss and roll around but the ground is hard. Twigs and small stones dig in their backs and the pearls swing against Karl's nose. They stand up and wipe off their clothes before sitting again, facing the sun. Danielle fondles her gift as daylight gives way to twilight.

"This must have been expensive. I've seen ones like this in our store and they're over two hundred dollars."

Karl mouths a silent thank you to his brother.

"So you like it?"

"Of course I like it. I love it. I love you."

"I love you too, Danielle."

They ride back to her house. Karl holds a faint hope her parents changed their minds. But the Chrysler is still there.

"Want to come in and say hello?"

"Ah, no."

"All right. Sorry again. I thought for sure they wouldn't miss the fireworks this year."

"I think they chose to create their own."

"That's what I like about your parents, Karl. They're polite to each other. They don't fight."

"Maybe they should sometimes."

"That's an odd thing to say." Karl shrugs, not sure why he said it himself. "Never mind. Listen, my folks absolutely, positively, will be gone tomorrow. What's even better is that they're going for dinner with our neighbours, meaning they're leaving me the car."

"So long as they get beyond the driveway."

"They will."

For once, Karl's glad they haven't gone far physically and feels happy and light-headed when they separate.

That feeling diminishes at the top of Hartzell Road at Queenston. Near the hospital, he nearly hits a parked car as an image invades his mind of Violet and his uncle, sitting on the Baxter sofa, together, arms around each other. Is it a real memory or made up? Probably real because the view is from below, from a small child's perspective. Other images follow, mental snapshots of his uncle's face, Violet's face, smiling, laughing, telling him to play in the Baxter's backyard while they clean the house, or make some other adult excuse.

Several blocks from home, he encounters the hunched over frame of Scott Toomer, a friend from school. Not so much a friend as a connection that can get beer and dope. At fourteen, Scott already could grow a convincing beard.

Lately Scott's been scarce. Rumour has it he was serving time in juvenile detention for possession. Well, he's definitely out now and doesn't look rehabilitated as he greets Karl with an open-for-business wink. Karl spent his last cash on the burger and Samuel's commission for Danielle's gift and it's doubtful Scott operates on credit but it's worth a try. Karl waves but suddenly the stoner ignores him, though there's no doubt in Karl's mind that wink was for him.

Now there's laughter coming from Samuel's schoolyard. Karl rides in through a laneway. Between the main building and the far goalpost, shielded from a yard by a thick and bushy fir tree, a kid leans on a fence with one hand, taking a whiz. When the boy zips up, Karl follows him to the paved play area by the school entrance. Three other boys sit in a circle, cross-legged. Upon seeing Karl, they shuffle about and squirm, all but Samuel who remains rigid while wearing a sardonic expression.

Though the other kids are older, Samuel is the biggest, the ringleader. Yet the others seem more menacing, almost feral. If they ganged up, Karl wonders, would Samuel join them, persuade them to stop, fight with his brother, or abstain? Karl points at Mitch Kalashuk, Marty's little brother, an obnoxious misfit in a dark jean jacket closest to the school wall.

"Move," Karl says.

The boy looks at Samuel who shrugs. Karl takes a step toward Mitch who then obeys, revealing two six packs, one Brador, the other Molson Extra Stock, neither opened, yet.

"Where'd you get the beer?" Karl says.

All eyes turn toward Samuel who's watching Karl.

"All right, all you guys, go home, scram," Karl says, in a calm voice, though his heart is beating rapidly.

They hesitate. One reaches for a Brador. A cough from Karl stops him. The kid is about to protest but then Mitch gets up and leaves. The others follow. When they're gone, Karl sits across from his brother, next to the beer.

"Do Mom and Dad know you're out?" Karl says.

"Who cares? It's not a school night."

"It's almost midnight, for crying out loud. Have you been out all this time?"

"Of course not. Dad and Mom think I'm in bed. I snuck out, like you showed me before."

Karl conceals an involuntary smile as he turns to take a bottle of Extra Stock from the plastic ring. He restores his stern expression and holds the bottle out in front of him, looks to the sky, then back at his brother whose eyes follow his movements like a cat. Karl digs out an opener from his backpack, pops off the cap, and gives the bottle to Samuel. He then opens another for himself and takes a swig.

"Go ahead, little brother."

Samuel, who was guardedly watching, puts the bottle to his lips. Before he has any, Karl grabs his wrist.

"You take one sip, just one, we drink all of it."

Samuel shrugs contemptuously, as if threatened by a feather. He takes a drink, swallows, and grimaces. As Karl suspects, recalling the bitterness of his first beer, this is his brother's initiation. It looks like Samuel wants to spit it out, but he manages to swallow and keep it in. With subsequent sips he makes the same face. He's no more than a third of the way through when Karl finishes his.

"Now hand over the other stuff."

"What other stuff?"

"I saw Scott. I know he didn't just get you beer."

"Scott who?"

Karl pauses to open another can.

"Don't make me search you."

Reluctantly, Samuel reaches into a coat pocket and hands Karl a sandwich bag. Karl counts five perfectly rolled joints. Karl digs through his knapsack for a book of matches, lights one of the joints, and takes a couple of tokes.

"I'll enjoy this while you finish that beer."

"We weren't going to drink it. We were going to sell it."

"Yeah right. Now drink."

Samuel continues to struggle. Karl feels a little sorry for his brother who's drifted into his own melancholic world. Odd. Karl always saw him as happy-go-lucky, with all his physical advantages. Maybe he's got problems too. Maybe Karl's being too cruel. On the other hand, he wouldn't put it past Samuel to be faking his dislike for beer.

Samuel takes a swig, stands up, and spits it out against the school wall. He ignores Karl's glare, tips the bottle as far as he can and takes another sip. He spits that out too. If he is acting, Karl thinks, he's pretty good. Finally, Samuel puts the empty on the ground and rolls it toward the school.

"You've made your point. Let's go home."

"Have I? Sit down. Let's compromise. We'll just finish one of the six-packs. It'll give us time to chat."

To confirm his part in the deal, Karl wraps the Brador in his dirty sweatshirt and stuffs it in his knapsack. Then he opens another Extra Stock for Samuel, which his brother accepts grudgingly.

"By the way, where'd you get the money for all this?"

"We all chipped in."

"Bullshit. Your friends wouldn't have left so quickly if they'd put their own money into this."

Samuel rolls his eyes but says nothing. Karl tokes away, patiently waiting for an answer. Then Samuel grins.

"So did Danielle like her gift?"

"What? Oh yeah, she certainly did."

"I figured as much. I did a damn good job on that, didn't I? Bet you'd never have found something that nice."

"You're probably right."

"So you gonna pay me for the beer?"

"You've got balls little brother, I'll give you that."

"Well?"

"You know what? Because of the necklace, I won't say a word to Mom, or to Dad. Rumour has it there are tickets for the Bills home opener circulating his office."

Mentioning their father along with the Bills has the desired effect as Samuel's face drops. He looks down, takes a small sip and then picks up a stone, which he flings high in the air. Karl can't be sure he aimed it or not, but the stone drops through the net-less basketball hoop.

"But you gotta give me something for the weed," Samuel says, his voice soft, pathetic.

Karl smiles, waves the baggie as if to weigh it, and then puts it in his knapsack.

"Let's make it an anonymous birthday gift for Danielle."

The afternoon breeze is picking up speed, collecting heat, and Karl knows tonight will be stuffy. That justifies standing like a fool at a bus stop on Geneva Street. By not taking his bike, he avoids arriving sweaty and dirty for what he hopes will be an uninhibited, uninterrupted evening with Danielle. Taking transit, which, sadly, is slower than biking, means one less excruciating hour to kill in this day that is taking forever.

First thing that morning, he took a long shower, capped with a splash of his father's Old Spice, before realizing he smelled like a forty-five year old man. He tried to wash it off but a trace still lingers—if he gets the chance, he'll get a cologne sample sprayed on him at the mall. The hair dryer cooperated for once and he managed to part his hair in the middle with little static. Picking out the right shirt to match his favourite black jeans posed a more difficult challenge. Back and forth he switched between long sleeves and short sleeves, eventually choosing a simple tan polo shirt. After all, he doesn't want to look like he's trying too hard.

By noon he was ready, leaving over four hours to kill. He was desperate to find things to occupy the time but it was as if everything conspired against him. His father had no office errands.

Even if he had, the car was unavailable as his mother was visiting old friends in Port Colborne. He was too clean to mow the lawn, trim the hedges, or weed the garden in the back. That also ruled out a bike ride to the beach or even a decent walk around the neighbourhood. He no longer needed to go to the bank either, as his dad had paid him for last month's work. Television offered nothing other than baseball, animal shows, and Star Trek repeats. PBS was televising a Monty Python marathon but Karl couldn't deal with those pledge drive interruptions. He wound up taking a risk and smoking a joint, then spending the afternoon in his bedroom, listening to New Order with headphones.

The red and grey Route Nine bus lumbers up on time. It will take him all the way without having to transfer. The few passengers onboard are older except for a young mother and her two boys about his brother's age, wearing matching plaid shorts. Karl takes a window seat in the far back, where he can be by himself. Sweat begins to trickle down his forehead. He slides open a window, which helps once they get moving.

The bus ambles south on Geneva, making no stops as it passes an elementary school, several modern churches, and a series of bungalows on deep lots with long driveways. At the intersection with Scott, the street opens up to become a busy and unattractive four-lane road with more houses on the left and high-rise apartment and low-rise commercial buildings on the right. It passes a ballpark and a Dairy Queen before stopping at the Fairview Mall.

Only the mother and two boys exit, while more than a dozen people board. With their shopping bags and buggies, the bus now feels cramped. Another mother, younger, with bickering toddler twins hovers an annoying fifteen seconds, at least, before taking up two seats beside him. Worse, a wheezing nut-bar lady, wearing a frumpy brown dress, and talking to herself, not only chooses the seat directly in front of him, but also closes the window, probably to protect her freshly permed blue hair.

It's unusual for Karl to be among so many strangers. He starts sweating again, second-guessing his transportation choice as the air-conditioned shopping centre is still an hour away. Seeing the jewellery store across the street improves his spirits, a reminder that Danielle's gift was a great success.

The bus passes under the highway bridge and the street narrows back to two lanes in an attractive older residential part of the city. Large trees arcade the main road and some of the side streets. Most of the houses are two-storey dwellings and the square footage increases with each block.

At Russell Street, a girl boards, the only other teenage passenger. She looks familiar. He keeps an eye on her as she scans for an empty seat. Her eyes make contact with his just as the nut-bar lady in front of Karl pulls the cord for the next stop. She vacates her seat and the girl rushes by a senior looking to change seats, ignoring his grumbling. She tosses her knapsack in and slides the window open before sitting down. She faces forward a few seconds but then abruptly climbs to her knees to face Karl, her arms spread over the top of the seat, her teeth showing a big-gummed smile.

"I know you."

"Hi Erica," Karl says.

Erica O'Brien, Erica the Red, as the kids in Grade Nine called her. Not just for her long straight strawberry hair, but also her constant blush over a face of freckles scattered like tiny jigsaw puzzle pieces. She's wearing a white windbreaker zipped up to her neck. It makes Karl think of the Canadian flag, or two-thirds of it. He barely knew Erica back then, but she acts now as if they're long-time pals, chewing gum with her mouth open, the fresh mint spearing his nostrils.

"It's Karl, right? Karl Stevens . . .?"

"Stevenson."

"That's it. So, where are you off to, Karl Stevenson?"

"To see my girlfriend."

It comes out as a rebuff or bragging, not at all what he intended. She nods without asking details. He asks her the same question. She unzips her jacket and spreads it open to reveal a powder blue and white striped uniform, then holds out her tightly braided hair until it's horizontal.

"Got a job at Wendy's. Don't I look like the original?"

To Karl, it's a startling resemblance only he can't be sure if her comment is self-congratulation or self-mockery. He doesn't know what to say. She drops her braids, re-zips her jacket, pulls out a pack of Spearmint, offers him a stick.

"No thanks."

"You and Tom Waryk are good friends, aren't you?" she says, after several chews.

The mention of his old friend flusters Karl. Instantly he recalls an image of them on their bikes, Tom with a cigarette in his mouth, as they watch a ship, a red laker, pass through one of the twin locks. The canal bored Tom who tolerated Karl's interest only to break for a cigarette or a joint. That time, upon seeing the colour of the ship, Tom made a crass comment about Erica and how she was a true redhead. Karl laughed at the time but now the recollection makes him cringe.

"So you do remember," she says.

Karl nods, momentarily speechless.

"Happen to know what he's up to these days?"

"Actually, it's been two years since I've seen him."

"Oh."

Her smile vanishes and she bites the inside of her top lip.

"He went to live with his father in Pittsburgh and that's the last I heard from him."

Erica nods, as if she already knows as much. She adds another stick of gum in her mouth and they get quiet again. She remains facing him, though leaning back more, glancing outside every few seconds.

Karl can see in her melancholic face what Tom found appealing, aside from the obvious. She's quite cute when she keeps her mouth closed and doesn't smile. That gives her a sultry, tragic look. He ought to find that appealing but something about her presence casts a pall over his mood, intrudes on his anticipation of the evening ahead. He's glad to see a transfer in her hand.

The bus rolls into the Academy Street terminal and pulls in behind another. While glad to see her go, Karl can't keep his eyes off Erica as she walks along the platform. She has a nice body and a sexy stride. Beyond her, a Greyhound bus pulls into one of the four diagonal bays at the Union Bus Terminal, no doubt destined for Toronto or Buffalo. It looks just as it did three years before. No way could he know back then he'd never see his friend again. He wonders about Tom occasionally. Does he have a girlfriend or another buddy like Karl? Erica turns to give him a little smile and wave but doesn't wait for Karl to respond.

A hydraulic hiss announces the driver's return. He steers the bus behind several others onto Carlisle Street, making a left at St. Paul. Downtown is virtually deserted, the citizens opting for malls like the Pen Centre, where Karl is heading. More than a hundred years before an old Welland Canal—Karl can't remember which of the four, maybe it was more than one—ran along Twelve Mile Creek in the valley below.

The bus drives past the arena where the Falcons Junior B team plays, then up to Westchester Avenue, the access for Highway 406. Three minutes up the highway would get him to his destination but on public transit it's another half hour.

Soon the bus coasts along Glenridge Avenue, perhaps Karl's favourite street. A predominance of German and English Tudor designs gives it a cozy European feel.

After crossing a narrow bridge over railway tracks, the bus turns onto Glen Morris Drive, passes the Catholic high school and a big field before stopping in front of Karl's school. It's strange to see it in summer without hundreds of students milling about. He transferred for academic reasons, at the expense of friends. He hasn't made many new ones, though Danielle is largely to blame for that. The bus quickly passes through more residential streets until it finally arrives at the Pen Centre, the largest mall in Niagara.

It feels like forever since boarding but it's still daylight and he's early. Good thing because he neglected one vital item. No big deal, a simple matter.

That's what he thinks until he pushes through a turnstile into the brightly lit drug store. There are few customers yet he feels increasingly self-conscious with each step toward the back, as if everyone knows his purpose. His hands shake as he yanks at one of the hanging packages, knocking over several others. He looks around, red faced, but no one's noticed. He kicks them under the rack with his foot and walks to the desolate prescription counter, hoping he can avoid paying at the front. No one's there but he'll wait; no way is he going to ring the little bell.

A woman in white, with a nametag that says Marjorie, appears. She's wearing deep purple nail polish and is about Violet's age. Her friendly smile causes Karl to suffer a brief internal panic. What if Marjorie knows Danielle? What if she spotted the two of them together before? Worse, what if she knows Dani's parents?

Stupid, stupid, stupid, he should have taken care of this earlier when he had all that time. The woman remains professionally disinterested as she drops the change into his clammy palm and hands him the white paper bag. He strolls out as casually as one can with his head down.

He finds an empty bench by a garbage can. Blindly he dips his hands in to remove the condoms. He throws out the box and the bag, stuffs the crinkly packages in his pants, six in each pocket, careful not to crush the joints he took from Samuel.

When he rises, the bulge is too noticeable. Reluctantly, he has to toss out half a dozen.

Danielle's department store is closing up, no one around to give out cologne samples. He heads to women's fashions but Danielle isn't there. He's about to ask another girl when he catches a glimmer of thick blonde hair thirty feet away in the jewellery department. He zigzags through racks of new fall clothes to surprise her from behind.

But she isn't alone; there's a commotion. Somehow, Danielle notices him and when she turns around she looks agitated. She also looks great, elegant in her grey pantsuit and light green blouse, too elegant; he feels a slight tinge of unworthiness. His gift matches perfectly with her outfit, except it's not around her neck but in her hands.

"Karl, you're here. You can help straighten this out."

"Who is this?"

Karl turns to the speaker, a matronly woman in a red dress with librarian glasses, to whom he takes an immediate dislike. It's clear the woman shares the same first impression of him. He wrests his eyes away from the accusing gaze to turn to Danielle. The woman's eyes stay on him.

"This is my boyfriend, Karl. He bought it for me."

"What's going on?" Karl says.

"I came over to help Julie cash out, anxious to show off my birthday gift. This is our boss, Mrs. Claxton, by the way. When Mrs. Claxton saw my necklace she said it was the one stolen here earlier this week. Not like it, but the very same one. I told her it was a coincidence but—oh, I hate to ask, but can you confirm it?"

A warm pain surges through Karl's chest, along with a sinking feeling in his stomach. He has to fight to keep his cool and avoid turning red. He looks at the necklace, then at the supervisor's unflinching face, afraid to talk, knowing that whatever he says will come out as gibberish.

"Karl?" Danielle says.

"Yes, yes, of course I bought it. But not here."

Inside, Karl swears at his little brother who gave him no receipt, no box. Then he swears at himself for not thinking of asking. Fear wells up and it's a struggle not to betray guilt under the woman's accusing eyes. But what proof does she have? If there is an identifying mark on the chain, the hag would have pointed it out already.

"You wouldn't, by chance, have the receipt with you?"

"Excuse me?"

He affects an indignant expression and tone to match. Mrs. Claxton studies him; Karl's face doesn't break. She addresses Julie and Danielle, excluding Karl, as if he no longer exists.

"Well, this is an odd situation," she says, ironically.

Everyone remains quiet until she leaves wearing a frown that turns to a smile when a new customer appears. Danielle thanks Karl and asks him to wait for her in the mall.

He's glad to get out of the store, until he sees Marjorie, the pharmacist, approaching. She's heading for the mall exit doors. He backs away and picks up a payphone, turning his head slightly so he can watch her walk to her car and get in.

Danielle reappears and they exit the mall holding hands. She's looking straight ahead when she lets out a short laugh.

"What a coincidence with the necklace."

"Yeah, strange."

She unlocks his door first. He climbs in and reaches for her lock. After clicking in their seatbelts, Danielle inserts the key in the ignition but doesn't start the car.

"It's true you didn't take it, right?"

He turns to her abruptly and realizes how hard it must be for her to ask, what a risk she's taking with her question. He takes her hand, pats it, and looks into her eyes.

"I guarantee you I did not take it."

"Sorry, it was just so upsetting. I believe you of course."

"That woman's a cow. Why would I steal from a store someone I knew worked at? I'd simply use your discount."

"I believe you. Still, I won't wear it to work again."

"No, please don't."

"Tonight though, I'll wear them the whole night . . ."

She starts the ignition. A minute later they head east on Glendale Avenue for the short drive to her house. At each stoplight and stop sign she plays with the pearls and for once Karl appreciates the New Yorker for its air conditioning.

"You're certain Jack and Trudy are gone?" Karl says.

"I guarantee it."

/6\

A Monday morning lemony scent left by the cleaners greets Karl when he opens the glass door. Yet it's stuffy inside. No one has turned on the air conditioning, meaning no one else has shown up that morning. His dad is the only one who can stand the summer heat, preferring to save on the electricity bill. Karl pokes his head into the only walled office.

"Anything else for me today, Dad?"

A balding head popping out of a tan business suit pores over a legal document and doesn't notice Karl. It's not like his father to ignore people; must be a complex offer. Karl steps away to check out the office.

All the individual desk calendars, including the popular drug store calendar with the Leafs team photo on the main wall, need to be flipped from June to July. Karl adjusts them, then plops his butt on Dirk Fuller's orthopaedic chair. He spins while twirling the puck with the Leafs logo Dirk supposedly caught ten years before off a Dave Keon deflection. Classical music plays on his small transistor radio, which Dirk always forgets to turn off. Karl turns the dial until he hears *Every Little Thing She Does is Magic*, by the Police.

His father emerges and looks surprised but pleased to see his oldest son. Never one for a wide smile, his mouth, like Venice, is sinking. Bands of sunlight streaming through the panel windows reveal crow's feet that run deep and long. Strange how as the years pass, his mother seems to get younger while his father ages. Isn't it supposed to be the other way around?

"Finished already?" his father says.

"Only two signs to remove, one to install. It helped that the ground was soft."

"Good. It's a quiet day. Let me take you to lunch."

Karl hesitates, his initial instinct to decline. He's daydreamed all day about taking Danielle to the Falls for an afternoon picnic, his dreams going as far as swapping cars with his dad to take his girlfriend out in style. That's a long shot, as the Benz is his father's pride and joy. A more meaningful success symbol to his father than the prominent Stevenson Realty sign out front, Karl suspects, though it pales in comparison to the pride Karl feels whenever he sees that sign.

"Unless you've got other plans?"

"No, just whatever needed to be done around here."

"All right then."

"But, hey, can we take your car? The wagon's too dirty from the signs and the Benz is much more comfortable. I'll drive. That way you can have a couple of beers, if you want."

The beer argument works, though his father nixes Karl's proposal to go over the river, citing the American holiday would likely delay their return. Karl in kind vetoes his dad's favourite Italian restaurant for which, in his faded jeans and t-shirt, he is grossly underdressed. They compromise on the Chicago gangland themed restaurant on Lakeshore Road.

It's not yet noon. The restaurant is empty and they have their pick of booths. They settle by a television broadcasting CNN, order drinks, and take in the latest on a North Korean jet crash in Guinea. Plenty of NASA coverage of Pioneer Ten and Sally Ride too. As the beer and Coke arrive, Karl begins to sense a deeper purpose behind this lunch.

"Your mom wants you to pick a date for a birthday dinner for Danielle."

That's not it, that's just procrastinating.

"How'd she know it was Dani's birthday?" Karl says.

His father chuckles. Karl laughs. Of course, his mother would know. Her fondness for Karl's girlfriend has become legendary, a source of family amusement. Samuel teases her from time to time by announcing Karl and Danielle have broken up. She fell for it the first few times and became annoyed with Samuel, but now she handles it well. The last time she got him back, telling Samuel she was negotiating with the Fosters to swap him for Danielle. Samuel thought this was hilarious but their mother expressed immediate regret and for days apologized for conceiving such a horrible idea.

While his father orders, Karl thinks of a date. Danielle is going away with her parents this weekend, and she's working on Thursday, so it'd have to be Wednesday, or the following week. His father has a scrap of paper listing available days in his mother's handwriting. Wednesday is at the top of the list and circled by the time the food arrives.

For Karl it's the Al Capone cheeseburger piled high with all the fixings and fries, while his father goes for the Dillinger deep-dish pizza, topped with pepperoni slices and bullets of bacon, along with another beer.

"Karl, I know you're not big on football, but you should go see your brother play once in a while."

Karl sighs. Another reminder of the deep bond between his father and Samuel. He only manages a half-hearted reply.

"How'd he do on the weekend?"

"Well, he ran for a TD and caught one as well."

"No kidding."

"But his best play came as a result of his worst play. On an off tackle run, he failed to tuck the ball, which allowed a defensive back to knock it out with his helmet. Without bobbling it, the DB then picked it up and ran with it."

His father pauses to wipe his hands and drink his beer.

"And what did Sam do? Did he pound the ground and get mad? No, he bolted up and chased the guy down. Not only did he tackle him, but he also knocked the ball out and recovered it. I've never seen anything like it. The little thief."

Literally, Karl thinks, but keeps it to himself. Samuel will always be his father's favourite. It's a fact Karl's learned to accept and in a way appreciate. Would he want that kind of attention?

In the silence of chewing and swallowing, Karl wonders about that some more. Maybe he isn't giving his father the credit he's due. Perhaps this lunch is a kind of attention personalized for him.

"Dad, you remember Violet Baxter?" Karl says, almost as surprised as his father at how abruptly it comes out.

"Your old babysitter? Yes, of course, I remember her."

Karl detects a trace of disapproval and almost chokes on a French fry.

"You don't sound happy to hear her name."

"It's silly, I know, but I'm still peeved about your uncle's funeral."

"Oh? What happened?"

"It's no big deal, at least not anymore. But at the time your mother and I wanted Violet to bring you home after the funeral. We didn't want you to be spooked by the cemetery. She never showed and we had to take you to the gravesite."

"I'm not easily spooked, Dad."

"That's true. We found that out—anyway what bothers me is we considered her part of our family. She knew your uncle well and I guess I thought she'd be there with us. You see, no one else, at least no one we knew, was at his funeral. It was kind of sad, really. Her absence only made it worse."

Karl's mouth opens. Doesn't his dad know about Violet and Uncle Douglas? It seems impossible for him not to, yet there's no trace in his voice or eyes he's concealing anything.

"Does, or did, Mom feel the same way about Violet? Not showing up, I mean?"

"Not so much. Your mother always liked that girl, much in the way she's fond of Danielle. She defended the absence, saying Violet was ill or something."

"Oh?"

"I accepted that and gave Violet another chance when I asked her to baby-sit you the day we brought your brother home. Of course, I misread everything because your mother wasn't happy about that."

"Why?"

"You know how your mother can be . . . unpredictable, at times. For some reason, she'd become disenchanted with Violet. I've never seen the girl since."

His father has some beer, suppresses a belch.

"Why do you ask? Did you run into her?"

Karl pauses. It seems pointless to mention his visit to Violet if his father doesn't know anything. Then again, he doesn't want to lie, especially now that they're talking in this way, man to man.

"Mrs. Baxter, that's who I ran into. Obviously, Violet's name came up. Her mother also seems confused about that period between Uncle Douglas's death and Samuel's birth."

"Funny you should mention Sam and your uncle in the same sentence. I've been thinking recently how in many ways your brother is like my brother."

"Oh?" Karl says, pushing his empty plate aside.

"In good ways, and not so good ones as well. You see, I'm troubled about your brother."

So am I, Karl says to himself. Are they referring to the same thing? Is this the true purpose of the lunch?

"Why do you say that, Dad?"

"Have you noticed anything?"

"Like what?"

"I don't know. His attitude, his behaviour, his friends. Is he in trouble of any kind?"

Karl shifts in his seat, cornered. Part of him is tempted to reveal the episode with the beer and dope, but that would be self-incriminating. The necklace? Can he accuse his younger brother without absolute proof? That could backfire too. Karl can recall his uncle's harsh opinion of snitches.

"Well, he's always been cocky, and maybe that's getting worse. His friends are little punks—"

"That's what I'm talking about. Sometimes I wonder if a change in environment would be good for him."

"A new environment? You mean a new school? Are we moving?"

His father shakes his head as he finishes his last slice of pizza and wipes his hands.

"Your mother and I have been bandying ideas about."

"Will I get a say?"

"Of course, though by the time we decide anything, you'll probably be at university."

"Do you want me to talk to Samuel? To watch him?"

"I'm not asking you to spy on him or anything. I don't want to make a big deal over it. I was just curious."

Karl finds his mother in the kitchen, wearing a full-length cotton apron over a burgundy tank top and beige golf shorts, facing the sink, peeling potatoes. Occasionally she wipes her brow to clear a bead of sweat. The heat and smell of breaded chicken seeps from the oven. He sits at the small table and passes on the message his father will stay at work for dinner and for them to eat without him.

With a sigh, she wipes her hands on her apron and calls the real estate office. Karl doesn't listen, doesn't have to, as he's heard both ends of this dialogue too often. It's as close as his parents get to arguing. They'll speak for a few minutes, calm and civil, and the end-result is always the same, his dad staying at the office, his mom content to have lodged her complaint. Perhaps she believes that if she does so often enough, something will change.

"I went for lunch with Dad, today," Karl says, after she hangs up and returned to her potatoes.

"Good, at least one of us can bear witness that he eats."

Karl gulps, thinks about going to his room to give her time to simmer down. On other hand, he's always heard fish are more likely to bite in stormy conditions.

"I never knew Dad didn't care for Violet."

His mother drops the peeler into the sink but instead of clanging around, it makes a dull thud.

"Violet. You mean Violet Baxter?"

Karl lifts the lid off a pot on the stove. It contains only water, presumably for the potatoes.

"Of course. Do we know another Violet?"

"Don't be smart."

She doesn't add anything to that and continues peeling.

"So anyway, I ran into her mom the other day, which got me thinking about my old babysitter and what she might be up to. When I mentioned her name to Dad, he seemed annoyed. I guess he's still sore about Violet not showing up at Uncle Douglas's funeral."

"That was so long ago, Karl. It's hardly important now."

"That's what I thought. So why would it still bug him?"

"You'd have to ask your father."

"You liked Violet though, right Mom?"

"Sure, of course. You know I did."

Karl digs through a cupboard until he finds a bag of chocolate chip cookies, already opened. The rustling and crinkling catches his mother's attention and, without slowing her peeling motion, she shakes her head, nods at the clock, and Karl puts them back.

"So you never got mad at her, like Dad?"

"She was a teenager. Teenagers have a habit of stirring you up from time to time."

Karl hesitates. Is she trying to be clever?

"But was it like Dad, where you were bugged so much you remembered it for a long time?"

"Karl, what's the point of these questions?"

"I'm just curious as to what happened to her."

At this, his mother stops peeling. It seems dramatic until he realizes she stopped because she was finished.

"Do you know what happened to her, Mom?"

She wipes her hands on the apron, hesitates as if to balance her response, like a trapeze artist without the benefit of a rehearsal.

"I have no idea what happened to her."

Liar, he thinks. His mother just told an out and out lie, a bald-faced lie that, to him, confirms a link between her and Violet. A disturbing link. Karl feels his heartbeat quicken.

"How about those two men we met at Uncle Douglas's funeral? Do you know where they are?"

"No."

"So you remember them?"

"Karl, your uncle had plenty of unsavoury friends. The farther they are from us, the better."

He can buy that she doesn't know where they are but her characterization seems unfair. He doesn't want to press the point. Instead, he reaches into his back pocket, takes out the scrap of paper from his dad, and puts it on the counter.

"Oh yeah, Mom, by the way, Dad and I worked it out. Danielle will come over on Wednesday for her birthday."

"That's only two days away."

"But Dad had this list—"

"—which he should have used before the weekend."

"Sorry, we can change it."

"It's fine. By the way, how is everything between you and Danielle?"

"Never better, Mom. We're eloping. Wednesday night. Right after we eat."

Behind the reproach in her eyes, Karl gets the sense that wouldn't be close to being the worst news she'd ever receive.

"I feel awful for not cooking," Karl's mother says.

Karl's not counting but it seems like this is her fifth apology. This time a loud sizzle from the barbecue nearly drowns out her voice. She's distracted, holding her white wine in one hand while flapping at a wave of smoke with the other.

"Don't give it a second thought," Danielle says. "To be honest, I prefer eating outdoors, at least in summer."

"Me too," Karl says.

His mother flashes an appreciative smile. They're sitting side by side in lawn chairs while Samuel juggles a soccer ball at the far end of the yard. Nearer the house, Karl's father, in a green and yellow Hawaiian shirt and powder blue Bermuda shorts, performs another series of burger flips, stabs a few to check for blood, then announces the meat is ready.

"Oh my, already?"

Karl's mom sets down her glass, declines Dani's offer to help, and rushes into the house, her light pink summer dress flowing. She returns with a bowl of potato salad, which she places on the picnic table between two platters loaded with stacks of hamburger patties and hot dogs. She rushes back in for buns, condiments and a stack of Velveeta cheese slices, napkins, plastic forks and knives, and sets them down hastily, somehow avoiding three plastic cups filled with pop, and his dad's bottle of beer.

The brothers and Danielle assemble at the picnic table, Danielle between Karl and his mother on one side, his father and brother on the other. Slim ribbons of sunlight shine through the branches of two maple trees while a pair of flies, tauntingly avoiding the swatter, try but cannot mar the idyllic family setting.

Karl likes how Danielle looks in her white denim shorts and the peach rayon blouse, a birthday gift from her mother. She's dressed up, but not enough to make him feel like a slob in his cut-offs and tank top. The pearls around her tanned neck accent her outfit. It's surprising his mother has remained oblivious so far.

"Nice necklace," Samuel says, nonchalantly.

Karl glares at him, painfully reminded of the part his little brother played in its alleged purchase. His mother glares at his younger brother too.

"Samuel, if you must wear that grass stained t-shirt, at least take off that awful cap while we eat."

"Aw, Mom."

"Sam, remove that cap."

Samuel obeys his father and tosses the cap toward the back door. Then his mother points at the necklace.

"Oh my, that is lovely. May I?"

"Of course, and thanks."

Danielle blushes as she undoes the clasp and passes it around for everyone to admire. Karl watches Samuel, fearful he'll say something stupid, by accident or on purpose. He and his brother have barely spoken since the beer incident at the school. Until this remark, Samuel has shown no sign of a grudge. If he's been biding his time to strike, this would be a perfect opportunity. No doubt he's unaware of what Karl discovered at the mall, but won't be for long if he opens his yap. Once the necklace hangs around Danielle's neck again, without a peep from his little brother, Karl relaxes.

Then it becomes a food free-for-all. Karl makes sure to let Danielle grab a burger and hot dog ahead of him. On his turn he grabs two hamburger buns and four patties and then assembles his meal, adding cheese, relish, pickles, onions and tomato slices, ketchup, mustard, lettuce, topping them off with a sprinkle of bacon bits, ignoring the looks he gets from his mother and his girlfriend.

Once both burgers stand without support, he surveys the remaining food, estimates how long it will take them to eat it all, and calculates how much time he and Danielle can squeeze in at the canal. With her going away on the weekend, every minute is precious. With every minute comes increased regret at not postponing this celebration. He starts when his mother reaches around Danielle to tap him on the shoulder.

"The necklace is beautiful, Karl. I adore the pearls. You're my son, and I love you, but I'd never guess you'd pick out a piece as nice as this."

Everyone laughs, especially Samuel.

"Yes, Karl, how exquisite," his little brother says putting on an impish grin.

"It certainly caused a scene at work the other day."

Danielle swallows a big bite of her hot dog and another before realizing they want to hear more. Karl squeezes his fat burger so hard a tomato slice slips out and relish drips down onto the table. The distraction only provides a slight delay before Danielle goes on to describe what happened.

As she does, Karl watches with great satisfaction as his brother's smile transforms into a guilty frown. Samuel has to realize Karl's figured out the truth now. To make sure, Karl stares at him and, as he expects, Samuel avoids eye contact. However, if his younger brother actually feels remorse, he hides it well and acts as if the story doesn't concern him. His smile even returns, which infuriates Karl.

Thankfully, the topic drifts off, as does the food. Karl never knows how, but his father has a knack for making the perfect amount. He's happy to see crumbs on all the plates, even happier for the silence that follows his father asking if anyone wants more.

The sun is setting now. The flies have retired for the night, giving way to the mosquito shift that chases the family and their guest inside. Karl's mother turns on the television to the Blue Jays game against the Texas Rangers.

"Isn't there something else we can watch?" Karl's father says, reaching for the remote control.

Immediately, Karl's mother yanks the box away.

"No, Danielle loves baseball."

"Well, I hate baseball," Samuel says. "Sissy sport."

"You don't have to—"

"Nonsense, Danielle. It's your birthday. In this house, unless it's Sunday, the birthday person controls the TV."

Karl's mom goes to the kitchen. At his father's nod, Samuel turns down the volume on the television manually. The lights dim and, to Karl's dismay, his mother comes out with a special milk chocolate and vanilla cake. The chocolate portion is sprinkled with bits of caramel and shaped like an opened baseball glove. In the glove's pocket rests a vanilla ball—actually two iced muffin tops attached at the base—with red liquorice strings as seams.

"Mom, it's almost nine, we should be going."

Karl points at his watch but Danielle slaps his shoulder with the back of her hand.

"Nonsense. This cake is too beautiful to rush."

Admiring, then cutting, then eating the cake—of course, Danielle has to have two pieces—takes another hour. Karl frets each minute, though he's sure he conceals it well. A pair of Jays tickets hidden underneath the cake helps. They're for a game in August against the Orioles, her favourite team next to the Blue Jays. Maybe they'll find a way to convince her parents, and his, to let them stay overnight, in a hotel.

It's not until after ten o'clock that he gets them out of there. To Karl's surprise, his dad offers the use of the Mercedes. But he has to decline. The risk is too high his father will discover what they're up to. With the station wagon he can leave the windows open through the night to let the smoke clear and then get rid of any evidence in daylight.

"What was your big rush?" Danielle says, while they're still in the driveway.

"What do you mean?"

"I was having fun. It was sweet of your mom and dad to go to all that trouble and make me feel part of the family."

"I guess."

"What's your problem? All evening, you've been acting like you didn't want to be there."

"Well, to be honest, I didn't."

"Thanks."

"I mean, I wanted to be with you, just not there."

She remains quiet. He can tell his behaviour put her off. Well, her question bugs him, and perplexes him. What's the rush? What kind of a question is that? This is their last time together until the following week. She's as aware of that as he is and should be have been as anxious to leave to maximize their time together. But he'll only waste more arguing the point. There'll be plenty of time to brood over it later. Alone.

"Sorry," he says, as he starts the car.

She smiles at him and he backs the car out. When they reach the stop sign at Lake Street, he flicks on his left turn signal, but then she puts her left hand on his thigh, moving it up slowly until he sits back. With her other hand, she flicks the turn signal to the right.

"I don't have to be at work until the afternoon."

He needs no further encouragement and drives north to Lakeshore Road and on to the canal. A left turn takes them to a dirt road that leads to a dark, secluded spot beyond the giant sand dunes, beyond the creepy water treatment plant, among discrete trees and other vehicles far below Lock One.

They shuffle into Wendy's, giggling, self-conscious, ordering with hands covering mouths to contain their giddiness. After getting two large fries and a large Frosty, they skulk to a table at the back. Outside, traffic on Welland Avenue is busy with cars exiting the last show at the cinema.

They eat the smooth cream with great deliberation, Karl using a spoon while Danielle indulges her craving for chocolate dipped fries. At one point, Karl snaps his spoon, causing the giggling to resume and escalates into hysterics. The dessert is almost melted before he returns to the counter for a replacement.

"Hi Karl."

Behind the cash register, looking very cute in a silly cap, stands Erica. Whether it's the dope or the unexpectedness of the meeting, her friendly smile affects him in a weird way, makes him think of her as somehow dangerous. He nods a reserved hello and shows her his broken spoon. She chuckles knowingly and gets him a new one. Before she hands it over, Erica uses it to point toward Danielle.

"Is she your girlfriend, the one you mentioned?"

"Yes, yes she is."

"She's pretty."

"Thanks."

"Sure."

Erica lets go of the spoon and he senses she held on to it longer than necessary. He's in no condition to be sure about such things and for the moment can't seem to move.

"See ya," Erica says, her voice echoing in his head.

She walks to the back and Karl feels his muscles relax at the same time.

"What took so long?" Danielle says, as he sits down.

"Nothing. Ran into someone I know who works here."

"Oh?"

"Yeah, an old friend I happened to run into on the bus the other day."

"Aren't you going to introduce me?"

"To be honest I don't know this person that well. What say we get out of here?"

To his relief, Danielle nods. She takes what's left of the Frosty with her, but leaves behind a clump of cold fries.

As they approach their traditional evening ending spot, Karl notices an upbound ship rising in Lock Five. It's about to reach its peak before gliding into the next lock. He drives on to Lock Six and parks in a gravel area. They remain silent for a while, looking at the ship. He glances over to see Danielle's melancholic smile, which mirrors the empty sadness he feels.

"I'll miss you this weekend," he says, declining a spoon of her melting Frosty.

"Of course, I'll miss you too. But I'll have my necklace around my neck the whole time, to remind me."

As she looks down, her spoon tips, dropping chocolate just below the necklace. Karl bends down to lick it away.

"That tickles."

"All right, I'll lick your nose then."

"Hey, I thought you didn't want any more."

"From your nose it's different."

"Well, don't you dare."

Normally he'd persist but Karl catches a subtle change in her tone, her mood. She won't be gone long but it seems eternal. A lot can happen in a few days and he dreads the interruption of the dreamy perfection of the past few days.

"Where is it you're going this weekend?"

"That's the third time you've asked in the past week."

"Sorry, keep forgetting, I guess."

She watches him a moment and then dips her spoon up and down inside the cup, finally taking out only a small spoonful, half melted, half solid. Even though he's just told her he doesn't want any, he wishes she'd offer again.

"Arnprior, to see my aunt and uncle."

"Right, Arnprior. That's near Ottawa isn't it?"

"Sort of. Under an hour."

"I see."

She stabs her spoon in the cup again, harder, scraping the wax paper.

"What do you see, Karl?"

Karl breathes in, lets out a nervous sigh. She stares into his eyes, ready for a challenge. She knows what he's getting at but is forcing him to say it.

"When you're there, will you see him?"

"Him? Who? Who's him?"

Fear grips Karl now, panic even. His mind scrambles for the conversational eject button. Too late. When he drops his gaze and looks toward the lock, Danielle grabs his chin and twists his head until their eyes met again.

"Who?" she says, her eyes wide and round, lips pursed.

"You tell me," he says, with faint fierceness, a last grasp at control.

"Tell you what, precisely," she says, firmer, louder.

"The guy you were with before, in Ottawa." Karl fights to keep his voice from shaking.

Danielle raises a hand, as if to slap him, but pulls it back.

"I don't believe it. I really thought we were past this."

"Maybe you are. Not me. Honestly, it's been tormenting me. You go on about not keeping secrets and here you are—anyway, it bothers me, and it bothers me especially now."

"Now? Why now?"

"You know, since we've been having—since you and I have been—you know . . ."

She pauses and looks genuinely baffled by his response.

"What the hell difference does that make?"

"I don't know. I figured that now you should tell me."

"Oh, you figured, did you? God, Karl . . ."

She puts her head in her hands. Mentally, he's working out a retreat with the slim prospects of a regretful Niagara Falls barrel jumper. In front of them, the southerly gates of Lock Six, the last of the twin flight locks, open and, without a word, he starts the car.

She doesn't look up until they reach her house. He gets an automatic kiss on the cheek and then her voice softens, but now it's more patronizing than tender.

"Karl, while I'm gone, you need to think seriously about this, about us."

She shuts the door, without slamming it. A hopeful sign of future peace even though the sound rips through his heart and paralyzes him. Probably a good thing because otherwise he might do something stupid like get out and run after her.

It's after two in the morning when he drags his heavy heart through a swarm of mosquitoes dancing under the porch light and into his quiet and dark home. Too quiet.

He's about to steal a beer from his dad but remembers the six-pack of Brador stashed under his bed. In this mood, he'll drink all six. The beer will be warm but at least he won't risk making noise.

About to head to the basement, Karl senses something not right. It really is too quiet, a background noise missing. He creeps up the stairs slowly, past the closed door of the master bedroom and the empty office to his brother's room. He goes inside to find the window open. Under the duvet, a football at the pillow and his brother's football uniform stretched the length of the bed.

When he gets to his bedroom, he reaches under his bed for the beer. Gone. In its place, a postcard of a city skyline, fronting a rolling countryside, taken from a hilltop across a river with many steel bridges. The card is addressed to him, in Tom's unforgettable scrawl. The message, also in familiar handwriting, comes from a different source, a younger hand.

"Thanks for holding on to my beer and not telling. Snatched postcard before Mom and Dad could see it. Now we're even."

It turned out to be a wonderful weekend in the Muskokas. All my fears and concerns vanished once I indulged in the beauty of still lakes shaped like puzzle pieces—not even that connection made me fret about Karl—bordered by swathes of evergreens looming over the tiny cottages. For the first time since, well, since my brother-in-law came to Canada, I experienced the joy of having John to myself for an extended time, without human distractions.

We returned Sunday evening to find Violet watching a Disney movie, Karl in bed. Something in her demeanour troubled me. She was nervous, didn't ask about our trip, and barely acknowledged the t-shirt we brought back for her. John headed to his little office to get paperwork ready for next week. After checking on Karl, I offered to make tea and watch the movie with her, but she seemed anxious to go.

That's when I spotted bits of ashes in the ashtray, as if it had been emptied but not wiped. Violet didn't smoke; in fact the only people in our house who did were John, rarely, and Doug. I inspected the ashtray, sniffed it while Violet watched guardedly. The smell wasn't tobacco, though, but something sweeter. I recognized it from the days when Doug would come home from his bar smelling of booze and this stuff.

"Were you smoking marijuana?" I said, more shocked than angry.

"No."

Her obvious lie irritated me. I ushered her to the door and out but made it clear we would discuss it later, to which she nodded meekly.

I went to clean the guestroom but found the bedding unused. I rushed to the master bedroom. Our bed was made but not as perfectly as I had left it. The room smelled different. Like sex. I tore off the ruffled duvet and sheets. More ashes and blond hairs. The first thing that came to mind was Doug but the idea of him and Violet was too preposterous. I took the linen to the basement and stuffed it in the laundry machine. I sprayed the bedroom with air freshener, and remade the bed. To keep my mind occupied and prevent myself chasing after the girl, I began vacuuming. That made John come out of his office.

"What are you doing? Can't that wait?"

"I'm sorry John, but—"

"But what? You'll wake Karl."

"You're right, I'm sorry. I wasn't thinking."

As I pulled the vacuum cleaner away, it hit something under the bed. I kneeled down and pulled out an unfamiliar book with a white cover entitled, *Twenty Cases Suggestive of Reincarnation.* I opened it and saw a name, Gareth or Garth. What a relief. I didn't know who this boy was but at least I knew who it wasn't.

I still intended to confront Violet but it seemed she was correspondingly intent on avoiding being alone with me. She couldn't outsmart me forever, though.

Often John would ask my help with his preparations for open houses. I would point out ways to spruce up the home to make it attractive to strangers. I got Violet to watch Karl one of those mornings after explaining John would be with me when she arrived. We got the work done early and came back. I suggested the four of us go for ice cream before the actual open house. She couldn't refuse once she saw Karl's eagerness to go. What I didn't mention to her was that Doug would meet us there to take three of us back while John went to attend his open house. I'd arranged it so my brother-in-law would arrive late enough after John left to leave a gap for a candid talk between us girls.

The weather co-operated, the canal did not. The bridge was going up for a ship and left us stuck waiting. It took forever to get across; the puffy languid clouds were moving quicker. My nerves were frayed by the time we reached the green expanse of farmland with its slight pasture odour. The dairy's white silos towered over the flat countryside against a blue sky. Several cars were parked by the picnic tables but, thankfully, not Doug's LTD.

Violet was acting normal in helping Karl pick his flavour while I let John choose for me so I could watch the road. No sign of my brother-in-law but I still sensed my window of opportunity was shrinking. We finished our ice creams and once everyone had gone to the bathroom, good old reliable John looked at his watch.

"Time to get going," he said, causing Violet to perk up, but she didn't say anything.

"Yes, it's okay," I said. "We'll be fine."

Violet watched with curious detachment but when John got into his car without us, she clued in.

"What's going on? Is Mr. Stevenson coming back?"

I guided Karl to the swings to have him play with some other kids while I took Violet aside. I did my best to restrain judgement in sharing my suspicions about what happened at the house while John and I were away. Her expression sank with each word; she listened intently but denied nothing.

"So who is this Gareth, or Garth?" I said.

"Who?" she said, now taken aback. I retrieved the odd book from my purse and she looked as if she was going to faint. I opened it and showed her the name. "Oh, Gareth." She still sounded unsure, confused.

"Are you in love with him?" I said, looking her in the eyes; this actually seemed to calm her. "Violet, you are much too young. I'm not your mother and maybe it's not my place, but I do consider you like a little sister. And as a sister, I urge you to be careful. Before something terrible happens."

"I will," she said, taking the book.

Doug showed up minutes later. The only one who acted happy to see him was Karl. Doug could not have missed the tension but paid no special notice to Violet or to me and acted his usual self with Karl. His indifference to our babysitter—a couple of times she playfully touched him but he backed away—seemed to bother her. Silly girl; I'd have to warn her about Doug too.

But I didn't have to. For all summer there was no inkling of anything between them beyond a minor infatuation on her part. If that helped keep this Gareth fellow at bay, as it seemed to do, then what was the harm? Doug still joined us at the beach on weekends and Violet once again became our regular babysitter; their paths rarely crossed. I trusted Violet had wised up about boys or, if she had tried anything with Doug, that he'd spurned her.

Then one Sunday in the fall, while Karl was taking a nap and Doug, John, and I were watching a football game, I asked John what we should do for Karl's seventh birthday. He scowled either at what I said or a bad call by the referee.

"What is it?" I said, realizing it was the former.

"I have a conference in Kitchener that weekend."

"Oh John, really."

"Helen, why don't you and Karl come spend the day in Toronto with me?" Doug said.

John and I exchanged glances. We'd never been to his new home. We'd never asked to go nor had we been invited.

"Sounds like a good idea," John said.

"I'll make sure it's a special day for the boy," Doug went on. "There's so much to do there, even in November."

"I don't really like driving in the city," I said, though otherwise warming to the idea.

"I'll need the car for Kitchener anyway," John said.

"Take the bus," Doug said. "It's only an hour or so and I'll pick you up at the station. It'll be an adventure for Karl."

While I wasn't keen on taking public transport, I knew Karl would be thrilled. It was his birthday, after all. When we put the idea to him, he wasn't sure at first. But when Doug told him about the Greyhound bus and subway he became so excited that all my misgivings evaporated.

The first half hour on the bus my son was abuzz with excitement to the amusement of the other passengers. But by the time we reached Oakville he was asleep.

"Ready for a busy day?" Doug said, as he helped unload a groggy Karl and assisted me down the bus step.

"Yeah!" Karl said, instantly energized again.

"Where are you parked?" I said.

"Car's in the shop, I'm afraid. Turns out it wasn't such a great vehicle."

Doug led us to Bay Street where he hailed a taxi. After helping us in the backseat, he took the front and affected the tone of a train conductor.

"First stop, Ontario Place."

"Why aren't we taking a subway?" Karl said.

"We will. Later."

At Ontario Place, which had opened that year, Karl stared in awe at the orb of glass floating in the water, connected to four pavilion pods on spindly supports. The place was closed for the season and I wondered aloud what was the point in coming here.

"A preview," Doug said. "Next summer, when it's hot, we'll come back to ride the pedal boats."

A walk along the waterfront was pleasant with the cool lake breeze, the choppy water, and so few people around. A brave sailboat jostled in the wake of a ferry to the Toronto Islands. I could have walked for hours but Karl was getting tired and cold. I suggested we stop for a rest and some food.

We found a modest restaurant. Doug and I each had a burger with fries and sodas while Karl settled for a hot dog and chocolate milk. I was starving and finished mine quickly. But Karl was taking his time, as usual.

"I wouldn't say no to a beer," I said.

"I was thinking the same thing," Doug said.

The place had gotten busier and it took a while for him to return with our drinks. When he did, Karl had finished eating. I expected my son to want to get moving but he seemed content watching the variety of people walking by. We drank our beers slowly. I was happy in my indolence and part of me hoped Doug would suggest another round.

"Time for our next stop," he said, instead.

"But I like it here," Karl said and looked at me.

"We could stay here, Doug, take it easy."

"Nonsense, I promised a subway ride, didn't I?"

This swayed Karl. We walked to Union Station, down the stairs, and caught a northbound train to Eglinton Station. A longer than expected bus ride took us to Don Mills Road. From there, a short walk to the Ontario Science Centre.

Karl showed no sign of exhaustion climbing in and out of rockets, pulling levers, pressing buttons, and running around the air-conditioned rooms. But as we stood in line to touch the Van de Graaff generator to get his hair raised, his energy and interest vanished.

"Maybe we should call it a day," I said.

Doug leaned down to Karl who was holding my hand.

"Would you like to see my pad, Karl?"

"Doug, what are you doing?"

"Relax," he said. "I thought this might happen, which is why we came here last. I live just across the street."

He pointed toward a dark brown high-rise, said his apartment was on one of the highest floors of the one behind it. Karl was starting to close his eyes again.

"Mom, are we going home?"

"We're going to your uncle's place first. It's close."

"I want to go home. To sleep."

"You can nap at his place. It'll be more comfortable than the bus."

Doug picked Karl up and hoisted him on his shoulders and held him up all the way to the elevator where he had Karl press a button for the fifteenth floor. Then he set him down.

My son leaned against me, his eyes shut. He would be asleep the moment his body hit anything soft, I thought, and now this detour seemed a good idea. Doug went to the kitchen while I found the bedroom and tucked my weary son in bed. Karl tried to say something but was asleep when I asked him to repeat it.

I returned to find Doug sitting on the sofa. The walls were covered with prints of paintings; he seemed to have an affinity for abstract nudes. Individually none were offensive but, collectively, it seemed in dubious taste. Books were piled onto the two lone chairs so I sat beside him. Then I saw the two frothy red drinks on the table in front of us. I was thirsty and picked up the one closest to me. He took the other and raised it in an informal toast.

"Whoa," I said, "this packs a punch."

"Sorry, too strong?"

"That's okay, it tastes nice. I'll drink it slow."

But my thirst betrayed my intent and the sweet drink was soon finished, and just as quickly replenished. Then I saw a familiar book on the table and picked it up.

"What's this?" I said, trying to act nonchalant, fighting to still my shaking hands.

"Ah, my book about reincarnation."

A coincidence. It had to be a coincidence. Reincarnation was a popular theme in this Age of Aquarius, wasn't it? This could be a best seller, for all I knew. Yet when I turned the cover I knew I would see that name, Gareth.

"Who's Gareth?" I asked, struggling to keep calm.

"A friend," Doug said, strangely. "From prison. He lent me that book, you could say."

I dropped it on the table. It made a crashing sound. Or was that the thunder of revelation in my head. Of course. I'd known all along but just didn't want to see. Violet's lover was not some boy named Gareth. No, it was none other than my brother-in-law. I grabbed my drink and swallowed it in a single gulp. Its sweetness soothed my throat an all too brief moment before the alcohol hit me.

"Are you all right, Helen?"

We stared at each other. Before I could answer, Doug took my empty glass to the kitchen. He was taking longer than before and I picked up the book, flipped through it. It was more scientific than spiritual. Then I saw the author's name and for some reason said it aloud.

"People think he's a relative. And by people, of course, I mean the ladies."

"You don't correct them?"

He shrugged as he sat down. I needed to keep calm, not to let on what I knew, not until I found a way to handle it.

"Have you even read it?"

"God no. Too academic for my taste."

"Women really fall for this?"

"Just the pretty ones. They do because they want to. It's like a lubricant that eases their resistance to my charms."

"Vulnerable teenage girls too? Like Violet?"

My accusatory tone came out limp and made him laugh. For some reason I laughed too. But it wasn't funny. I was mixed up.

Everything was mixed up. He then took the book from my hands, pushed it to the end of the coffee table.

"Of course, such an unsophisticated ruse could never work on a woman like you, Helen."

I had to get up, step away, but I was thirsty. I took my drink to the balcony to take in a cityscape of high-rise apartments, roads, and parks. Below, a woman was entering a taxi, carrying a child. I wished they were Karl and me.

"I often wonder how things might have been different if I'd come to Toronto instead of St. Catharines."

"My parents lived in Toronto before I was born," I said, watching the taxi drive off, suppressing an urge to wave.

"You don't say?"

He then began rubbing my neck. I tried to shift away, but his grip was strong. A pair of cars were circling the front driveway. Or were they still and was it me circling? I looked away to watch some kids tossing a football to each other. When one missed and the ball skipped off the lawn and onto the road, the wooziness set in. I felt a hand slide down my back to support me.

"It's okay Helen, lie down, you're tired."

I obeyed and let him take my glass and settle me on the couch. The room spun for a moment until I started watching the walls and felt myself steadying, yet also emptying.

What a strange place, all those naked women on the walls, and now I was about to join them. What?

He had already unbuttoned my blouse and slipped off my bra—so expert, so smooth, those hands—now he was undoing my skirt. I resisted but he forced it, tearing the fine material. That brief flash of horror abandoned me once I was naked and he was too. Then he was on me and I wanted to submit my body to those hands while I concentrated on that gorgeous face.

"You're a beautiful woman," a voice said.

"I'm a beautiful woman," said another voice, mine.

"And we've always been meant for each other, no?"

I couldn't say anything to that, not sure if it was true or not, but fearing it was. My throat betrayed me and let out a small sigh. Those lips of his, every part of his gorgeous body pressed over me, on me, in me. I let it happen. I let it happen because it felt wonderful, as never before . . .

*

I awoke alert but nauseous, with a headache, and a soul full of self-loathing. I realized instantly where I was, that I was naked, but couldn't remember what happened. No, that was a lie. I didn't want to remember what had happened. I dressed and rushed to the bedroom where my son lay asleep in his uncle's bed, oblivious.

"Karl, wake up." He rubbed his eyes and looked at the ceiling and I could see fear in his eyes. "Come on, get up."

"Where's Uncle Douglas?"

His question arrested me for a moment; I didn't want to know.

"No questions, let's go."

My tone in turn curtailed his resistance. He followed me out the strange room, down the strange elevator and out to the strange dark street. I wasn't sure where we were. I headed to the left but Karl pulled me back.

"We came from that way, Mom."

We walked to Don Mills Road where the vision of the Science Centre reactivated my nausea. I looked at my watch: ten-fifteen. Would the last bus to St. Catharines have left yet?

Several minutes passed before a taxi came. It ignored us. I cursed after it, drawing a stare from my son. We found a bus stop where we waited ten minutes before one stopped. I boarded and asked if it was going to the subway. The driver pointed across the street and made no attempt to conceal his annoyance at having to stop for someone not getting on. We crossed just in time to wave down a taxi.

"To the Greyhound bus station and please hurry."

The cabbie turned around and stared at me.

"You all right, Ma'am? I can take you somewhere else, a place where they can help you."

His concern was touching but his perceptiveness scared me. I shook my head and pulled Karl to my side.

"No, just the bus station."

"As you wish."

Calmness returned with the motion of the car and the curving of the highway until the lights of the downtown skyscrapers came in view.

"Excuse me, how much would you charge to drive us all the way to St. Catharines?"

"St. Catharines? Well, I was hoping to go home after—"

He must have seen something in my face for he then said it would be a hundred dollars. I fished around my purse and found ninety. He looked at the money, then at me, then at the dozing Karl. He took the bills, shut off the meter, and sped up. I sat back with my son's head in my lap.

I hoped Karl would sleep the entire way but he regaled the amused taxi driver with his impressions of Toronto. Each time he mentioned his uncle, I cringed. That wasn't nearly as bad as trying to quell the sickening feeling growing in my stomach, the same feeling I felt after Karl was conceived.

/7\

Office buzz is music to John's ears. Ringing telephones, squealing fax machines, humming photocopiers, all signs of a busy week for Stevenson Realty. Busy weeks are profitable weeks. Which is why he never asks Maggie to shut his office door behind her, though he wishes he did this time after she gave him the registered letter.

As John hopes, it's from a client, Mrs. Preston, a widow who promised him Bills tickets as a token of appreciation for his personal handling of her property sale. He slits it open with the monogrammed, gold plated letter opener, Helen's lovely gift at the office-warming party last year. Inside he finds not two, but four tickets for a game against the Colts. It's still weeks away; the NFL strike should be over by then.

A pang of guilt attacks his conscience as he looks out at the desks of his best agents, Sarah, Ralph, and Nelson, all worthy of sharing such a bonus. The pang lifts once he tucks the tickets in his briefcase. He has others in mind for this occasion, in particular his two sons, and Karl's girlfriend.

What a pleasant surprise to discover Danielle was not just a baseball fan, but a fan of all sports, including football, CFL and NFL. He'll forgive her preference for teams from Baltimore, even the Colts. It could be worse, the Jets or the Dolphins or that team from Boston. Wouldn't it be great if her enthusiasm rekindled Karl's interest and sparked a family rivalry like the one he shared with Doug and his Cowboys? True, she might convert Karl into a Colts fan but John can risk that.

The office music/buzz is winding down, agents on their way home, with detours for showings or, with luck, offers to process. It's not the same but the peace of a quiet office is also enjoyable. A pleasant atmosphere to wait until Karl returns from his tasks; he can't wait to tell his sons about the tickets.

John looks at his watch, six o'clock. His oldest is consistently prompt with his responsibilities, almost religiously so. He opens his briefcase to look at the tickets again. That's when he notices a sheet with them, Karl's list of instructions, addresses, and other details: untouched. He calls Helen, but she's surprised too.

"Karl's not with you?"

"I haven't seen hide nor hair of him today, Helen."

"I thought he'd finished early because the wagon's back. Now I'm not sure it ever left."

"Goddamn it," John says.

He swears again when Helen says Karl is supposed to pick up Samuel from hockey game, that she's too busy to do it. He looks at his watch, at the sheet.

"Everyone here's gone and this must get done tonight. Now I have to pick up Samuel too."

"Meaning?"

"Meaning, I doubt I'll be home for dinner. Without Karl's help, I'll have to come back and take care of his tasks myself."

She grows silent, no doubt thinking how easily he jumps at any chance to stay at the office. Only he's as annoyed as she is. He wants to be home for dinner so that he can speak to Samuel about his poor marks and school absenteeism and whatever prompted the Vice Principal to request that special meeting next week. He plans to persuade Samuel to promise improvement in his special fatherly way, cementing the deal with the tickets.

"Do you have any idea where Karl might be? Have you tried Danielle?"

"I spoke with her earlier. She's working tonight."

"This is so unlike him."

"I know, John. He's been acting dodgy lately, kind of like he did a few years ago."

Dirk Fuller, one of the more difficult to manage agents, leans in and taps the inside of John's door, enters part way. He's got a coat on and looks in a hurry. John glances at him, then at the phone. Dirk backs up, but only a step. John lowers his voice.

"It must be Danielle. Remember that brief break-up in the summer just after her birthday? Maybe it happened again."

"That was months ago, they're fine now. You saw how close they were last Sunday."

"Then what do you think—forget it, Helen, it doesn't matter because I need to get his tasks done, somehow."

"All right, John, I understand. Just do me a favour and pick up Samuel first, before you forget."

"Okay, I will."

Then he notices Dirk is out of sight. He tells Helen about the football tickets and his plans to take the three kids.

"Other than Danielle, I'm not sure they deserve it, do you?"

Helen's parting words echo all the way to the hockey rink. As a parent, he has to agree but, as a dad, and a football fan, he'd be punished too. There has to be another way.

Outside the rink, a couple of kids wearing sneakers, still in their Screaming Demons blue and white jerseys and black hockey pants, casually shoot red street hockey balls against a wall. Their giant hockey bags act as goalposts. The shooting is poor. Unlike his gifted Sam, they probably need to practice every moment they can.

He decides to wait in the car, hoping his son is inside, changing and showering, as John just cleaned the interior of the Benz on the weekend. A van shows up and the kids stop playing. John opens his window.

"Hey, do you know Samuel Stevenson? Is he inside?"

The boys look at each other, shrug. A third kid, coming through the double doors, destined for the van, overhears and points John to the other end of the building.

"Try over there, mister."

"Thank you."

John parks the car and walks. As he turns a corner, he makes out a pair of silhouettes by a dumpster next to a mound of snow.

John recognizes the hulk of his son and the barely wearable Bills cap John detests, though he's long forgotten why. Strange how he can see their breath as they talk because it isn't that cold out.

Samuel is still in his gear, a giant compared to the other boy, a skinny kid with long hair, wearing jeans and a scruffy jean jacket. It's Mitch, a boy Samuel brought to their house for dinner once, but never since.

"Hey, Sam," John calls out.

Both youths turn slightly, as if not trusting their ears or that they're too cool to respond. Each boy is holding a thin cylindrical object between their fingers and, seeing that, John freezes. Samuel says something to Mitch and both drop their butts, step on them, brush-kick them under the bin like bulls. Mitch says something to Samuel and takes off.

John approaches and his son turns to face him. It's hard to tell what's on the boy's mind by his blank expression. Guilt and shame certainly, but behind it, stoic defiance. John points to the car and walks ahead. Like a trained dog, Samuel meekly follows.

Close to home, John stops at a convenience store for a pack of peppermint gum, which he gives to Samuel.

"Chew this, clear your breath."

"Sorry Dad. It was my first time, honest."

The pathetic, insulting lie hits John like a linebacker, but he chooses to absorb the blow and say nothing.

"I thought Karl was picking me up."

From the tone, as if he only regrets being caught, John infers Karl might have tolerated the smoking. Both of his sons have disappointed him greatly tonight. Yet why does he feel like the guilty one?

"Are you okay, Dad?"

"Not really, Samuel. Not really."

"You're upset about the cigarette."

"I'm upset about the cigarettes."

His son leans back, pouts—a good sign—and stares out the passenger window, twisting that cursed Bills cap back and forth across his skull.

"Take off that goddamn cap while you're in this car."

Without a word, Samuel obeys, releasing his growing golden locks and opening up his startlingly handsome face. John suddenly notices how much his youngest son shares Doug's tragic good looks, now that he's let his hair grow out. With that cigarette in his mouth, Samuel's posture is spookily similar to that of John's dead brother.

The streetlight above the decrepit brick building has burned out. That, along with a gloomy drizzle, camouflages the three rummies loitering in front. A neon Las Vegas style sign over the windowless tavern's doorway—McCready's—has its first and last letters out. The place looks sleazy and old, as if it's been operating since the first Welland Canal.

The rummies watch Karl with vague interest. While his body's no longer sweating, his hands are clammy. For a brief moment, as he secures the bike lock around the lamppost, almost certain his Targa will be gone by the time he returns, Karl considers bailing out, riding down to Secord Woods to be with Danielle instead. The moment passes and he enters.

It's darker inside than out. As his eyes adjust, a nostalgic odour of stale cigarettes and beer assaults his nostrils. Whether concealed by the dense layer of smoke, the numbing drone of the rockabilly music, or general indifference, no one pays attention to the underage teenager.

He strolls past unoccupied stools along the length of the heavily varnished bar, avoiding eye contact with a bartender who shoots him peripheral glances. Tacky beer company mirrors reflect at least a hundred bottles of vodka, gin, rum, scotch, rye and other whiskeys; they comfort him in showing his internal shaking isn't outwardly noticeable.

Tom is there, lounging in a booth, wearing the old dark brown leather jacket. It seems to have outgrown him rather than the other way around. His collarbone is visible through a white t-shirt. He's smoking a cigarette with one hand while dipping a clump of wedge-shaped fries in a mound of ketchup with the other. They size each other up before Tom shoves the clump into his mouth, chews and swallows, and then nods.

His friend's angular face is thinner, older, almost emaciated. Karl feels strangely broad compared to him, how Samuel might feel next to Karl possibly. Tom's casual, unimpressed expression hasn't altered, his long black hair still droops, though his bangs are shorter and no longer conceal his eyes. It's in those eyes where Karl sees the biggest change. Before they flitted about indifferently to his surroundings; now they are hardened with a determined aspect that belongs in a bar, this type of bar.

"Was wondering whether you'd show."

"You're the one who's too shy to talk at school."

"Trust me. It's better for you that we meet here."

"If I'd known I was coming to a bar—"

"Good to see you again too, Karl."

Tom stands up, steps forward, startling Karl who thinks it's to hug, until Tom sticks out his hand. A ropy vein that seems ready to burst runs along his arm from wrist to elbow. His grip, despite his slight frame, is as strong as Karl's dad's. Karl slides in the seat across from his friend.

"I can't believe you're back."

"I'm back."

"But I got your postcard three or four months ago."

"Yeah, well, things took a while."

"A long while. I'd given up. When I saw you at school this morning, I thought I'd seen a ghost, or smoked a bit too much of the good stuff."

"No ghost. And dope's bad for you. Alters your sensibilities."

Karl watches his friend for a sign he's joking. It doesn't come. Instead, Tom waves his empty glass in the direction of the bar to get someone's attention. Karl waits until he stops.

"Speaking of sensibility, at least my little brother had enough to grab that postcard before my parents saw it."

Tom chuckles.

"It's not funny. You should have put it in an envelope."

"Never thought of that. I suppose my name's mud in the Stevenson household."

"You have no idea. The moment I came home—no, the moment I was met in Buffalo by my mom, I was grounded. For almost two years, my parents would interview my friends and their parents before consenting to let me go anywhere. I lost the desire to go out for the longest time. Naturally, they outlawed me having any contact with you ever again."

"I figured as much, which is why I didn't write anything on the card. It was more of a warning."

"They'd have figured it out if not for my—warning?"

"That's right. To be honest, I never intended to contact you. That's why I chose to go to another school. How the hell could I have known you'd transferred there too?"

Karl becomes speechless, not sure how to express the hurt he feels from this. A waiter appears, barely older than them. He studies Karl with security guard superiority. When Tom requests four glasses of draft, the waiter snickers.

"It's okay Tom, I'll just have a Coke."

"No, you'll have a beer."

"I'll need to see your Age of Majority card," the waiter says.

Karl taps his pockets, shakes his head as Tom mimics the waiter's demand behind his back.

"I'm afraid, I—"

"Show some ID before I serve you."

Tom slams a palm on the table.

"Never mind his fucking ID, just get our fucking beer."

The waiter locks into a staring contest with Tom. After several seconds, Tom looks away and flutters the back of his fingers, as at a lackey.

"Keep up the attitude, you'll both be out of here, forever."

"What a dick," Tom says with a snort when the waiter is out of sight.

"Why didn't you just let me get a pop? I'm sure we'll get in trouble now. We're not even eighteen."

"We will be, next week."

"Yes, but the drinking age is nineteen."

"Listen, in here, when you're with me, we are nineteen, and beer is our drink."

Karl recognizes the frenetic look from the weekend in Pittsburgh, knows it's pointless to argue. That doesn't stop him worrying about what will happen though. The manager or even the police could arrive any second. Several minutes pass and nothing happens. Tom scans the bar impatiently and seems ready to cause a commotion. It's a good time to ask what happened in Pittsburgh after that weekend.

"That night, seeing his JD gone, he pounded me good."

"You never told me your father was violent."

"He wasn't. Before then. Maybe he was sore about having to keep me. Or because I was drunk and laughed at his pathetic Steelers losing. Maybe he just needed a hobby."

After another impatient look toward the bar, where two bikers now sit, along with a thin, older man, Tom continues.

"He kept me under wraps pretty good after that, though he didn't hurt me, much. Never enough for the hospital, just enough to keep me awake at night. Eventually, I got fed up and began lobbying my mother to take me back. She's not strong enough to beat on me anymore. Mind games are her forte. Quite a parental tag team there."

Tom reaches into his shirt pocket for a cigarette, offers one to Karl who refuses but is unable to keep from staring at his friend's pale yellow fingers, which shake slightly.

"So, which parent do you prefer?" Karl says.

"The one I'm not with."

"Too bad you're not old enough to be on your own."

"What for? With them, I have a place to sleep and they don't make a fuss when I steal money. In that sense, I guess I've got it pretty good, paradise."

Karl can't tell if Tom is being intentionally ironic. The same waiter returns with a tray holding four small glasses filled to the top with beer. He sets all four down. Tom takes a mocking sip from one, as if testing for poison, followed by a longer one. He smacks his lips in approval.

"That's better," he says, looking up.

Karl glances at the waiter. He's never seen such hatred in a pair of eyes before.

"What just happened?" Karl says, after the waiter leaves.

"Look at this dump. How many customers are here? A dozen? Including us. Trust me, they need our business. So be a good contributing citizen and drink up."

The glasses are ice cold and the beer tastes better with each sip. It seems as if the weekend in Pittsburgh was two days before, not two years. Karl relaxes and has no trouble keeping up with Tom as more trays arrive. The beer hits him hard as he hasn't eaten anything. Then he remembers Erica.

"I ran into an old girlfriend of yours. She asked about you."

"Really? Which one?"

"Erica O' Brien. You know, back in Grade Nine. Erica the Red, you called her, you know, because—"

"Yeah, yeah, I get it. Can't say I remember her though."

"Kind of cute, but lots of freckles—"

"Karl, there were many girls then, several redheads—oh, right, Erica. Not the prettiest, but at least she—"

"Actually, she's not bad looking now."

Tom's lewd grin offends Karl as he pictures Erica in her Wendy's uniform, pig tailing her hair. Now he wishes he hadn't brought her name up.

"You think she's pretty, Karl?"

"See for yourself. She's working at the Wendy's at—"

"Nah, never mind. It'd be pointless."

The bartender comes this time, with a tray of fresh beer. He clears the finished fries and empty glasses and replaces Tom's ashtray. Did they get the waiter fired? Tom leans back and stares at the ceiling. He lights another cigarette, takes a long drag, and exhales little grey-white circles. Karl, fairly drunk now, struggles to keep his eyes off those circles.

"I remember what you said in Pittsburgh. It stuck with me."

"What did I say?" Karl said, his eyes beginning to spin.

"Remember Western Pen? The prison? We were talking about death row? You said there's not much difference between life and death row. That's precisely how I feel."

"I said that?"

"The profoundest thing I ever heard? Of course I'd remember who said it, and when, and where."

"Not sure I'd say that now, since my life . . . hey Tom, since we're talking about death, what about reincarnation?"

Tom takes a big slug of beer and leans forward, his eyes wild and intense.

"That'd be the poisoned icing on the cake, wouldn't it? You work your way through death row, get your needle, get free of this planet, and whammo, you're back."

"You wouldn't want to come back for another chance at life, to do things better?"

"Well, since earth is a cruel punishment for humans, coming back would be extremely cruel punishment."

"Come on, you don't honestly believe that."

"Of course I do. Read some Nietzsche. Eternal recurrence, that sort of thing. I've been punished. You've been punished. It's like a board game where you move your piece up and, bang, all of a sudden, something happens and you have to start over again. That's cruel. Therefore, reincarnation is cruel."

For an entire cigarette, they're silent, Tom alternating glances between Karl and his beer. Then his eyes light up.

"Sounds like you believe in reincarnation," Tom says.

"Believe may be too strong a term. I'm interested in it and I've looked into it."

"That's it?"

"All right, I used to believe in it, when I was a kid."

"Come on, come on, out with it," Tom says, pushing a full glass of beer in front of Karl.

Before realizing it, Karl is telling Tom about his uncle's book, how it led to his childhood theories of his brother's connection to his uncle. Karl watches Tom closely for signs of mocking but only sees his friend listening with a mix of amusement and interest, encouraging Karl to go on. It feels good to have someone to share this with. Karl ends by cataloguing the similarities he can recall.

"But I realize now that Samuel couldn't be my uncle."

"Why? They seem to have so much in common. Too much to ignore."

"Maybe, but then it would have come out by now."

"All right, if that's the case, it doesn't mean your uncle won't reincarnate, does it?"

Karl chuckles but Tom remains serious.

"You know what I think, Karl. You haven't gotten over your uncle. You're still holding out hope that he'll appear."

"That's nonsense."

"First you tell me you believe in reincarnation, then, when the most obvious candidate doesn't pan out, you just give up?"

Karl wavers as he finishes the last of his beer glass.

"You should read my book. I'd love to hear what you think."

"Sure, I'll read your book. It might reveal the mechanics of how this tormenting cycle works."

"Last call," a voice yells out, which is followed by grumbling and scuffling chairs.

"Are we getting more?"

Tom shakes his head. Karl is disappointed at first but then relieved. He reaches into his pocket for cash. Tom shakes his head and produces a wad of bills. Karl stares at it in wonder, until he recovers, grabs his knapsack, and gets up.

"See you at school then," Karl says. "I'll bring the book."

"It'd be better if we just met up here."

"All right."

"Speaking of school, your girlfriend, she's pretty sweet."

"Danielle? You know Danielle?"

Tom grins, mouth wide, white teeth showing, a sudden reminder of the Ottawa trip . . .

"Danielle. Is that her name?"

"Yes, how do you know her?" Karl says, struggling to contain the quivering in his voice.

"Relax, she's in one of my classes and I overheard her talking about you."

"Oh."

"So, you two done it yet?"

"You look like shit."

Karl shuts his locker, tries to smile, but only feels worse when facing Danielle's red-cheeked cheeriness. She's clutching a binder to her chest, a paper bag dangling from her fingers. He knows he should say something but in his condition answers are risky.

"Those jeans fit you nice."

"Uh, thanks. You going to be all right, Karl?"

"Eventually, I hope."

"You probably should have stayed home today."

Of course, I should have stayed at home, Karl thinks. Does she not realize he's hung over? If so, why isn't she pestering him with questions? In a way, he's dying to tell her where he was, who he met. No reason not to, he's done nothing wrong. Not as if he was with another girl. Yet for some reason it feels wiser to keep quiet. Her and Tom, two incongruous worlds best kept apart. Then there's the risk of her mentioning Tom to his parents, and if he asks her not to, she'll get suspicious. So he just nods.

"Want to go home, Karl? I've got a quarter to call you a cab."

"No."

"Maybe you should."

"I said no. Let's have lunch together, at the mall."

Danielle looks at her watch. "All right, we'll have to be quick, I don't want to be late for History."

"History? With Mr. Atkinson? He's a jerk, and a terrible teacher too. I'd be doing you a favour if I kept you late."

"I agree, he's a bit of a pill, but I like the class."

"You're crazy."

Holding hands turns out to be a tonic as they walk past leaf-covered lawns, the autumn colours having a soothing effect on his eyes. With each step under a sunny sky, and a cool breeze behind their backs, the nausea is replaced by a ravenous, welcome hunger.

They cross the road, stepping back to let a city bus pass, before crossing the giant parking lot and entering the mall. The air conditioning refreshes his face and body but then hits his head, reactivating the throbbing he's felt all morning. Danielle grabs a table in the food court while Karl scans the kiosks before lining up at Kentucky Fried Chicken.

He watches Danielle delicately unpack her lunch bag to retrieve a sandwich—ham and cheese on whole wheat, two pickles on the side, no doubt—and an orange juice in a small cardboard box. A plastic cup of blueberry yogurt follows. She jabs the straw into the orange juice, takes a small sip, but then puts it aside; she's waiting for him. Those jeans do look great on her, too great, as he detects other guys checking her out. A nudge from behind moves him forward.

Danielle gives him a wry smile when she sees his three pieces of chicken, fries and large Dr. Pepper, but says nothing until he's wolfed down half of it.

"Feel better now?" she says, as he sips from his pop.

"Much better," he says, belching, then apologizing.

"Good."

"You know Danielle, I can't get over you liking a class taught by Atkinson. Especially History."

"Speaking of History, let me tell you about this creep in that class. God, I never thought I'd see that character again."

"Creep? That doesn't sound like you, Danielle."

"I know but it applies. I ought to know, I went to junior high with him. With Tom, Tom Wark, something like that."

"Ottawa?"

"No, it's Waryk. Tom Waryk."

Hearing his friend's name numbs Karl. He struggles to finish swallowing a French fry, before speaking.

"What's so creepy about him?"

"He's mopy, quiet, intense and, ugh. Creepy just sums it up best. In Ottawa, he always had girls hanging around him. I have no idea why because he's as ugly as sin. A Rasputin."

"But why are you telling me? Why is it such a big deal?"

"I don't know. I guess in case you meet him. You're an easygoing, chummy guy. I wouldn't want you feeling sorry for him and becoming his friend."

"Like with you?" Karl says, amazed he gets out the joke.

"Ha, ha, ha. So you haven't told me what made you so tired. I know you're working for your dad, but I can't believe he's that much of a slave driver."

Karl almost chokes on a chicken thigh. Those errands completely slipped his mind. As pretty much everything else did the day before, from the moment he saw Tom at school and read the note his friend slid in his locker. He does recall his mom saying his dad is furious about something. Now he knows what.

"Cat got your tongue, sweetheart?"

"Sorry. It was a late night and I got caught in the rain a few times, which is why I feel crappy today."

"The rain made you look like that? Bullshit. You're hung over. I figured your dad rewarded you with one too many."

He looks up from his drink. She's smiling, not looking at him, not waiting for an answer. He chuckles.

"I wish. I didn't even get my work done for him, which means I'll get the car tonight . . ." He pauses. After letting his father down, this is actually doubtful, but he'll figure out a way. ". . . anyway, let me take you to a movie."

She finishes the last bite of her sandwich and opens the yogurt.

"Not tonight, I'm going to see an old friend."

"Who?"

"No one you know."

Touché, Karl thinks, desperate to grill her but able to restrain himself while he finishes the pop and noisily sucks at the ice. He learned his lesson in the summer.

Back at school, he goes to his locker while she heads to class. This separation, which occurs several times a day, now leaves him feeling a void. Instead of opening his locker, he backtracks to try and convince her to skip class and spend an afternoon at the mall. His chances are slim but he has to try, if only because the faint hope makes him feel good.

He turns the corner and spots Danielle with her friend, Christy, entering the classroom. Tom is following, oblivious to the pretty girls in front of him. Danielle drops a pencil, which rolls behind her. Tom stoops to pick it up, hands it to her. She takes it and thanks him, curtly, but with a smile lacking the venom shown when describing Tom earlier.

Karl's lucky he got the wagon. The farther south he drives on the canal road, the harder the rain pelts the windshield, the more his good fortune sinks in. The car became possible due to a heartfelt apology to his father after admitting to having a few beers, without mentioning Tom, then suffering a lengthy lecture on responsibility and vowing to finish the work he neglected yesterday immediately. Luckily his father overestimated the complexity of the tasks and Karl dispensed with them within two hours after school.

A red light at Glendale Avenue makes him think of Danielle. It's a short drive to her house. But would he find her there? She's been vague about her plans to meet her old girlfriend. Did she say girlfriend, or just friend? Once beyond the sprawling lawn of the St. Lawrence Seaway Authority complex, the car climbs the escarpment. He overtakes an upbound ship at Lock Seven and turns away from the canal into downtown Thorold.

He parks several blocks from McCready's on a dark side street lined with trees, some still holding on to their leaves. The houses are quite attractive here. The cool air, as he walks from the car to the tavern, relaxes him but his anxiety grows when he reaches Front Street and gets closer. So easy the first time, he's bound to run into trouble now. At least no one's hanging about the door.

Karl walks straight in, unchallenged, as he did the night before. His confidence grows until he finds the same booth occupied. Not by Tom but by an old man he's sure he's seen elsewhere. He has silver hair and is wearing a green cardigan, while sipping a glass of white wine. Karl circles the tavern, checks the bathroom, and the poolroom in the back: no sign of Tom.

"Your friend hasn't come in today."

The gruff voice compels Karl to turn. He recognizes the bartender from the other night by his red flannel shirt. He's staring at Karl, no doubt annoyed by the spaced out kid standing in the middle of his place. Karl sits on a barstool. The man pours a glass of Coke and gestures to Karl it's for him. Karl sucks the pop back quickly and reaches for his wallet. The bartender refills the glass, refusing Karl's cash.

"Don't you recognize me, Karl Stevenson?"

Hearing his name frightens Karl, though the man's face seems genial. He's not older than Violet's boyfriend but his features are more wrinkled. It's the sparkling eyes that make him look younger. Their liveliness looks out of place in the dour surroundings.

"How about that fellow, do you know who he is?"

The bartender points to the older man in the booth who looks back at them, lifts his glass to acknowledge their attention. At the same time, his silver medical bracelet shimmers. Karl glances back at the bartender, then back at the man, and he gets a chill that's accompanied by a vivid snow-filled image.

"My uncle's funeral."

"Let's go join him."

The bartender leads Karl to the booth. He shakes hands with the men who introduce themselves once again as Craig McCready and Gareth Underwood. Craig excuses himself and returns with a tray containing a Coke for Karl, a glass of white wine for Gareth, and a frosted beer glass and two bottles of Molson Canadian for himself. Craig sits beside Gareth and motions for Karl to sit opposite them.

"Tough times for the Magpies, lately, don't you think? But I believe Kevin Keegan will bring them back to the top."

Gareth's eloquent accent throws Karl. These men have been in his mind from time to time over the years, always as interesting people, like his uncle, but darkly mysterious. Now their clothes, their drinks, these two could be his father's friends. Karl can't help feeling a bit of a letdown.

"I remember my mother didn't like me talking to you."

They seem amused by this. Karl wants to wait for them to speak, ask why he's hanging out in a bar, but they keep quiet.

"So how did you two know my uncle?"

Gareth looks at Craig who takes a sip from his beer before speaking.

"I met Dougie when he joined GM. He would come to my bar with guys from his shift. He'd tire of them and sit with me. We got to talking, became friends, and he described living with your parents. Sounded like things were claustrophobic. It so happened I needed a roommate so he moved in with me. It was great until that Angeline girl came along and started all that trouble."

"Trouble? Who's Angeline?"

"That was the name of the girl."

"What girl?"

"You know, the assault that turned into manslaughter, a ruined honeymoon . . ."

"What are you saying? Uncle Douglas killed a girl?"

Gareth shakes his head quickly.

"No, a friend of the girl's. You do know he spent time in prison, for manslaughter?"

"Five years, in Kingston," Craig adds.

Karl freezes in his seat, his gaping mouth providing his answer. Then Gareth begins to talk.

"That's where I met him. He had a fifteen-year sentence but with my help he stayed out of trouble long enough to get parole. I got out a year later. He introduced me to Craig here and the three of us became good friends."

"I can't believe no one's told you."

"I'm not surprised, Craig. It happened before Karl was old enough to truly know his uncle. I imagine Doug's sister-in-law believed she could maintain a heroic image of Doug indefinitely."

"Which is crazy. The boy would have found out the truth. Eventually. Who could hold on to a secret that long?"

Karl raps his glass on the table.

"Hey, I'm still here. I'm not a child anymore. Why'd he go to prison? Who'd he kill?"

Craig looks at Gareth who nods at the empty glasses. It prompts the bartender to get up for refills, leaving Karl alone with Gareth.

"Tell me. Like you say, I'll find out eventually."

Gareth laughs.

"Maybe so. But not necessarily from us. I see now why your mother treated us as she did at the cemetery. She was adamant we didn't reveal anything about Doug's past."

"If you don't tell me, I'll conduct my own research, this time knowing there's something to find."

Gareth sighs, sits back, like he's considering the request. Karl leans forward anxiously, his heart beating quickly. After a few more seconds, Gareth shakes his head.

"It's not our place to say any more. A lot happened back then and, well, it'd be better if you found out from your parents."

Though frustrated, what the man is saying sounds reasonable to Karl, until he pictures sitting in the kitchen with his mother and her stoic, impassive face as she deflects his questions.

"Okay, how about I bring my mom here and ask her?"

They have to know he's bluffing, Karl thinks, yet he can see anger in Craig's eyes. Gareth doesn't look pleased either.

"What the hell, let's tell him," Gareth said

Craig nods and coughs to clear his throat.

"Keep in mind what we're going to say happened before you were born, when your uncle was younger, wilder."

"I will."

"Good. Now things between your father and your uncle were tenuous but they always managed to work it out. The real trouble began when your parents asked Doug to look after you while they went to Paris on a delayed honeymoon."

"A honeymoon delayed by Doug's immigration process in the first place," Gareth says.

"Right. Doug readily agreed, figuring he owed them at least that much, which he did. Besides, Doug was good with kids, especially you. Your mom had misgivings and was proven right on the evening before they were supposed to depart."

"Supposed to?"

"Doug was spending a lot of time in Toronto in those days. At heart, your uncle was a big city man, not small town folk like us. Whether he'd mixed up his dates or whatever, he went partying with this girl, Angeline, who he had met years before on the plane to Canada from England."

"I saw her once," Gareth says. "She was gorgeous, with pitch black hair and these haunting green eyes—"

"What'd he do?" Karl says, barely getting the words out.

"The way I heard it, he and Angeline were at a bar when a guy comes up who recognizes her. While she's in the toilet, the guy claims he's her boyfriend, suggests Doug take a hike. Doug refuses, even though he's alone with this lunatic and his friends. They provoke Doug until, in a rage, he kills the guy by stabbing him with some knife he finds. Cops show up and Angeline's vanished. So no witness to support his story."

"Instead of being in St. Catharines on departure day, he's in a Toronto jail," Gareth says.

"This is insane. I don't believe a word of it."

Karl shakes his head but the two men shrug.

"Your parents cancelled the honeymoon so your dad could come to Toronto, a truly unselfish act that almost cost him his marriage."

"No, impossible."

Not once in his life has the thought of his parents not being together entered Karl's mind. Yet what they're saying rings true for some reason. Why would they lie? The two men are watching him so Karl nods for Craig to continue.

"Your dad got Doug a great lawyer. True, they found him guilty of manslaughter and gave him fifteen years, but he wasn't deported. In England, apparently, he hadn't been a saint either. Everyone was pleased with the outcome."

"Except your mother," Gareth says.

"Why?"

"She'd had it with him, wished he had been deported, and hated him from then on. Her resentment was hard on Dougie, especially as you got older. He wasn't able to see you again until you were five or six years old."

At this point, Gareth takes over.

"While at Kingston, your dad visited quite a bit, always alone. He'd bring pictures of you as you grew from a baby to a toddler. A few he let Doug keep, including one of you assembling your letter blocks to spell your uncle's name. It was obviously staged but Doug treasured that shot, bragging about how smart his nephew was. I'm sure it helped him keep his cool in prison until he got parole.

"He moved to Toronto, but sometimes came to Niagara to visit. Though your mother suspended her animosity, her kind of probation, she never pardoned him. She knew him well because then he got into that other trouble—"

"Violet," Karl says, without thinking.

"Ah, you know about that."

What strikes Karl is how readily he believes everything he's hearing now, how it all makes sense, how it all fits and connects with the disparate details he's accumulated over the years.

"I always thought of my uncle as a hero."

"Of course you would," Craig says.

"But he was a criminal, and he hurt my mother."

"That's true," Craig says, and looks at Gareth who nods.

"Karl, no matter what he did that made people angry with him, or disappointed, or even feel betrayed, he never did it to you. You were special to him, you have no idea. To the point of making us sick he'd describe the things you two did together. How he taught you to swim and his pride at your natural talent for it. The puzzles, playing with football, baseball, soccer ball, going for walks at the lake and so on. We heard it all. To us he was a crazy partier, a risk taker, but he was different with you. Don't discount your memory because of the experiences others had with him."

"I remember," Craig says, "how excited he was when you and your mom visited him in Toronto. It wasn't easy convincing her to take you, but she finally gave in. He had all sorts of plans for the day, including the Science Centre."

Karl smiles; he likes hearing this, likes the memory.

"I remember a long drive along the lake and seeing all these skyscrapers from the highway. I had to stretch my neck to see the tops of the buildings. And all the gadgets, all the buttons, all the levers at the Science Centre and like the static made my hair frizzle and stick out."

"And his apartment?" Gareth says.

"Yeah, I guess, no . . ."

"He lived across from the Science Centre," Craig says.

"I'm sure he'd have invited you in," Gareth says.

"Maybe. I know I was tired, but no, that part's a blur."

"Too bad."

"What Craig means is, immediately after that weekend we noticed a change in Doug. He quieted down in his ways, settled, as if he'd had an epiphany."

"We feared he'd gotten religious on us," Gareth says.

"I don't remember any of that," Karl says.

Something in their questions and their tone nags at Karl, but he can't pinpoint what or why. Whatever it is, it inspires him to open his knapsack to pull out the book.

"Hey, you guys might know about this then."

"Well, well, well," Craig says.

"Never thought I'd see that thing again," Gareth says.

Karl's heart beats faster as Gareth takes it from him and flips through the pages, smiling nostalgically.

"This was mine until Doug *borrowed* it when he got out."

Gareth then points to his name written inside the book.

"Oh, you want it back?"

"It's okay, you can keep it."

"Thanks. So you used to believe in reincarnation?"

Craig scowls but Gareth smiles.

"Used to? I'm a genuine hippy still."

"So do I, maybe."

Karl reveals his theory that his uncle will return but stops at sharing his belief his uncle came back as Samuel.

"It's possible," Gareth says, while Craig shakes his head.

"You think my uncle would have believed in it enough to predict his own return?"

Craig laughs and, to Karl's dismay, Gareth chuckles too.

"Listen, Doug's interest in spiritual things only went as far as they could help feed his appetite for the ladies."

"I don't understand," Karl says.

Gareth and Craig exchange a smile.

"Women liked to think he was related to the author, and Doug was more than happy not to contradict them."

*

His eighteenth birthday.

Karl is an adult now, he can vote, get into more movies, even drink in certain provinces and states. Yet here he is, in the living room, bored, watching a soap opera on television.

Even though everyone's home, the house is quiet, other than the television and the ticking grandfather clock. His brother is at the dining room table in his hooded hoodlum grey sweatshirt, busy with schoolwork, or concocting some scheme. His mom is in the kitchen, dutifully preparing his birthday dinner, coming in every few minutes to see what Luke and Laura Spencer are up to, occasionally lingering for a dramatic exchange. Upstairs, his father works away in his bedroom-turned-office, door closed.

Then the door opens. His father's heavy steps descend then reverse when his private line rings. He answers and his voice grows progressively louder, angrier. The fallout from Dirk Fuller's screwed up deal that rippled through the office, even affecting Karl's workload and income, continues. What frustrated his father most was finding out about the incident after rewarding Dirk with tickets to a Bills game. The end of the NFL strike compounded the misery by taking away the karma of the gift proving worthless.

Like Pavlov's dog, Samuel taps his pencil to drown out his father's voice. For a tough kid, authoritative tones upset Karl's brother, just as Samuel's way of dealing with them bothers Karl.

His mother comes into the living room at that moment and turns up the television in time to hear Luke and Laura argue about an infidelity. Just as the actors heat up, the water for the corn begins bubbling loudly. His mom rushes back, but too late. The sizzle of hot water on the stovetop drowns out the television argument. By the time the kitchen is under control again, the unresolved discussion has given way to a feminine hygiene product commercial.

A sharp double rap at the back door before it opens.

"Hi everyone, sorry I'm late."

Dani enters the living room, still wearing her new suede jacket, carrying a large shopping bag. She's cut her hair and styled it differently, kind of like Debbie Harry but curlier. She's not wearing the pearl necklace but still looks radiant as she hugs his mother who rushes to greet her, patting her hand on her apron, tied over her navy blue pleated skirt.

Karl can smell his birthday meal, a T-bone steak with roast potatoes and corn on the cob. His stomach rumbles; he hasn't eaten since a Snickers bar at lunch.

"Can you believe it?" she says, addressing Karl, before giving him a quick kiss.

"Believe what?"

"You're pregnant?" Samuel says.

"Shut up, moron," Karl says.

"Ooh, touchy, touchy," Samuel says.

"You haven't told them?" Danielle says, to Karl.

Her tone, a mix of judgement and bewilderment, puts him off. Did she discover he skipped his afternoon classes to ride around searching for Tom?

"What?" Samuel says, yanking at his hood strings.

"Let's wait until both your parents are here," she says.

"Dad, your adopted daughter's here," Samuel calls out.

His father comes downstairs, having changed from his suit to twill pants and a knit sweater.

"Now you can tell us your news," Samuel says, turning the television sound down.

"What news?" Karl's father says.

"There was an arrest at school," Danielle says. "A big one."

"What for? Drugs?" Karl's mother says.

"No, much bigger, murder," Danielle says.

Danielle pauses for effect. Other than a questioning glance at Karl, she's relishing her scoop.

"Who did it? Who'd they murder?"

"Sam, hush, let her tell the story," Karl's father says.

He motions for everyone to sit down, then for Danielle to continue.

"I was in History class, just after lunch, when we heard sirens. Police sirens, getting louder and louder until we could no longer hear the teacher. Mr. Atkinson flapped his hands about to keep us in our seats but we ignored him and rushed to the windows. The flashing lights were dizzying at first but then I saw cops rushing through the main doors while others ran to the sides and the back."

Danielle pauses, this time to catch her breath.

"Go on, go on," Samuel says.

"Then behind us the classroom door opened. Principal Grant came in with three cops, two in uniform and one in a suit. Well, we all knew who they'd be arresting, and we were right, though none of us would have guessed it'd be for murder. He killed both his parents, in cold blood."

Karl's parents gasp in unison. Then silence. Now Karl understands Danielle's surprise at his ignorance and it's no longer possible to act blasé. Out of the corner of his eye, he senses his girlfriend watching him. What troubles him is the malice in Dani's voice, as if she's revelling in Tom's troubles.

"Who'd they arrest?" Samuel says.

"Anyone we know?" his father says.

"I doubt it. His name's Tom Waryk."

Despite his premonition, Karl's jaw falls, but he closes it when his mother and father look at him, displeased.

"Waryk? Isn't that the boy from Pittsburgh?" his mother says, while his father nods vigorously.

"Yep, that's Karl's friend, oops," Samuel says, and then covers his mouth and looks at his brother, with regret.

Karl feels his face turn red but then the blood seems to rush away, leaving him cold throughout his body.

"You're friends with that guy," Danielle says, her voice throaty with disgust. Karl nods. "You didn't tell me? Oh my God. For how long?"

"We were friends in Grade Eight."

"And you never said anything when I . . ."

The room spins and closes in on him from the intense stares of four sets of eyes. Samuel's glitter in wonder, his father's in bewilderment, his mother's and Danielle's in reproachful shock.

"He's not 'some guy,'" Karl says, a bitter surge of truth piecing together into an epiphany about to release. "You knew him too."

"Yes I know him. He's in my class. I wasn't friends with him."

"No, I mean you knew him. In Ottawa."

"I already told you that. A loser then, a loser now. Just like anyone who'd be his friend. Are you satisfied?"

In the absence of a rational response, a surge of anger stoked by hatred and betrayal fills Karl and gets his heart beating rapidly.

When his breath becomes normal, it's his voice that speaks, but it's some other entity commanding that voice.

"No, Dani, I'm not satisfied. How well did you know him?"

"What?" she says, her hands on her hips, her eyes cold, locked on his, glaring with the comprehension and clarity of a guiltless conscience. Too late, the words cross his lips.

"It's an act, isn't it? Being so disgusted by him, shocked by his arrest, you not wanting me to be friends with him, all an act. What you don't know is I was in Ottawa when—I figured it out. He was the one, wasn't he? The one you slept with before me. That's why you wanted me to avoid him. It explains everything, you sl—"

He halts, unable to complete the word, because he truly loves her. Unconditionally. Other than the clock and a slow bubbling sound from the kitchen, utter silence and looks of dismay. Karl steps toward Danielle. She steps back, points at him.

"Stay away. Don't touch me."

Her command freezes him. She picks up the shopping bag and turns as if to leave. Instead, a sad whimper comes from her mouth. She wipes tears from her cheeks.

"That's it, Karl. I can't take it anymore. Sure, it was him, why not? If you want to believe I'd sleep with someone like that. If you want to torment yourself and insult me. Be my guest. Only I want nothing to do with it, or with you."

Before anyone can respond, Danielle is in her shoes and out the door. Karl's mother rushes after her but stops when the New Yorker's tires squeal. Samuel joins their mother on the porch and together they look out to the street before coming back in.

"For God's sake, Karl, what the hell is going on?"

He glares at his mother. How dare she give him grief, after all she's kept from him for so many years? Instead of answering, he walks to the backdoor and puts his shoes on.

"You've got some explaining to do," she says.

"You're a fine one to talk," he says.

"Karl!" his father says, standing up.

Karl grabs his jean jacket and is outside, on his bike, a moment later.

*

Entering McCready's, Karl feels awkward, as if he's arrived at a party hours after the exhausted hosts have ushered out their last guest. Gareth sits on one of the barstools, alone, reading a Robert Ludlum novel. Karl has to tap the older man's shoulder to get his attention. When Gareth sees who it is, he spills some wine.

"What the hell are you doing showing your face here?"

"What do you mean?"

He puts down the book, grabs Karl by the shoulder, drags him to a dark booth in the back, beyond the pool tables, near the kitchen, and shoves him down, firmly, not violently.

"I'm sure you're aware of the trouble your friend is in."

"That's why I came."

"An unbelievably stupid thing to do."

"Why?"

Gareth sighs, as if the question is even stupider.

"Has Tom been here at all since last week?"

"No."

"Then what's the problem?"

"What's the problem? Someone told the cops he hangs out here. Craig's at the police station now, not his favourite place as he has a record. He'll be lucky to keep his liquor licence."

"Why?"

"Serving minors."

"It was only the one time."

"Only the one time. For you. What about your friend?"

"Oh."

"Listen, Craig'll be okay. He's clean and he'll co-operate. Out of respect for your uncle he'll keep your name from the cops. You were never here. Got it?"

"Why would the cops care about me? Tom would never say anything."

"You have more faith in your friend than I would. Even if you're right, his silence means nothing if the cops find you here now." Gareth leans over, his ruthless face showing no trace of sympathy. "Want the police asking you about Tom?"

Karl shakes his head and gets up. Gareth grabs his arm at the bicep and makes him sit down again.

"Since you are here, be honest. You know nothing about it, do you? I mean, this wasn't some bizarre teenage scheme you brewed up between you two, is it?"

"Scheme?"

"Just tell me you had nothing to do with it."

"I had nothing to do with it."

Karl says it in a monotone, as if swearing an oath. Gareth nods, satisfied, then leads Karl through the kitchen to an exit door that opens onto a dark and chilly November evening. Karl expects the door to slam behind him but hears nothing. He turns to see Gareth still there, his indignation replaced by a sympathetic but grim smile.

"Good luck, kid," he says.

Disoriented, it takes Karl a few minutes to locate his bike. Under swirling grey skies, a drizzle starts as he realizes he has no destination. Nonetheless, his feet push the pedals robotically and take him through Thorold back to St. Catharines, down the steep sweeping curve of Burleigh Hill Road, in the direction of home.

But home is too far off and not a desirable option. He could visit Violet, except Roy will probably be there. Besides, that's also quite far from where he is now and too near his family.

Another possibility is the Thorold jail to see Tom. That would be dumb. Aside from not knowing how to get there, they'll never let him see Tom at this hour. As Gareth pointed out, the cops would talk to him and that would make things worse. Besides, does he even want to see his friend, his sad, changed, friend?

Near the bottom of the wide and steep road, he turns right on Glendale and stops at the Mountain Road, close to the remains of the second Welland Canal. He recalls the evening he gave Danielle the necklace. If the ground wasn't so wet, he might indulge in further self-torture and go reminisce in the dark among the trees.

Instead, he stays on Glendale, crosses Hartzell, and rides along an industrial stretch before Secord Woods to where his unconscious will is guiding him. He's in no condition to plead, let alone reason with her. But this might be his last chance to salvage their relationship.

The New Yorker isn't there. A deep melancholy sets in and for the first time since he can remember he wants to cry. Yet no tears come and the unsalted rain is a poor substitute. He rides north along the canal as far as Lock Three, slowing by all their favourite spots, all empty.

He hasn't eaten anything since lunch but his stomach is so tied up in knots, the notion of food puts him off. But he should eat something. Maybe a Frosty. It could help him feel better and provide nourishment. At Wendy's he might see a friendly face unaware of his troubles and screw-ups.

He gets there as they're closing. Erica wasn't on shift tonight and the staff regard him with suspicion when he asks where she might be. He'll, he'd be happy with a fake address if only to have a direction.

He's tempted to return to Danielle's house and wait it out but then thinks of the mall where she works. It's a bit of a ride but it's somewhere to go, somewhere neutral. He takes Glenridge, past the houses he admires, spookily protected by trees in the grey, misty light. The rain no longer bothers him and a second wind powers his pedalling. He reaches the mall in good time. He circles the shopping complex slowly. Plenty of vehicles at the theatres but no sign of the New Yorker.

Since he's there, a movie might be a good diversion, a refuge. At least it will get him out of the rain, which is once again picking up. He goes in, leaving his bike against a wall, unlocked. Whoever wants it can have it.

The *Big Chill* is playing but he's already seen it with Danielle. *The Right Stuff* looks inviting but he wants to see that with her too.

What is he thinking? He forgot his wallet, he has no money.

A faint aroma of garlic triggers his hunger, draws him to a restaurant. Maybe he'll attempt a dine-and-dash. No, he wouldn't have the guts. Samuel might, not him. He goes in anyway and sits at the bar, ready to order a glass of water when the bartender, busy chatting with a couple of waitresses, gets around to noticing him.

A ruffled copy of today's paper is on the bar, the cover showing a colour photo of two hockey players fighting, their arms cocked, streams of blood running over a player's cheek. The Falcons thrashed the Blackhawks, literally, as well as on the score sheet. They'll have a juicier cover tomorrow, a real news story, and Karl's friend will become famous, infamous.

At the request of a man who just entered, the bartender turns on a television above the bar.

"The alleged murderer, seen being arrested here, faces a legal challenge from the District Attorney of Pennsylvania, as the slain father is a U. S. citizen and resident of Pittsburgh. It turns out the accused has dual citizenship. Pennsylvania still exercises the death penalty but in Canada it now only applies to the murders of police officers and prison guards. No talk of extradition so far. Since the crime occurred in Canada, it is unlikely Mr. Waryk will face the death penalty, at least not until completing his sentence here, if convicted."

Apparently, the police found a packed Duffel bag, a bus ticket to Pittsburgh, and other clues. These could imply Tom intended to murder both parents, beginning with his mother, not expecting to find his father there, let alone in bed with her.

"One theory being explored is that upon the unexpected sight, the young man went into shock, which accelerated his plan. Then, perhaps in a stupor, he casually went to school."

Gareth's question about playing a part in the crime troubles Karl. He couldn't have guessed Tom's plans, could he? Though of anyone close to the situation, even of the entire world, perhaps only Karl could conceive a plausible explanation.

The news story continues with repeated video of his friend, head down, face obscured by drooping hair, hands cuffed behind his back, escorted by two uniformed officers from the school into a police car.

In the background, he recognizes Mr. Atkinson's classroom by the two ancient globes in the window. Faces are staring above the globes. He spots Christy's face but Danielle's is obscured.

Where could she be? Does he have a right to ask?

"Get you anything?" the bartender says, daring him to ask for alcohol.

Karl shakes his head, leaves the restaurant, having never felt so alone in all his life.

Three-quarters up the steep road, approaching Lock Seven, Karl hears a snap, a metallic clink and now he is pedalling air. The chain's broken. When he realizes this, he loses balance and falls off the bike onto the road. Fortunately, there's no traffic. He drags the bike up to the quay, south of the lock, tempted to toss it in the water. Instead, he lets it drop and sits next to it on the damp ground, his back against a bollard.

"What next?" he says.

No one answers, not even an echo.

The water is still, the sky dark, except for red, green, and white signal lights around the lock. He hangs his head in his hands for some time, numb to the cool air and drizzle, until he drifts off.

It could have been minutes or hours before the whiny, siren-like hum of idling engines stirs him. A ship is rising in the lock. He knows without looking it has to be the *D. H. John Henry*. The giant vessel levitates from below until it looms over him and becomes the tallest object on the escarpment. It's too dark to tell whether the hull is mostly black or red as the paint is wearing off. The ship bobbles slightly, as if anxious to bust out of the gates, but patient too, like a well-behaved Kentucky Derby thoroughbred.

The gates open slowly, quietly slicing through the water. Another brief siren blast and the ship edges forward until it clears the gates. From here to Lake Erie it will be a long, flat run, with one last lock in Port Colborne before it's freed from the canal.

A familiar, sickening stench of cigarettes and stale beer issues from somewhere. He rises to look around but is still alone; it must be coming from him. He sniffs his jacket and the putrid smell is stronger, as if he's still in McCready's.

Never mind the cold; he has to remove the jacket. But when he does, the smell worsens, as it has penetrated to his shirt. So he removes that too.

A wonderful fever now courses through his body. Only briefly, as it turns on him and makes his stomach muscles flex and contract.

He slogs toward the water but the retching starts before he gets there. Painful as it is, doing so makes him feel better, refreshed, but extremely lightheaded, as from the best dope he's ever smoked.

The ship is moving slowly but steadily away, its slight wake calmed to nothing. The moon casts a shiny glow on a point, a beautiful inviting light.

Karl peels off his shoes, socks, then strips off his pants and underwear. He takes a deep breath and dives, breaking the surface cleanly, wiggling his feet. The soaking coldness wraps him like a blanket and miraculously all his aches and sores disappear. Within seconds, he is no longer aware of the temperature, unaware of anything other than an unwavering desire to pursue that ship.

He floats to the surface, swims and swims. As long as the ship remains in sight, his arms and legs work, furiously at first, before settling into powerful, controlled strokes and kicks.

He is gaining . . .

I wasn't against having another child but I was against having that child. The biological possibility it was John's existed—I ensured the circumstantial possibility immediately upon his return from his conference in Kitchener—but I knew better.

It was easier to arrange an abortion than to make the decision. A daytrip to a clinic in Buffalo, that would be that. Only I'd have to wait six weeks until the middle of January. That meant hiding my secret—hoping I wouldn't suffer the same degree of morning sickness I suffered with Karl—until the Super Bowl, all the while resisting the inevitable doubts along the way.

I had not forgotten about Violet whom I hadn't seen since the day I tricked her with the ice cream. After dropping off Karl for his afternoon kindergarten class one day, I drove to her parents' bungalow. Luckily, the carport was empty and Violet was home, alone, her parents off to play bingo.

"How did you figure it out?" she said, not shocked at my discovery.

"Dear, you've always had a crush on him," I said. "I only just realized the extent of it."

"I see," she said.

"If it hasn't already, it has to stop, now."

Her face twisted into a strange look, her eyes widened with contempt.

"You're in love with him too, aren't you?"

I wanted to slap the girl. Instead, I took the blow of her accusation. My lack of response only made it worse.

"I knew it," she said, her voice calm but firm. "He's in love with you too. The way he talks about you. He'll never love me the same way. I'm just a vehicle for him."

"Vehicle?"

"I'm pregnant."

"Oh Violet." I wanted to hug her then, sister to sister, and admit my own predicament. But I was the elder here, the adult. "You're more sensible than that. How could you let it happen?"

She told me how Doug would come over on the days she watched Karl, to fool around, but they didn't have sex until the weekend John and I went to Muskoka. She insisted he use a condom but he began talking about reincarnation, about how he used to have a brother named Walter that he wanted to come back to the world.

"It sounds stupid now," Violet said, "but the way he put it. I mean . . ."

"You agreed to be his surrogate?" She looked at me, as if unsure what the word meant at first, then nodded. "My brother-in-law is a sick man." This only drew a shrug from Violet; it was clear I hadn't made my point. "There's no such thing as reincarnation."

"You can't prove something like that."

"I can prove there's no Walter Stevenson."

"Oh God," she said, and began crying.

I took her hands in mine, told her to trust me, and then asked who else knew about her pregnancy.

"My dad wants me to have an abortion. But once I do, he'll kick me out of the house."

"What about your mom?"

"Same as my dad."

"What about . . ."

"He doesn't know."

The poor girl was so scared there was no choice for me but to help her. That's when I decided to keep my baby, and that it was John's baby. I only hoped he would be happy with another child as we had planned to stop with Karl.

"Violet, I'll help you. Let me take care of it. Only keep away from my family. It may be months, it may be years, but that's important, you understand? And for God's sake, don't mention this reincarnation nonsense to a soul."

Her vigorous nodding told me she was only too willing to follow any direction I gave her.

The absence of my brother-in-law thereafter was conspicuous, particularly on Sundays. Which ought to have made life easier for me but I couldn't bear witnessing John watching his NFL games and Karl doing his puzzles with such despondence. I could only take an hour or so of it each time before I had to get out.

It was on one of those aimless Sunday drives I found myself stopping by Port Weller. Soft snow was accumulating in the eerily empty parking area. I looked south and saw the *D. H. John Henry* entering Lock One, its last downbound lock for its last navigation of the canal for the season.

Watching this particular ship always reminded me of the day John proposed, its presence a poignant symbol of my pure love for him. Before his brother showed up.

I brushed off the snow and sat on a bollard. The water looked murkily grey under a cloudy sky, a sombre backdrop for the black ship whose movement was agonizingly slow. Then I noticed tugboats and men with radios and realized it wasn't on its way to Lake Ontario. No, it was being guided into dry dock for repair. Or for scrap. Two derricks on shore looked ready to dissect it piece by piece onto a conveyor belt leading into a long, grey shed.

More likely it was in for a paint job, or an engine retrofit. I'd seen ships navigate the canal in far worse condition than this. But a fresh coat of paint would certainly conceal the blemishes in its black hull, possibly give it a spiritual new start. For this vessel had plenty of life in it, even it that life was destined to be unexciting.

It came to me then what I had to do for John, for Karl, for me, for my family and its future. It was so clear, so foul, but so necessary to repair a ship christened, *Helen Stevenson*, to brace it for a burden it would carry forever.

I kept my emotions in abeyance as I wrote a deceitful letter to Douglas, urging him to accept John's invitation and join us for the Super Bowl. I intimated I was not angry and even hinted a desire to see him again. I baited his ego and it bit.

"You were right, he couldn't skip the Super Bowl," John said, to me, as we watched Karl and his uncle sculpt snowmen outside. "Did you say anything to him to get him to accept?"

"What would make you think that?"

"I don't know. Things have been tense between you two, and with the baby—"

"John, please don't mention the baby just yet."

"But I'm excited about it. Look at my brother with Karl, he'll be thrilled."

"Just not yet, John, not today, all right."

His look of unconditional empathy broke my heart, so it was a relief the other two came in then. John went to fetch a beer for himself and his brother while Karl went to fetch a puzzle. Douglas seemed happy to oblige his nephew while avoiding me. Just as well for I was frazzled inside; any word or gesture on his part could have unnerved me enough to abandon my mission. Somehow I kept myself together until game time.

"What about the puzzle?" Karl said, looking at the half-finished farm scene.

"Tell you what," Douglas said. "You finish it before halftime, I'll give you anything you want."

"C'mon Doug," John said, "you can't promise a little boy that, not one with an imagination like Karl's."

"A drive to the canal?" Karl said.

"You're on." Douglas said.

John laughed. "Son, I'll have to teach you some things about negotiating."

Karl set to finishing his puzzle while we watched the game. Dallas was winning and Douglas was celebrating more than usual; apparently, he'd bet plenty on his team. His mood was infectious and even had John cheering for the Cowboys. I played along though I couldn't tell if my act was successful because my brother-in-law rarely looked my way. My son finished the puzzle long before halftime save for an empty spot in the middle.

"Uncle Douglas, you took the last piece again."

"Don't know what you're talking about."

"Yeah, you do. Give me it. Give me it."

Douglas laughed at him and shrugged, which made Karl leap at him. They wrestled as John watched with amusement, until just before the halftime whistle blew and the piece fell out of Douglas's shirt pocket. Karl picked it up, fit it in, and let out a loud yell to proclaim his victory.

"Karl, settle down," I said, and he dropped to the floor, exhausted. I got him to bed before the second half started.

The rest of the game was quieter and seemed to take forever, a test for my nerves. At last, the final whistle blew and Douglas got up, as if to leave. I nearly panicked.

"Where are you going?" I said. "Stay for another beer."

"The guys are waiting at McCready's. More importantly, so are my winnings."

"So go get your money and come back," John said.

"I don't know," Douglas said.

"Karl barely got to spend any time with you," I said, and then moved next to him and put my hands on his shoulders.

"True," Douglas said, and he looked confused. "What if I wake him and say goodbye."

"No," I said, now fearing I'd overplayed my hand. "He's out for the night. But he'll be full of energy in the morning."

"Stick around," John said, who I'm sure was as surprised as his brother at my insistence, "it's been a while."

"You want me to stay?" Douglas said, looking directly at me. No mistaking the meaning in his eyes. I had him. I nodded. "But I still have to go to the bar."

"Take John. You two go and have a good time, stay out as late as you want."

What a relief to watch them drive off. But then it took merely minutes to get everything ready. Karl's already being in bed and deeply dozing eliminated a major distraction, but at the expense of a time-killing option. It was agonizing. I felt my nerves would burst every ten minutes. I would reach for the wine bottle each time to calm myself but only once did I give in to that temptation; I needed to stay alert.

It was past one o'clock when the back door opened. I rushed to bed and listened closely. I heard beer bottles opening, followed by the calm chatter of the two brothers. My weariness started to win out and I was tempted to just go to sleep and forget all about it. Then I heard those familiar steps amble up the stairs. Minutes later, my husband was snoring a calm rhythm. I waited, afraid I would hear the sound of a car door; instead it was the creak of the basement door. It was time.

I slipped out of bed, out of my nightgown and into my grey old bathrobe I should have discarded long before, but would after tonight. The carpet felt ticklish on my bare feet.

My heart dropped when I stepped into the hallway and saw my son's bedroom door open. He was a restless one, a wanderer, but why now? I looked in, saw the bed occupied, and felt better. I pulled back the covers to be sure and found several teddy bears and Tonka trucks huddled underneath. No little boy. I retreated to the master bedroom to wait.

Finally his soft footsteps came up the stairs. My son was muttering something about the canal. Don't make it worse, dear, I mentally pleaded, as he closed his door. I waited several minutes until I heard my son sleeping with the pattern of breathing that ensured he wouldn't wake for hours.

But my tests didn't end there. I nearly abandoned my mission at the bottom of the stairs upon seeing the living room. It was a mess. How could Douglas and John have done that so quickly, and so quietly?

Out of habit, I began cleaning up and, while doing so, thought about backing out several times. Each time that happened I would stop until it came to a choice of one or the other. I regained my nerve and left everything as it was and headed to the kitchen.

There my resolve returned. I calmly retrieved the bottle of Ipecac from the cupboard above the fridge. I rehearsed carrying it and the two beer bottles, setting down one bottle and opening the other while creating a distraction to allow me to add the emetic.

My erratic efforts and constant attempts to find a method that would work best made me regret not practicing all that time they were at the bar. Eventually, I had to settle on one and I did.

Then I made my way down the dark basement stairs . . .

*

. . . there I stood outside my son's bedroom door, in my dirtied, dishevelled robe, doing my best to contain the violently rumbling morning sickness from the new life inside me, trying not to allow the gravity of what I'd just done to overwhelm me, let alone keep me from focusing on a single objective: get Karl to school.

/8\

Twilight falls on the serene and ancient Bosphorus, a calm haven amidst the exotic urban clutter of Istanbul, a laneway separating two continents, linking two seas. Save for the wake of an occasional ferry or fishing boat, its placid waters remain motionless, blackening toward the horizon. Beige abodes dot the dusky Asian hillside from which a bright ball of light ascends, a giant globe, raised by a heavenly crane. Up and up it rises until the sphere reaches a starry point high above the minarets of the Blue Mosque. "I've never seen the moon this close, this big," he says, her response lost in a din. A crowd of passengers, in black, await the formal night dinner seating, equally captivated by the horizon, paying no heed to the newlyweds. A scraping and shuffling comes her deckchair as she sidles it next to his. The movement excites him, then mortifies him once he perceives his own nakedness. She rolls off her chair on top, her bikini bottoms already off. "Let's go for a swim," she says, using their pet euphemism, "right here in the Bosphorus." She removes her top, her large, beautiful breasts plunge, blocking out the sea and sky as . . .

"Did his eyebrows just flutter?"

"Probably dreaming. He does that a lot."

"Does he know he's going home today?"

"Oh yes, we got the news this morning. All his stuff is packed and ready to go."

The two female voices, one on his left, the other on his right, both familiar, both friendly, neither the one he wishes to hear. His deck chair is now a narrow bed barred on both sides, the discomfort in his groin the only souvenir from Istanbul. Where is he? Prison?

The smell of antiseptic orients his awakening. For nearly a week, since regaining consciousness, the dream has taunted Karl. But he never wakes with visitors in the hospital room, only a sense of imprisonment. With horror, he wonders how long they've been watching him. He keeps his eyes shut.

"Should we wake him? Bet he's anxious to get home."

"You're the nurse, Violet. You advise me."

His mother then giggles, self-consciously, as if to clear any contempt hidden in her words.

"I'd prefer to not surprise him."

"I agree."

"He'll be happy to see you. I'm happy to see you again, even under these circumstances."

Karl yearns to open his eyes. Their reunion is touching. Nice that they're friends again. Only the unexpectedness of it prompts a troubling feeling within.

"I feel awful for how I treated you these past years. I'm sorry about that."

"You had no choice. I understand. It's a small price for how you helped me with my situation. For that I will always be grateful. If you hadn't changed your mind—well, I'm not sure I could have done it on my own."

Silence. Karl opens one eye to scan the room. The ladies are huddled near the door, alternately glancing at him and whispering to each other. He shuts it, then hears clacking heels and shuffling flat shoes and the door opening. He rubs his eyes before letting them see. On the other side of the frosted glass, he makes out two blurred heads: Violet's is mostly still but his mother's is animated. Impossible to tell whether she's cross with Violet or just talking.

Violet's revelation last summer drove him to the conclusion his mother her Violet get to Buffalo. Now he's convinced of it beyond any doubt. But what did Violet mean about his mother changing her mind? Was Samuel an accident.? What would have changed her mind?

Instead of shock or curiosity, a horrible emptiness fills Karl as he imagines life without his brother, his troublesome brother, his irritating brother, his obnoxiously charismatic brother. But what, exactly, would he miss? Hard to say but there's no doubt he would miss him. He feels an urge to see Samuel again, even though his brother just visited yesterday. In fact, he's visited every day after school, giving up friends and sports. A tear falls down Karl's face, which he hastily brushes away when the door whooshes open.

"Well, well, well, there he is, the mighty Mark Spitz."

Violet is wearing a pair of tight black jeans. A crimson sweater over a white, collared shirt makes her look dowdy. The sweater has a ruffled collar with a strip of evergreens across the chest. Christmassy. His mother follows, smiling, and in contrast looks youthful in her denim skirt and pink flannel blouse.

He gets a sisterly hug from Violet before she reaches to the ground to pick up a large package she hands to him. It's heavy, wrapped in blue paper, and tied with a neon pink ribbon.

"Kristen helped me wrap it. She insisted on the ribbon. Her favourite colour is pink, the brighter the better."

His mother keeps quiet, but wears a satisfied expression, telling Karl the two did all the catching up they needed outside the door. Now their stories are bound to be straight, that path to past secrets blocked forever. Oddly, this comes as an immense relief.

"Come on, Karl, open it," Violet says.

Ripping the thin wrapping reveals a cardboard box for a stereo receiver. He gives a quizzical look before opening it. Under the Styrofoam and packing paper is a picture, no, a puzzle. The pieces are larger than normal, forty or fifty in total, already fitted together.

He holds it out to view it better. Doing so puts a strain on his weakened arms. The image is a panorama of the Welland Canal, looking upbound, captured from the Garden City Skyway. The scene takes in the third lock and the twin flight locks. He counts three, no, four ships at various points. He's seen similar images countless times from the highway, albeit impeded by concrete barriers.

"Wow," Karl says.

"Roy—remember Roy?—he works at Port Weller Dry Docks and has a friend who paints and makes jigsaw puzzles out of scrap metal."

Karl lifts one of the puzzle pieces. It's weighty, thicker than normal, impossible to bend, break, or force in any other place than the correct one. He takes out several others. His mom taps him.

"Don't forget, you're going home today. As soon as you get dressed, we can go. Everybody's at home waiting—"

"Danielle?"

"I'm afraid we still haven't heard from her. God knows we've tried."

Since he regained consciousness, no one has mentioned the events of his birthday, let alone Tom. No one has given him the slightest reproach for his actions and their consequences. For that matter, Karl has no desire to bring them up either, and that surprises him. The exception is Danielle, but on that subject, they can only say she is out of contact, at least for any inquiries from the Stevenson family.

"That's okay, Mom. Say, can Violet come with us?"

After a quick glance to his former babysitter, his mom nods without hesitation.

"I've already invited her."

"I'm looking forward to seeing your new house."

"Me too," Karl says, though with less conviction.

Instead of the north end home he's lived in all his life, in the city he's lived in all his life, they'll drive south to Port Colborne to a house he's never seen. No photos since they moved in only two weeks ago and the camera is still packed away. Not even the listing photo as his father scooped it up before it went public.

Port Colborne, the Lake Erie entrance and terminus of the canal, the place his mother grew up. He knows little else about it. When younger, he would visit his grandparents but that was too far in the past to remember. A few months ago, Karl would have protested such a drastic move but now he has to admit, at least to himself, a new start will be good for all of them. It's helped Samuel, according to his parents.

There's a light snowfall and all the cars in the hospital parking lot are powdered white. Violet walks at his pace, her hands ready at his elbow. Despite his many therapy strolls in the hospital, his legs are wobbly on the uneven surface. His mother brushes the snow from her car, revealing the Honda Civic she's been raving about for a week, a useful topic for conversation lulls.

They help him get in the backseat first, and then his mother and Violet sit together up front. The women gab as if eleven years have been a day. He cooperates by remaining a quiet child, except to ask his mom to head east along Queenston, which draws a wary look.

"It's not to stalk Danielle. For all I know, she's moved."

They reach the canal road, turn south to drive along the waterway. It's empty for winter save for some puddles. They climb the escarpment alongside the twin locks. His mother can guess the reason for the detour but doesn't protest when he asks her to slow down at Lock Seven and park on the dirt and gravel quay. He opens his window and points to a spot beyond the gates where water fills the canal again.

"That's where I dove in, Violet."

Violet's reaction is a morbid smile. He decides not to ask them to get out and both women seem relieved. Next he asks his mother to follow Pine Street to Beaverdams Road and turn left. The flat farmland is covered by a thin layer of snow while the wind raises dusty white clouds, sweeping the pavement clear. Another left takes them to a bridge that crosses the canal. Karl has his mother park. He gets out and beckons Violet to follow while his mom stays behind. He guides Violet to a small, steep pitch of dead grass, twigs, branches, and litter that borders the canal. Behind them, beyond two poorly maintained baseball backstops, two kids are playing catch with a football.

"There, that's where they found me," he says, pointing to a spot about thirty metres north of the bridge.

Violet gasps, and looks to the distant north.

"That's what, five kilometres? You swam all that way?"

"There was a strong wind that night, kind of like today. So I had help. I don't recall much about the swim itself, but I do remember the bridge because it was being raised. But that's the last thing I remember before . . ."

"Before the hypoxia, the coma, the pneumonia, I know about it. I was on shift when you were brought in and over heard some

Emergency Room nurses talk about a reckless kid who jumped in the canal, bare naked, and swept up on shore, passed out."

"I didn't jump in, I was swimming."

"I'm just saying what I was told."

Violet gives a nervous glance toward the car where his mother sits patiently, staring off. Still, she whispers.

"But once I saw it was you, I checked on you whenever I had a chance. You can't imagine how hard it was seeing you lying there, unable to move, unable to talk. So helpless. I'm just thrilled everything's all right now. Isn't it?"

"Sure. You and my mom seem to be buddies again too."

Violet smiles and that smile tells Karl the conspiracy between the two women is sealed tight.

"Are you going to tell me why you did it, Karl?"

"Probably not."

"I get it. It's okay to have secrets, things you don't share. Too often past events are brought forward and are taken out of context, misunderstood."

"Are you trying to tell me something?"

"Perhaps just clarifying what I've said before."

Karl nods and they get back to the car. After clicking in his seatbelt, he directs his mother on the best route.

"How do you know this area so well?" his mother says.

"Uh, Dani and I sometimes drove here to get away."

Violet giggles and the mood in the car lightens. They cross the bridge to continue south along the east side of the canal. The flat horizon is broken up by farm buildings and small industries. It's like a foreign land to Karl. A community welcome board, with the city's coat of arms and colourful logos of various social clubs, heralds their arrival in Port Colborne, his mother's hometown. Karl feels homesick for the Garden City.

He loses track of the streets but soon they are alongside the Welland Canal and reach the double-length Lock Eight.

Karl informs Violet that, unlike the other seven locks, this is a control lock, no lifting or lowering, no drama. A dozen ice chunks float there like lazy swimmers in a pool. In two or three months, downbound ships will enter and upbound ships will exit the canal here. Karl tries to picture himself riding his bike and stopping to watch, as he did in St. Catharines, with little success.

At Clarence Street, they cross the canal over an ornate bridge and drive through a cramped downtown area of small, buildings and houses. Soon the houses become bigger, newer, and fancier. They turn again and ahead of them lies Lake Erie.

Karl finds the vision of whitish blue endless water with tiny whitecaps soothing. He's disappointed when they veer right several streets before the shore. Just prior to the lake vanishing from his view, Karl spots a ship, perhaps stranded for the winter.

The image stays with him until the car slows at a large white brick bungalow situated on a very wide lot. Baby trees dot an enormous front lawn broken up by a large driveway that can hold at least four cars. His mother parks her Civic next to his father's freshly washed Mercedes. No sign of the station wagon.

Karl steps through a double door entrance. Ever since leaving the hospital, in the back of his mind, he's held on to a faint hope of a surprise, of seeing Dani. Instead, he finds a spacious, ceramic tiled foyer and Samuel. His brother has on a brand new oversized Bills jersey that makes even him look small. He surprises Karl with an unexpectedly warm bear hug.

"Welcome home, big brother. What took you so long?"

"We made a couple of detours."

Karl introduces Violet and Samuel, happy to have her there as they seem to share outsider status. They enter the living room. His dad—in too dark jeans that could use a few stone washes—greets Violet with a brief, sincere hug, before putting out a hand for Karl. But Karl shocks his dad with a full embrace.

"Who won the Super Bowl?" Karl says, as they let go.

"Couple of weeks early, son. Check this out. Even you'll want to watch it on this baby."

Karl follows him to a room off the living room, containing his dad's brand new La-Z-Boy that's like a throne between two leather loveseats. Two wall panels slide open, revealing a giant television screen flanked by a stereo system. His father picks up a remote control unit the size of a book and presses two buttons. A pair of giant, attractive, heavily made up heads of women appear on the screen, arguing over the paternity of a baby. Almost frantically, he presses more buttons, until a motocross race appears.

"ESPN on satellite, and also MTV, HBO, you name it."

"What about blacked out home games?" Karl says.

His father and brother share a conspiratorial grin.

"Dad bought season tickets for next season. He says you and I can go to the home opener together."

"Great," Karl said.

"Want me to take you two on a tour of the house?"

"Sure," Violet says.

"Maybe later," Karl says, and lets them go off.

His attention is drawn to a giant bay window. Between two houses across the street is a gap that provides a glimpse of Lake Erie. Through a thin mist, he spots the ship he saw minutes earlier from the car. He stares at the ship until the tour ends when he joins the others in the living room.

His mom has laid out cookies and cinnamon rolls, along with several cans of pop and a glass of milk for Samuel. The discussion covers the neighbourhood, the amenities, and his brother's school. They move on to weather, regional politics, and the future of the Bills. His mother eventually brings out a Welcome Home cake, double chocolate, with no corny theme. It's delicious but after eating a piece a bleak weariness comes over Karl.

No one objects when he excuses himself for bed. He detours to pass by the bay window. The sky is blue and the mist has cleared, giving a better view of the lake. Much as he strains, he can no longer see the ship.

His steps are wobbly and he has to walk gently down to the basement. He finds his bedroom furniture—bed, desk and chair, bookshelves, lamps, speakers and stereo stand—arranged just as it was in his old one room.

He shuts the door behind him. Nailed to the back is the picture of Istanbul, stabbing him with such sadness, he has to turn away or rip it down. The framed Taj Mahal puzzle, which loomed above his headboard in his old room, seems insignificant on the wider wall. The bed, on the other hand, is newer, bigger, and far more comfortable than the one at the hospital.

The door swings open and his brother enters just as he pulls the bed sheets down.

"I need to rest."

"So, you think I'm Uncle Douglas, eh?" Samuel says.

Instinct makes Karl search for an evasive response but he's too tired to come up with one.

"How'd you figure it out?"

"Who do you think got stuck packing your junk? I can't believe you kept all those puzzles. When one of the puzzle boxes didn't rattle, well . . ."

"You little shit. You shouldn't go through my stuff."

"Did you know our uncle spent five years in jail?"

Karl nods.

"For murder?"

"Actually, it was manslaughter."

"How'd you know that? Dad said he never told—"

"Dad told you?"

Samuel nods.

"Right before I discovered your secret experiments."

Samuel points to a cardboard box next to Karl's bed, still packed and taped.

"You didn't show anything to him, or Mom, did you?"

"Nah, I figured I'd keep that info for another time."

With a pen cap, Karl slices open the tape and rummages through books and records, down to the bottom, until he finds the Taj Mahal cover that matches the picture hanging above him. Karl studies it for a moment before taking it out and handing it to his brother.

"Show them, I don't care."

"Just tell me what it was about," Samuel says, refusing to take the box.

"All right. For a long time, since I can remember really, I didn't think Uncle Douglas died. I thought he went away to India. I was certain he'd return one way or another. I ended up believing he was reincarnated as you."

"Well, that explains the weird things you've done over the years. But what would make you think that?"

Karl pulls the box back, takes out the souvenir photo from Niagara Falls, which he hands to Samuel.

"You have the same blond hair, similar facial features, not to mention many of the same mannerisms."

Samuel grabs the reincarnation book and flips through the pages until he finds the sheets filled with Karl's notes.

"That's it? What about these?"

"What about them? Nothing came of it so it's not true."

"What's not true? Reincarnation in general, or me being Uncle Douglas?"

"The latter."

"You got that right. I may look like Uncle Douglas, but I'm not him. I'm not going to jail."

"Not yet."

"Not ever."

Karl shrugs and Samuel gets up and walks toward the door. Before leaving, he turns around, his face serious.

"I'm really glad you're going to be okay, Karl."

Alone, Karl sifts through the rest of the box's contents. At the bottom, he finds two postcards. One is from Tom with the view of Pittsburgh; the other from his uncle. A shot of the Science Centre in Toronto, along with an invitation for his birthday, his seventh birthday, the last birthday he shared with Uncle Douglas. He inserts them into his uncle's book and throws the book in the wastebasket.

He takes out the picture of his uncle, wipes some dust from it with his shirt, and leans it against the wall on his desk. Then he rips up the puzzle box and throws that away. Next, he takes down the puzzle from the wall and slides it under his bed. In its place he tries to hang the one Violet gave him but finds it heavy so he sets it down and decides to put the Istanbul picture back.

A light, barely perceptible knock on the door as the alarm clock clicks to eight-seventeen. The small window, which has no curtain yet, belies the darkness outside, except for a faint glow of moonlight shining on the picture against the door.

Another knock.

"Come in," he says.

Istanbul vanishes; Danielle appears.

"Am I dreaming?" he says.

She shuts the door and approaches the bed. Her face is fuller, softer, kinder. She's gained weight and cut her hair even shorter than before. Loose bangs obscure her forehead. She's wearing the black angora turtleneck he gave her last Christmas. It would look better with the necklace.

He alternates glancing at her and at the Istanbul photo. She turns to see what he's doing, recognizes the picture, and smiles. She sits at the edge of the bed and bends down to kiss him softly on the top of his head.

"I'm sorry I haven't come to see you till now, though I had my reasons."

"You don't have to explain a single thing to me."

"Actually, I do."

"Listen, Dani, I'm so sorry about everything—"

"Don't."

Her tone isn't harsh. There's a long silence during which they stare at each other. Karl tries to search behind her eyes, but the light isn't good. Then she strokes his forehead.

"Can I at least say how happy I am to see you?"

"I'm glad you're going to be okay."

"What about us, Danielle? Can you ever forgive me?"

"I can forgive you, Karl. As for anything else . . ."

"So you came out of pity?"

"No."

"Then why did you come?"

"Under different circumstances, I might not have."

"What are you talking about? What circumstances?"

Tears stream down her face and her lips tremble, as she takes his hand and moves it onto her belly. Karl looks up and she nods. Then he sits up, rubs his hand and moves it up under her sweater. She lets him. Fortunately, his hands are warm. So is her stomach.

"This changes everything."

"Not so fast. There are other options."

Karl lets go and slides back on the bed, afraid to say anything. Danielle walks to his desk and sits in the chair.

"When did it happen?" he says.

"Either the night after Halloween when my folks were out, or the weekend before your birthday. We took one too many risks."

Karl sighs, partly in agreement, partly in relief.

"I'm due in summer, if I decide to keep it."

Her eyes are intense, as if expecting a response. Instinct prods him to analyze the timing, but another voice, one previously weak and quiet, yells to keep quiet, to trust. This voice holds sway and, as if rewarding him, Danielle smiles.

"Will you?" he says. "Keep it?"

Her smile does not go away; if anything, it brightens.

"You know, I wasn't going to tell you anything, except Samuel tracked me down. Somehow he found out. He pestered me, and even persuaded my parents, that I should see you before making a decision. He's quite something."

"My little brother, what a hero."

Danielle's unexpected laugh is glorious.

"A prospective uncle *should* be a hero—hey, who's that?"

Her finger is pointing at the Niagara Falls souvenir photo but Karl can't tell at which head she's pointing.

"That's me, with my uncle. He died a long time ago."

"You look so happy with him."

"I was."

Acknowledgements

For geographical, social, and historical aspects of the Niagara Region, several books were particularly helpful in filling gaps and identifying flaws in my recollections: *St. Catharines, Canada's Canal City* by John N. Jackson and Sheila M. Wilson; *The Ships of Port Weller* by Skip Gillham; *The Welland Canals Corridor, Then and Now* by Robert M. Styran and Robert R. Taylor; and *St. Catharines Transit, The First Forty Years* by Mark Dobell. The free pamphlet, *The Welland Canal, Niagara, Canada*, provided an informative and well-written overview of the waterway.

Twenty Cases Suggestive of Reincarnation, by Ian Stevenson M. D. is published by University Press of Virginia. This interesting volume was more than a prop and inspired not only reincarnation aspects of the novel, but also certain plot elements.

Many thanks to the friendly, knowledgeable staff at the Welland Canal viewing platforms in St. Catharines and Thorold, Marnie Woodrow, and Frank Warman.

For her enthusiastic, constructively supportive readings, and willingness to help on many trips to the canal and all around the Niagara Peninsula, I am especially grateful to my wife, Yolande.

About the Author

Peter Hassebroek published the first edition of *Upbound* in 2008. In 2010 he published, *Melange and Other I. T. Stories,* a collection inspired by his pre-writing career, which was followed by a second novel, *The Dancer's Spell*, a year later.

A diversion into screenwriting resulted in a screenplay collection published in 2016: *Greenplays, 3 Scripts by Peter Hassebroek*. A fourth script ultimately turned into a third novel, *Thylacine,* published early in 2017, and marking a rejuvenated return to fiction writing.

This edition of *Upbound* improves on the original in revamping the prose and correcting errors. More importantly, it now incorporates Helen's perspective, in her voice, adding a degree of depth and insight readers may have found lacking in the original.

Peter lives in Whitby, Ontario, Canada with his wife, Yolande.

To contact Peter, as well as to learn more about his other books, please visit the website:

www.peterhassebroek.com

www.ingramcontent.com/pod-product-compliance
Lightning Source LLC
LaVergne TN
LVHW091042080826
845145LV00002B/590

* 9 7 8 0 9 8 6 6 6 4 0 8 3 *